Ride the Rough String

Other novels by Alfred Dennis

Chiricahua
Lone Eagle
Elkhorn Divide
Brant's Fort
Catamount
The Mustangers
Yuma
Rover
Yellowstone Brigade
Sandigras Canyon
Shawnee Trail
Fort Reno

Ride
the
Rough String

by

Alfred Dennis

WCP

Walnut Creek Publishing
Tuskahoma, Oklahoma

Ride the Rough String

ISBN: 978-1-942869-03-0
First edition, Paperback
Published 2015 by Walnut Creek Publishing
10 9 8 7 6 5 4 3 2 1
Library of Congress Control Number: 2015936079
1. Western 2. Action/Adventure 3. Historical Fiction

Books may be purchased in quantity and/or special sales by contacting the
publisher;
Walnut Creek Publishing
PO Box 820
Talihina, OK 74571
www.wc-books.com

This book is dedicated to my wife Jimmie Dell. A small woman with a big heart. Quite a cowgirl, best woman bronc rider I've ever seen on a bad horse and a great barrel racer. Thanks for the many good years and helping with the bad ones.

Chapter 1

Men dressed in every attire, from cowmen to farmers in overhauls, to well-dressed bankers and storekeepers, line the top rail of the pole corral. They watch the dark-complexioned, young man as he pulls the cinch tight on a large, roman-nosed palomino gelding that another cowboy is holding, snubbed to his smaller horse. Tall, slender, and broad through the shoulders, the man standing on the ground works calmly with the rigging sitting atop the bug-eyed gelding. Suddenly, with no warning, the big palomino lunges sideways into the smaller pony horse. He knocks him to his side, throwing his rider to the ground under the plunging horse's feet. Quickly, with one smooth stride, the younger man steps forward, pulling the downed cowboy from under the two scrambling horses, away from the dangerous flaying hooves.

Limping, as he backs away from the crazed animal, the rider throws up his hands then leads his spooked horse from the corral as he grumbles under his breath. "That's it, no more. You people ain't paying me enough to get myself or my horse hurt on that loco outlaw."

The dark-complexioned young man, standing alone in the corral, holding the palomino's lead rope, is Cam Mitchell. Barely past twenty-five years old, he cannot count the times he has been in the same situation. Every town has at least one outlaw horse they know no one can ride. There is one thing for dead certain though, plain as the nose on a man's face, the palomino he holds is a pure bona fide bronc. Many a rider tried their luck but no local cowboy or any other challenger could stay aboard the powerful animal. Thick through the body and standing over sixteen hands tall, the dark yellow horse is huge, weighing at least fourteen hundred pounds, dwarfing most horses in the territory.

Every town, village, or hamlet across the southwest has a bad horse the local townsfolk are proud of because of its bucking prowess. Being loaded with a chest full of civic pride for their city and horse, knowing they will make easy money wagering on the outlaw. They are ready and eager to bet against any newcomer coming into town, willing to try to conquer the beast. People know there is always somebody willing to try their luck with the palomino. Today money changes hands freely as the watchers push eagerly forward to lay down their bets and see the challenger stomped into the dirt and filth of the huge corral. An older man dressed like a horseman or buffalo hunter, holds in his right hand a folded piece of paper with a stub of pencil. In his left hand, he holds the money as he keeps busy covering all bets.

"You boys hurry now and get your bets down." The leathery face of the money holder, weather beaten and covered with grizzled grey facial hair looks about the crowd trying to place one last bet. Looking over into the high corral, he grins and nods the go-ahead signal to the tall youngster in the corral. "I reckon you boys are through. Maybe you know best. That old yellow plug doesn't look like much to me."

"That's your opinion, you old horse thief," a bystander laughs. "Old yeller is gonna toss your boy into next week, or his grave."

"Well, that may be true enough, but you know dumb as I am boys, even I'm smart enough not to bet on that yellow piece of crow bait."

Dark scowls and frowns settle on several faces as the old horse trader scoffs at the palomino's bucking abilities. They wave their hands at the older man but no further bets are offered by the gathered crowd.

Just as the better starts to give the go-ahead signal, a well-dressed man in gambler's garb and a derby hat steps beside the older man holding the bets. "Wait up one second, Caintuck, you old reprobate. Just how much are you willing to wager on your rider?"

The horse trader, the man calls Caintuck, scratches his chin thoughtfully and looks at the gambler, shaking his head with a grin.

"Doc Mills, why I haven't seen you since you cleaned me out in Bisbee, nigh on three years ago."

"You're seeing me now, old-timer." The well-dressed man grins. "I've got five hundred dollars says your rider can't ride that old yeller plow horse."

"Five hundred; I don't know Doc, the boy is green." Caintuck shrugs with worry showing in his grizzled face. "You must know that palomino well to layout that kind of chicken scratch on him."

"Matter of fact, I do and that's a certainty. I've seen that outlaw buck off every man that's been foolish or drunk enough to climb aboard him," Mills admits, holding out his money and grins. "Put up or shut up, you old horse thief."

Caintuck counts what money he has left in his hand and looks over at the gambler. "I've got a thousand left, Doc. No one else here seems inclined to bet anymore on the palomino, so I'll tell you what. I'll bet the whole shebang on the kid."

"You've got yourself a bet." Mills points at the pad and pulls out another roll of bills. "Jot it down quick, before that yeller horse buries your man there."

"It's down Doc, but I doubt there'll be any burying done here today." Caintuck grins slyly, like a fox slipping into a henhouse. "Unless, old yeller there dies of fright."

"I reckon we're fixing to find out."

"That we are hoss, that we are." Caintuck pockets the paper and a large roll of money plus silver.

Nodding through the high corral poles at the tall youngster, Caintuck watches as his nemesis pulls the yeller horse's head around to his shoulder, stepping smoothly into the saddle, in one fluid motion. All eyes focus on the palomino gelding in expectation as he explodes into the air, jackknifing sideways, then rolling back on his haunches, trying his best to dislodge the hated human on his back. Caintuck smiles as the final bet from Mills will add to their bank account in the Gila Bank. It will be all they need to buy the land on the Pecos to start their horse ranch. The old horse trader has no doubt the young man will ride the yeller horse. He knows, on any given day, any rider could be thrown, but Cam Mitchell is the best he has ever seen on a bad, bucking horse. Nine times out of ten, the youngster will still be aboard when the dust settles. No rules exist when man and horse are matched against each other in the boiling dust of a dirty corral. It is a contest of the fittest, sent down from the ages. Ride or get bucked off is the only outcome as to who wins the contest.

Born with the long-legged physique of a rider, combined with no fear, natural balance and determination to stay aboard a bucking animal, most times the youngster is still riding when the horse stops bucking. Caintuck knows their ranch depends a lot on this one ride. Today can possibly have a different outcome, but the old trader has faith in Cam Mitchell. He wagered all the money he had on the youngster, knowing if the young man is thrown, they will have to wait longer to earn the money they need for their ranch.

For five years now, since taking the young man under his wing, Caintuck taught Cam every trick he knows about horse-trading and the tricks of riding bad bucking horses. He saw many bronc riders in his time, traveling from town to town trading horses, but none had the natural balance, tenacity, and ability to ride a bad horse like this youngster possesses. No fear, not in the least, exists in the youngster. Normally, he loves horses, but Caintuck sees that love temporarily turn to hate as the man and beast go at it with no fear or quit in either one. Caintuck watches as the big yeller horse bucks across the corral kicking his hind legs high in the air, snapping them out, catching the rider hard in the small of his back. Rolling his head and neck sideways as he hits on his front end, the gelding bawls and tosses his head in rage with every leap. Caintuck watches the ride with a trained eye. He knows Cam is sitting a tight saddle. Even though the contest has barely started, he knows the yeller horse is already finished. He will not unseat the hated rider on his back today. Smiling, he watches as the yeller horse makes his last lunge, then sulls and quits cold in the middle of the corral. Today, as the dust clears and settles over the corral, the disgusted crowd starts to walk away as the old horse trader nods happily. He knows their horse ranch is paid for.

Doc Mills frowns over at the old man. "Well Caintuck, I reckon you got your money back this time."

"For a fact Doc, but you'll get another chance at me, I reckon."

"You're wrong about that old friend."

"How's that?" Caintuck looks hard at the man. "Where you headed?"

"I'm headed east on the first stage out of here, come morning." The gambler shrugs. "Providing I can get in a game around here and get some money to travel on, which I doubt."

"You in a tight, old friend?"

"Right about now, I reckon I am, for a fact."

Caintuck looks at the money in his hand and offers it to Mills. "You need a stake Doc; you broke?"

"I am now." Mills looks down at the money Caintuck holds out to him. "I can't take your money, old friend."

"Yes you can and will, Doc." Caintuck presses the thousand dollars Mills wagered back in the gambler's hand. "I remember a few years past when you got me in the horse business, even if you don't."

"I remember those days." Mills nods. "They were plenty lean years for us working men."

"Then you take this money and welcome." Caintuck smiles. "It makes an old friend happy to help out a man that's been as good as you have to me over the years."

"Thanks Caintuck." Mills looks at the money and shakes hands with the horse trader. "I'll get it back to you, quick as I can."

"No rush." Caintuck looks over at the corral gate as it squeaks open. "Anything else I can help you with?"

"No old friend, not this time." The Gambler shakes his head sadly. "I killed the wrong man back in Tombstone, the brother-in-law of a local rancher. The town law advised me to leave Arizona on the first available train or coach out of the country."

"Behan?"

"Yep." Mills shrugs. "It was a fair fight, but I was in the wrong place and heavily outgunned."

"I know you weren't afraid of that popinjay." Caintuck spits.

"No, not of Sheriff Behan I wasn't. There were too many cowboys from the Slash Knife Outfit, just itching to pump me full of lead."

"Where you headed?"

"East I reckon." Mills looks over at the corral. "Healthier climate so I've been told."

"Well, Doc good luck to you." Caintuck sticks out his hand. "Tell me, was it over a woman or cards."

"A little of both I reckon, don't matter much now though," Mills laughs lightly. "He's a goner and so am I."

"You ever get down to the Pecos country, thirty miles south of a town called Willowmook, look me and the boy up." Caintuck smiles. "There'll always be a place for you to lay your head."

"Willowmook, what a funny sounding name. What are you going into Texas for, to raise prairie dogs?"

"Horses Doc, horses and lots of them," Caintuck laughs. "Me and young Mitchell are going into the ranching business."

"Well, y'all will do fine. He's a real ring-tailed terror on a horse." Mills nods as Cam walks up. "Never seen better and you know horses better than any man I know."

"Cam Mitchell, meet Doc Mills." Caintuck introduces the two men as Cam approaches.

"So you're Doc Mills. Caintuck has spoken of you many a day."

Cam heard Caintuck speak of Doc Mills, the gambler and gunfighter, on several occasions while sitting around a lonely campfire or passing through a town. He can tell, as the well-dressed man shakes his hand and speaks, he is no doubt a well-educated and cultured man. After shaking hands with the man, both Cam and Caintuck watch as the gambler ambles away, his shoulders square, a proud man.

"There goes the last of a breed, boy."

"Was he that good?'

Caintuck nods his head and spits a stream of tobacco. "I'd put him up there with Holliday, Earp, Masterson, even Hickok. He just don't have someone writing about everything he did, fact or lie, but he was that good."

"Where will he go now?"

"Hell. I figure that's where most of his kind wind up, eventually." Caintuck shrugs. "Take heed boy, settle down and plant some roots. Don't end up like old Doc there."

"That bad, huh?"

"Those boys had their time in the sun. They shined, but sadly like me, they grew old and it's over for them or soon will be."

"What about us, Caintuck?" The tall youngster looks down at the old trader. "Where we headed now?"

"We'll head for Gila Town in a few days by way of Garden City and the Mogollons. We need to add the money we won today to our nest egg." Caintuck pats the bulge of money in his vest-pocket and smiles. "I let Doc have a grubstake same as he would have done for either of us."

"So now we'll have to work a little longer before settling in on our new ranch?" Cam questions.

"A little while is all boy, we got the land money. Now all we need is a little working capital, but we got plenty of time." The old horse trader smiles, "You don't mind do you?"

"I don't mind at all." Cam shrugs. "Young men coming along now, owe men like him and you. Y'all made this country."

Caintuck smiles. "For a fact boy, but few young people your age would say that."

"Will our little valley wait or will someone else beat us to it?" Cam watches as Doc Mills goes into the local saloon.

"It'll be there for a spell yet." Caintuck looks over at the palomino, changing the conversation. "Well, old yeller can't brag to the other horses, he ain't been ridden now, can he boy?"

"Reckon not, that is if horses brag."

Caintuck grins. "I 'spect they do, hoss."

"You've heard them?" Cam shakes his head. "Actually brag, I mean?"

"They're like a man, boy. It's the way they carry themselves with pride and the way they look you in the eye with that, devil-may-care twinkle." Caintuck nods. "They brag alright, but in their own way."

"He was a lot of horse." Cam's eyes wander over to the corral. "I was lucky to ride him today."

"No, you were better than he was today." Caintuck nods his head. "He was game for sure."

"Yep, he was at that." Cam looks away. "I kinda feel sorry for him."

"Don't!" Caintuck shakes his head. "If it turned out the other way, he would have thrown you then kicked your brains in. He'd brag to the local yahoos and they would still be laughing."

"Yes sir, those boys were really enjoying themselves, but with that old horse, it wasn't nothing personal. He was just doing his job."

"I'm going across to the Hogshead and wet my whistle." Caintuck looks across the street at the nearest saloon. "You wait here boy. There's some pig farmer that sent word he wants to look at that team of Grays. Take care of it, okay?"

"Alright." Cam lays his saddle in the back of their battered covered wagon. "Just wet your tonsils, don't drown them, you're carrying a lot of money."

"Smart aleck kid." Caintuck spits, grumbling as he trudges toward the saloon. "I was nursing my own self when he was whelped."

Several horses stand hipshot, swishing flies in an adjoining corral, as Cam walks among them, stroking each one as he passes. All are good horses, sound and prime horseflesh. Caintuck's reputation stands behind every horse he sells or trades. In this country, a horse trader has to. His reputation and good word, precede him in every town. The wide strung western ranches and farms depend on good horses for their livelihood and even their lives at times. Acquiring a bad reputation, by selling lame or wind broke animals, means a horse trader traveling the countryside will soon be out of business, if not hung outright for lying. Caintuck has been a horse trader for many a year and still his reputation flourishes. Almost everyone in Arizona and New Mexico respects and likes him.

In the past few years, since meeting Caintuck, the two traveled across Arizona, New Mexico, and parts of Texas. Almost to the New Mexico border in West Texas, is where they accidentally found the small valley loaded with deep grass and plenty of water. In the vast, rough, dry Pecos Country they crossed for miles, they suddenly came to an old grown up road, leading down into a small canyon which spread out into a beautiful valley. Seeing the glimmering water of a clear creek, beckoning them at sundown, they made camp and explored some of the valley before dark came upon them. The next morning, they accidentally stumbled on an old log house with a caved in roof and crumbling corrals a short distance from where they pitched camp. The buildings were old, rundown, and weather beaten. Apparently, whoever originally occupied the valley was probably long ago dead by Indians, outlaws, or by time itself. However, the picturesque valley with its pristine creek and tall bluffs, hasn't changed over the years, making both men think they are standing in paradise. The air is so clean and pure, neither man, young or old, can draw enough of the sweet fragrances of the flowers and hemlocks into their lungs. Tracks of every kind of wild critter show plainly in the soft dirt or along the beautiful clear running stream where they come to water. Grass, tall as a man's waist in places, is abundant, a natural feeding ground for cattle and horses.

It is an isolated valley, many miles from the nearest civilization. The valley borders two states, reaching almost to Old Mexico, making it the perfect location for a horse ranch. They took one last look at the valley before riding out of the canyon. Their dream was to begin saving enough money to return one day with the deed to the land and horses to stock the vast canyons and its grasses. The valley and its supine beauty are all that is on their minds or tongues around the many campfires of the evening.

At the nearest town of Willowmook, some thirty miles from the valley, they enter the Federal Land Agency and study the rough maps of the area. At one time, long ago, a trapper or buffalo hunter built the old cabin and put up pole corrals. Now, years later, no one has paid taxes or ever laid claim to the huge valley covering almost ten thousand acres by the maps estimate. The Land Agent scratches his stubble of beard and shakes his head in disbelief as Caintuck places his finger on the exact spot on the map.

"Gentlemen, that land ain't fit for nothing but Gila monsters, rattlers, scorpions, Apaches or Comanche." The agent looks over his spectacles. "Depending on which one of them bites you first."

"Well then, it should be cheap, we want it." Caintuck taps the map. "How much will it take to hold it?"

"That's government land, only cash for back taxes. For that land, cents on the acre will buy or hold anything the government lays claim to out there." The old agent smiles and shakes his head. "Don't worry Gents, I'll guarantee it's too far, too dry, and too dangerous for anyone in their right mind to risk their necks wanting that chunk of sand."

"So we can't put money down to hold it, is that it?" Caintuck growls and frowns, looking at the short man. "We'll be back, mister, count on it."

"Sorry old-timer, but that land will be here years from now. I'll always be here 'cepting Sundays." The agent peers over his wire rimmed glasses as they pass back through the door. "Only a crazy man would want that land anyway. Could be that pair might just fit the bill."

Cam looks peculiarly at Caintuck as they leave the Land Agent's Office. "How they gonna know how much land we will have to pay for?"

"Its simple boy, they guess. They write us out a bill of sale from point A to point B then we own everything in between." Caintuck nods knowingly. "How's that sound?"

"You're right, they'd have to be guessing." Cam shrugs. "I'll guarantee that little fat man sure didn't ride a horse all the way out there and he ain't about to either."

"Amen to that, Cam Mitchell."

Cam strokes the neck of a well-made bay saddle horse, speaking softly to the animal, but his thoughts are of the beautiful valley and flat grassy canyon they discovered. He never thought of owning anything, especially his own ranch, but the valley haunts his every waking moment, beckoning him to hurry and return. The beauty of the land calls to him, pulling him back to its peaceful, rolling grasses, small creek, and timberland, crossing the entire canyon. Many nights, he wakes with the nightmare that someone else laid claim to the land.

"Young man." The voice is deep and gruff, calling from outside the corral. "Mister."

Cam turns to find a large, middle-aged man in farmer's bib overalls, looking through the cedar posts of the corral. "Yes, sir."

"Sorry to disturb your thoughts young feller, but my name's Johnson. I'm looking for Caintuck. I hear he's got a fine matched pair of gray, work animals for sale." The farmer looks around the corral. "I expect it's them two there."

"That's them alright; they belong to Caintuck." Cam is a little embarrassed the man caught him so deep in thought. "Step in and look them over."

"Where is the old horse thief?" Johnson looks around as he climbs through the poles. "He sent word he'd meet me here today."

"He's bathing."

Johnson looks curiously at Cam. "I've known old Caintuck since the early days and never known him to take a bath. What's the occasion?"

"His tonsils were dry."

"Oh yeah, I know what you mean." Johnson grins and looks back at the wagon where a woman and a young girl sit quietly. "We heard someone rode the palomino over there. Would that be you?"

"He'll be along directly." Cam's eyes look to the wagon where the women sit. "Yes sir, I rode him."

"Man said it was some ride you put on him. He said you seemed glued to the saddle." Johnson shakes his head. "Sure wish I'd of been here to see it."

"I got lucky is all." Cam is embarrassed in front of the women. "Tomorrow might have a different outcome. Maybe he'd be the lucky one."

"Those cowboys sure weren't happy."

"Don't expect they were. Most bet an entire month's wages on the horse."

"Anybody think to bet on you?"

"Just old Caintuck."

"May I introduce my wife and daughter Felicia." Johnson has seen the young man's eyes drift to the wagon then turn away abruptly.

"Yes, sir." Cam tips his hat and his face blushes as he is introduced. "It's nice to meet you, ladies."

"Nice to meet you, young man." The older woman smiles while the younger one sits frozen, her eyes staring at the tall, handsome young man.

"Abe Johnson." Caintuck tips his hat to the women as he passes the wagon and pulls up in front of the farmer. "Hope you ain't been here long."

"Would it have mattered, Caintuck?"

"No, sorry, but I have pressing matters to attend to across the street."

"Dry or wet matters?"

Caintuck grins over at Cam then motions toward the corral where the two workhorses stand chewing on some rough hay. "A magnificent team of grays, perfectly matched, not a blemish or a scratch on them, and they'll pull a heavy load. These boys, I'll guarantee won't sull and they are easy to catch."

"You guarantee they're one hundred percent sound?"

"Abe, you find anything wrong with them, you just bring them back for a complete refund of your money."

"Plus my expense money, of course."

"Abe Johnson, I swear." Caintuck shakes his head. "You want the grays or not, cause we're heading out."

"Don't get yourself stirred up, I'm thinking." Johnson runs his hands over one of the big horses. "Do they ride?"

"Ride, what for?" Caintuck spits as he watches the younger woman climb down from the wagon and run her hands over the horses. "Shucks Abe, they're work animals, not cow ponies. They're too broad backed to straddle and you'd have to get yourself a ladder to get on them."

"If I have to go to the pasture and bring them in, I sure ain't walking back." Johnson looks over at Caintuck. "Do they ride?"

"They're work animals Abe, but if they do ride, they'll cost you another hundred."

"Okay, you old thief, I want to trade this lighter team of mules in on the deal."

"Mules, shucks I don't trade for mules," Caintuck frowns at the small black team, hitched to the wagon. "You know that."

"If you're a wanting to sell those grays, you're trading for mules today." Johnson grins.

Caintuck walks to the wagon and looks the team of black mules over closely. Turning, he walks back to where Johnson stands by the grays. "Those long-eared jackrabbits don't weigh nine hundred pounds, soaking wet."

"I know that you old horse thief, that's why I'm willing to trade them off. They're too light to pull a plow all day in rough ground," Johnson growls. "I'll tell you this Caintuck, there ain't a better team of garden or wagon animals in the state. Now how much do you want difference?"

"Five hundred."

Johnson blinks. "Plus my good mules?"

"With the mules or without the mules." Caintuck spits. "You get the drift? I don't want them things."

"I do."

All eyes turn to where Cam stands holding the lead ropes of the grays. "What you want them things for, boy?"

"I'll give a hundred for them." Cam looks over at the girl. "Each."

"Alright young'un, but I think you've done gone and lost your senses." Caintuck nods. "I reckon we'll trade with you for three hundred Abe."

"What about my harness? It's the best brass knobby harness made."

"Well Abe, you put that knobby harness on the grays and I'll keep mine."

"Caintuck, you know full well, my harness won't fit them work-horses." Johnson shakes his head. "You're getting to me again."

Caintuck pockets the pouch of gold coins Johnson handed over without counting it then starts unhitching the mules. "You ever rode a mule, boy?"

"No, sir, never had much truck with them things or even tried."

"Well, don't. They'll suck that big head clear out of sight and leave you riding nothing but air out there," Caintuck laughs. "Tell me, if you don't want any doings with them long-eared jackrabbits, why did you trade for them?"

"You'll see soon enough."

Johnson looks to where his young daughter is staring holes at Cam as he hitches the grays to the small buckboard. Walking over to where the huge draft horses dwarf over the small spring wagon, making it seem even smaller in size, he pulls the young woman from the wagon. The girl is so engrossed in making eyes at Cam, she doesn't see the farmer has come up beside her.

"Felicia, you get over to the store with your ma. I'll pick you up there."

"Yes Pa, good-bye Mister Caintuck and you too, Mister Mitchell." The brown eyes flash as she smiles coyly at him. "Nice to meet you."

"Ma'am." Both men touch their hats.

Shaking hands, Johnson frowns as Felicia turns one last time to stare at Cam before entering the mercantile store. "You have a very pretty daughter, Abe."

"Yes, she is Caintuck, young and headstrong." Johnson sticks out his hand. "See you boys next year."

"See you." Caintuck watches as the girl lingers in the doorway of the store a second then turns his attention back to Johnson. "You find anything wrong with those animals, bring them back and I'll make it right."

"At your prices, you old thief, there better not be anything wrong with them." Johnson grins, wrapping his huge hand around Caintuck's smaller one. "They'll do fine; I need them."

Johnson stops and looks back where Cam is stroking the mules. "They are good mules, young man. They're just a little hard to catch."

"Yes, sir."

"Well, boy you get the horses ready and I'll get supplies, then we'll head out."

"Where we headed now?"

"We'll head east, toward Garden City. Maybe trade some with the local ranchers on our way."

"Sounds good. Do we have enough money for the ranch?'

"Almost." Caintuck pats his pocket. "It'll only take another few sales like this one today and by the time we get to Gila Town, we should have it."

Chapter 2

Rough cut cedar poles and heavy timbers make up the entranceway of the ranch. Turning off to the south and passing across a vast flatland covered in stunted small trees, there are cactus and thorn bushes of every kind. Little grass shows on the arid, sandy land this high but down lower in the canyons, the grass becomes abundant.

Caintuck pulls in his gelding and studies the strands of barbwire passing as a makeshift gate. "Reckon we'll head down and pay old Shadrack Hammer a social visit, while we're this close."

"Wanting a hot, home cooked meal are you?" Cam looks up at the afternoon sun. "You timed it just right. We'll be there about suppertime."

"I could use a bite to eat. His woman cooks up a right tasty pan of biscuits. Besides, we may even sell a horse or two." Caintuck rubs his flat stomach. "Kick them up, boy. I'll open the gate for you."

The Hammer Ranch is one of the smaller ranches in size, in this part of the state, but the ranch buildings are almost five miles from the gate they passed through. The horse trader never passes up the hospitality of his old friend Shadrack Hammer. Even if he doesn't trade off one single horse, the free grub is worth every mile of the ride.

Clucking to the team, Cam frowns, remembering the redheaded Hammer girl that smiled at him so friendly on their last visit. The problem is, he also remembers the hateful glare he received from Obe Wilson, Hammer's foreman, who already branded the pretty filly as his own. He remembers the angry scowl and challenging, jealous stare of the big man as they left from their last visit. "This could get interesting old man."

Caintuck spits, but does not look back at the wagon. He knows exactly what the young man is saying. "Leave that gal alone and it won't."

"I ain't done a thing and you dang well know it." Cam shakes his head. "That red headed girl scares the by Jiminy out of me."

"You must have done something, the way she was hanging onto you." The trader grins. "That Double H, foreman sure didn't get his hackles all standing up over nothing."

Cam tightens his jaw, but utters nothing further in his own defense, refusing to listen as Caintuck teases him. The girl was either overly friendly or she was trying her best to get Obe Wilson jealous. Whichever it was, he is determined to stay clear of her this time and not let her drag him into any lover's spat. Yes sir, he will stay plumb clear.

"I should have waited on you at the gate." Cam shakes his head and looks longingly at the gate. "I can feel it."

Caintuck grins. "Where's your fighting spirit, boy?"

"Fighting spirit? I sure ain't fixing to fight over a woman I barely know and sure don't want to know."

"Well, hopefully Obe will see it that way too."

"Funny." Cam knows the older man is just teasing him, as older men are prone to do about girls. Trouble is, Caintuck doesn't see the seriousness of the situation with the Hammer girl. On their last visit, the jealous boyfriend, foreman, had a murderous look in his eye. The same look Cam had seen in many outlaws. No sir, last time they rode out just in time and this could turn into a similar situation. It isn't funny to him, not in the least.

Shadrack Hammer, all six feet six of him, stands like a giant oak waiting on the front porch. A wide grin is plastered across his large face as the wagon and horses pull to a stop in front of the house. Several huge staghounds, almost the size of the giant, surround their master's enormous legs. Stepping lightly from the porch, for a man of his bulk, Hammer lifts Caintuck bodily, like a baby, from his horse. Then he bear hugs the old trader until Cam thinks every bone, in his partner, is going to break.

"Caintuck, old friend, am I ever glad to see your old hide."

Caintuck is still trying to get his wind as Hammer is pounding on his back. "Get your hands off me, you overgrown oaf. You dang near squeezed the life from me and probably bruised my ribs for life."

Throwing back his head, the giant man laughs deeply. "You ain't hurt so bad. You don't need a good meal, do you?"

"I didn't say that." Caintuck grins and shakes hands with Hammer. "No sir, I didn't say that at all. A good meal may fix me up real quick."

Hammer looks up to where Cam is holding on tight to the wagon seat. "Take your animals to the barn young man and turn them into the biggest corral. Put your stallion in the smaller corral by himself. There's corn and plenty of hay in the feed bins."

Seeing the redheaded daughter of Hammer emerge from the house with a huge smile on her face, Caintuck turns for the wagon. "Maybe I should help him."

"Nah old friend, he can do it by himself. He's young and strong," Shadrack laughs, grabbing Caintuck by the arm. "Let's go inside and have us something to lift our spirits. He'll be back quick enough."

"I'll help him, Pa." Betsy Hammer races by the older men, climbing onto the wagon quicker than a squirrel could climb a tree. "Ma's got supper almost finished and she don't need me."

Scottish Highlanders by heredity, the Hammer family migrated to New Mexico from the backwoods of Tennessee. Family traditions, close blood ties, and backwoods beliefs, were brought with them to this new land. Caintuck knows Obe Wilson came west with Shadrack Hammer as a youngster. He also knows her father promised Betsy to Wilson. As she climbs into the wagon, he watches the girl move close to Cam, smiling up at him shyly. Caintuck knows she is toying with Cam, pretending to shine up to him, to stoke the hotheaded Wilson's jealousy. All the while, she enjoys the power she holds over her fiancé and his emotions. Caintuck swears as he watches the girl carry on, wishing now he kept to the main road as Cam wanted him too, not stopping to trade horses with Hammer this time. The girl, Betsy Hammer, doesn't have sense enough to realize her riding in the wagon with another man could turn out bad or does she? He looks over at Shadrack questionably as he walks beside the big man into the house. The giant of a man from

Tennessee knows the jealous nature of his family and the other men from Tennessee, where fighting is a part of their life.

Caintuck starts to protest again but stops short as Shadrack Hammer laughs and propels him into the house. "My soon to be son-in-law has to prove his love for the girl and that he will protect her."

"I don't want the boy hurt Shadrack." Caintuck knows the rough and tumble nature of these mountain people from the backwoods and mountains of Tennessee.

"He won't be. I give you my word." Hammer motions to a chair. "They're to be married next week, if Obe shows grit and fights for her. Now their love will be strong. It'll just be a little fistfight at most. It may be nothing at all if your lad doesn't show fight."

"It better be, old friend." Caintuck touches the butt of his forty-five. "I mean it Shadrack. I won't see the Lad harmed in any way."

"You have my word, Caintuck." Hammer shrugs. "Obe must prove he cares for her before she respects him."

"At Cam's expense?" Caintuck takes the extended glass of home-made liquor. "You do all your guests this way?"

"I know it's a bad deal for a guest but your boy is the only outsider that's been around here in months." Shadrack smiles down at Caintuck. "I promise you old friend, it won't be much of a fight. Maybe they won't fight at all."

Caintuck knows Cam and he knows the youngster will fight. "Oh they'll fight alright but it may not be to your liking."

"Your young man's pretty rough, is he?"

"Rough enough." Caintuck thinks back to the licking Cam gave Emmet Folsom.

"Good, we ain't had much fun around here in months." Hammer roars, his loud booming laughter sounds clear to the barn. "It's been downright quiet for some time now."

As Cam watches Shadrack and Caintuck disappear inside the house, he groans to himself, clucking to the team and starts for the corrals.

Sliding tightly up against him, the girl smiles into his red face. "I was surely hoping you'd be coming back this way real soon, Cameron Mitchell."

Trying to move away from the swell of her round hips, Cam finds the seat rail catching him like a mouse in a trap with no place to retreat. "Yes, ma'am."

"Ain't you glad to be here again, Cam?" Betsy runs her hand through the crook of his arm, her hand brushing lightly against his leg. "Didn't you miss poor little old me, just a wee bit?"

Cam looks up at the barn in dread as several men, unsaddling their horses, spot the wagon and gather in a knot, watching them. He knows the fat is in the fire for sure. He is sitting in plain sight, tighter than two lovebirds on a limb, atop the wagon bed with another man's intended. There isn't a thing he can do about it. "Yes ma'am, I reckon I missed you a little."

As the wagon and a string of horses pull up beside the corral and stop, Obe Wilson stalks over and stands straddle-legged beside the wagon. His face is beet red and puffed up like a toad as he looks up at the two of them. He knows the other Hammer riders, men he works with every day, are watching to see what he will do as it is Highlander tradition. Every eye waits and stares in expectation, first at him then at Cam. Wilson is caught in the trap too, the same as Cam. Betsy Hammer snaps it shut tight, with both men ensnared in a situation neither can get out without losing face. One has to show her in the traditional Scottish way, he deserves her hand and will fight to win it. The other, well win or lose, has nothing to gain except maybe his head. He is just in the wrong place at the wrong time.

He can read the signs of jealousy all over the big foreman. This is not going to end well for someone. Caught wedged against Betsy in the wagon seat with her arm clutching his like a pair of fire tongs, he cannot budge. He feels like a child with his hand caught in the cookie jar. Finally, succeeding in prying her hand loose, he smiles sickly over at the grinning riders and starts to climb down from the wagon.

"You want to leave here with all your teeth Mitchell you best stay on that wagon and git." Wilson walks toward the wagon all puffed up like a Banty rooster, ready to fight. "You Betsy Hammer, you get yourself off that wagon right now."

"I like it here just fine, Obe Wilson." The girl grabs again for Cam's hand. "You ain't my boss yet and Cam is such a sweet gentleman."

Cam can only groan, as the foreman's face turns redder. "Maybe you better get down, ma'am."

"Don't pay any attention to Obe. He's just a spoiled brat." Betsy sticks her tongue out at the foreman. "He ain't got a claim on me, yet."

Cam notices several riders grinning in expectation of the upcoming fight. They have watched more than one newly, hired ranch hand run off the ranch after taking a sound whipping from Wilson when Betsy showed them too much attention.

"Now mister, I ain't got any interest in this lady." Cam looks over at the pouting girl. "Not at all."

"Don't look that way at me." Obe growls as he glares at their encircled hands, which Cam quickly tries his best to become unsnarled. "Not at all."

"You've got this all wrong, mister." Cam is still trying to extricate himself from the redhead's clutches. "I'm telling you."

Obe moves closer to the wagon and kicks the oak, wheel spoke. "Mister, I'm warning you for the last time, you best unhand my fiancé, quick like."

Cam can hear the cowhands in the back, snickering. He knows Betsy Sue Hammer is enjoying all the attention the men are paying her, especially Obe Wilson. He does not intend to fight over the redhead for her egotistical needs. For the life of him, he doesn't know how to get out of her conniving mess that entangles him.

Lifting the girl from the seat bodily, he dumps her unceremoniously from the wagon into Obe's outstretched arms. "You wanted her Wilson, there she is and you're welcome to her. Good-bye."

"Obe Wilson, are you going to stand there and let him insult me?"

"Not so fast, you Yankee scum." Obe grabs the lines. "Now you've done up and insulted a Hammer woman."

Cam knows the fat is surely in the fire now, as the Hammer riders start closing in all around the wagon. Looking down at the sullen group of men, he knows there is only one thing left to do, 'cause he sure can't run with all the horses tied to the wagon. Landing squarely on his feet in front of Wilson, Cam connects with a solid right, knocking Wilson senseless into the dirt before the foreman knows what is happening.

Everyman freezes in shock as their toughest fighter hits the ground after only one punch.

Betsy rushes to Wilson's side and kneels beside the prone man, looking down into his face. "You've killed him. You've killed my fiancé, Cameron Mitchell. You big bully."

Cam shakes his head as he watches five upset Hammer riders move in on him. "He ain't dead Betsy, just asleep, but you started it."

"Maybe I did, but I didn't mean for you to kill poor Obe," Betsy sobs. "I was just having some fun."

"I'm telling you, he's just asleep. He'll be fine in a minute or two."

Cam backs up against the wagon as the riders converge on him, swinging with both hands. The cowboys are so eager to land blows on the lone man, most of their fists miss their mark, some landing even on their friends. In the dust and savagery of the attack, Cam picks his shots as several blows rain down on him. A hard side kick sends one fighter to the ground, writhing in pain and holding his knee. A hard fist doubles Cam over as another just misses his head. Holding on to the wagon as he rises, Cam kicks out with both boot heels landing against a man's head, tearing a large gash along his forehead. With all the dust and viciousness of his attackers, Cam is not aware of the girl's screams until the roar of Caintuck's pistol goes off like a clap of thunder. Suddenly, the blows stop as the three men left standing back away from the wagon.

"A little fistfight, huh Shadrack?" Caintuck glares at the big rancher. "I ought to shoot you."

The big man stares quietly at the carnage around him and shakes his head in awe. "Peers to me like your man got the best of the fight, but you can shoot me if that'll make you happy."

Cam wipes the blood from his face and looks down at Obe Wilson. "No harm done, Caintuck."

"Yeah there is, let's go."

"Now Caintuck, we've been through a lot worse than this." Hammer pushes forward. "Let's all go to the house and have supper."

"You're right Shadrack, but I won't be having supper with you tonight." Caintuck holsters the forty-five. "We'll be heading out, right now."

Cam knows the two men have been good friends and doesn't want them to end their friendship over a simple fistfight. "Now Caintuck, you can miss supper if you're a mind to, but I've done worked up an appetite wrestling with these gentlemen."

"Now there's a man speaking sense." Shadrack Hammer laughs and pounds Caintuck on the back. "Mrs. Hammer fixed you a dinner fit for a king, Caintuck old friend."

Finally, as his temper cools, Caintuck backs out of reach of the big man's pounding and grins. "You boys talked me into it."

Cam watches as Caintuck and Shadrack Hammer start for the house without a backward glance. Obe Wilson is lying on the ground with the girl still holding his head. He knows Caintuck wasn't bluffing when he fired his pistol, but for now everything appears to have settled down. He has never seen the old horse trader as infuriated in all the time he has known him. Unhitching the team, he leads them and the other horses into a large corral and turns them loose. All is forgotten as the Hammer Riders wash their faces, help their injured friends get to their feet, and stand alongside the smaller corral. Now they are admiring the well-built Steeldust stallion Cam turned loose in the corral. Finishing with feeding the stock and the Steeldust, he glances over to where Wilson finally regains his feet and with the girl's help, finds a wooden box to sit down on to recuperate his senses. Cam shakes his head and starts for the house.

"Whew for a minute there I thought I was fixing to miss one of Mrs. Hammer's fine suppers." Caintuck smiles at Hammer as they sit down at the long table. "That was close."

Hammer grins back. "That boy of yours is pretty rough. Weren't any use missing a meal on account of him."

"I reckon." Caintuck sips on a cup of Mrs. Hammer's coffee. "He's been alone for many a year and had to learn to take care of himself."

"Well Caintuck, he's done learned real well," Hammer laughs. "I do believe, if we hadn't stopped it, he would have whooped all my boys."

"I wouldn't doubt that for a minute, Shadrack."

Caintuck nods, remembering the day Cam whipped Emmet Folsom in front of nearly the whole town of Garden City. Until that day, Folsom was the town bully, whipping almost every man in town. Now, after the beating Cam put on him, Emmet Folsom is rarely seen in town and when he does come to town, he avoids trouble and doesn't bother a soul. He grins, as he is proud of the boy because he holds his own and doesn't start any trouble like some toughs.

"I should have stopped it sooner old friend." Shadrack is serious. "I apologize for my poor manners."

"Well anyway Shadrack, I'm glad that it's over now."

"Obe didn't do so well, but at least he showed he cared about Betsy." Shadrack pulls out a Mason jar of clear liquid. "That's what counts."

Caintuck and Cam stay at the Hammer Ranch until well past midmorning the next day. They trade off two good cow horses, several horse blankets, and ropes, then pull out after eating a good breakfast. Obe Wilson never shows himself, but Betsy Hammer is her usual self, primping and preening in front of Cam when her father isn't watching. Finally, Caintuck and Cam shake hands with Hammer as their trading concludes and Cam turns the wagon toward the ranch gate.

Closing the wire gate behind them as they leave the Hammer Ranch they turn east on the larger road. Cam looks over to where Caintuck leads several of the saddle and work animals, then to where more are tied to the tailgate of the wagon he drives. Saddles, blankets, bridles, work harness, and all kinds of leather goods, made for the working cowman or farmer, completely fill the wagon. Even a few walking plows and horse collars sit in the oak floor of the battered old wagon. It rattles and groans noisily under the weight as it rolls across the rocky road. The gray stallion prances alone beside the wagon. They keep him far enough from the other animals to keep him quiet and stop him from fighting with the other geldings.

"Where we headed now?" Cam dabs black salve on several bruises on his face.

"We're gonna camp just ahead at sundown and throw together a hot meal." Caintuck looks at the youngster's puffy face. "Sorry about that little set-to back there last night."

"Weren't your fault."

"Yeah, it was. I should have listened to you." Caintuck spits. "Next time I will."

"Next time that little spitfire should be married and defanged."

"From what I seen the other night, Obe Wilson ain't man enough to defang that redhead."

"Shucks, I should have listened to me," Cam laughs. "It's over with now, ain't no damage done that won't heal up quick."

"There's a small pool of water ahead. We'll let the horses water up and graze, and I'll cook us a hot meal."

"Sounds good." Cam nods. "I'll soak these bumps and lumps."

"Keep the Steeldust in close boy." Caintuck nods at the gray stallion. "I sure don't want to lose him."

"I'll do that." Caintuck looks at the stallion trotting alongside the wagon. "He's a beauty, ain't he?"

"He's one of a kind, Cam." Caintuck nods. "He's the difference between success and failure for our new ranch."

"I believe it," Cam agrees. "Those boys back at Hammer's were sure impressed with him."

"They're good horsemen, they know horses."

"Are you looking for trouble out here?" Cam watches the older man studying the far hills and the east trail as they pull in next to a large pool of water.

After unsaddling and hobbling the horses, Caintuck kicks together several dry sticks and looks about at the scrub brush and the near mountains. "Out here you never know. Trouble could be just a short ways away. An animal like that stud will draw attention like stink draws flies."

The night is still and quiet as Cam and Caintuck finish their hot meal and sip on their coffee. Lying back on his blankets, Cam listens to the peaceful sounds of the night. He can hear the horses moving about in their hobbles, their molars nipping off and grinding on the heavy grass growing abundantly around the large spring fed water hole. Sitting back on his war bag, Cam looks off into the dark at the shapes of the grazing horses, then up at the brilliantly lit heavens above him. A man cannot help enjoy a night like this with the beautiful stars twinkling in the night and the sweet smell of the open range. Only the occasional yip of a lonely coyote breaks the silence of the night. Cam doesn't smoke, but he enjoys the smell of Caintuck's pipe as its aroma floats on the air around their camp.

"We're heading on to Garden City tomorrow?"

"Yep, I don't think we'll stop this side of her."

"Are you still thinking about the trouble at Hammers?" Cam smiles as he remembers Betsy, cradling Obe's head after the previous night's fight. "I hope Wilson is okay. I hit him hard."

"I didn't see him around this morning."

"Me neither."

"I figure he's okay. That girl wouldn't have been shining up to you this morning if he wasn't."

Cam shakes his head. "I sure wouldn't want to be him and married to that redhead."

"Amen to that too," Caintuck laughs. "A woman can be your worst nightmare one minute and your best friend the next. You can never tell about them."

"Have you ever been married, Caintuck?"

"Tried it once and that was it."

"What happened?"

"She forgot to mention she was already married. When I returned from a hunting trip, her other husband showed up and was eating my food at my table."

"You're joking?" Cam is about to burst out laughing at the look on Caintuck's face as he tells the story.

"Weren't nary a thing to joke about." Caintuck shakes his head. "It got mighty ticklish there for a minute or two."

"Well, for Pete's sake, spit it out."

"I shot the smart aleck, gathered my traps and possibles, and lit a shuck out of there." Caintuck puffs on his pipe. "That's all there was to it."

"You kill him?"

"Nah, but I figure he'd be mighty sore for a few days." Caintuck grins.

They travel along the winding road as it leads through the timbered mountains. Only the soft, muffled noise of many hooves, the trace chains jingling from the line of plodding horses, and the squeaking wagon disturbs the peaceful serenity of the early morning. Jays scold from the limbs and surrounding brush as the horses pass at a jog trot through their territory. Clouds start gathering to the west, just ahead of the wagon. Caintuck pays little attention, as any rain at all in this dry parched land would be welcome. A drought settled on several counties bordering Arizona and New Mexico for the summer. Not a drop has fallen in almost three months, making travel along the sandy roads a dusty and dry proposition at best.

Caintuck pulls his roan gelding to a halt and studies the fork in the road ahead. One road leads straight on, along the saddle back ridge road, while the other dips off the mountain and trails downward, leading down to the valley where buildings are barely visible far below. Caintuck picks his leg up and wraps it nimbly around his saddle horn while he pulls the makings from his vest pocket. His scraggly grey beard and lean brown face make the horse trader seem old, but the sharp, hard blue eyes of the man and the easy way he sits the slick saddle defy his age. Waving his arm, Caintuck motions Cam forward. Scratching a sulphur match against his worn chaps, the old trader looks over as the youngster pulls in the team of horses.

Cam pushes back his worn, dusty Stetson hat, letting a mop of unruly, black hair fall around his broad forehead. "Yes, sir." The dark brown eyes of the young man study the far distant buildings in the lower valley. The voice is soft with a pleasant and friendly drawl, which seems to match the quiet country they are passing through.

"Cam, we're gonna pass up Garden City this year." The blue eyes watch the clean face of his companion for a moment then look off down the road.

"Why Caintuck, you figuring there could be trouble?"

Nodding, Caintuck unfolds his bony leg and replaces it in the stirrup. "Maybe, you know the Folsoms. They ain't about to forget the whipping you gave Emmet Folsom last year when we passed through."

The dark hair blows in the slight breeze as the head bobs. "Yeah, I know the Folsoms, but that fight weren't my fault."

"No matter boy, it almost came to a shooting and selling a few horses ain't worth it." Caintuck blows a column of smoke from his mouth. "I don't want any more trouble after the Hammer incident."

"There's always been a good market in the valley for our horses."

Cam looks at the older man. "While we're traveling through the different towns, we're bound to find someone wanting trouble."

Caintuck nods and flips his burned-out smoke onto the road. "True enough, but not this time. We'll pass Garden City and move on, give the locals time to forget."

"Yes sir, you're the boss."

"You take the horses on to Sand Wells about five miles up in the mountains, water up and make camp." The older man hands the manila rope tied to the first horse in line and watches as the youngster dismounts the wagon and ties the rope off to the wagon. "I'm fixing to ride in and get us some more coffee and beans then I'll catch up with you about sundown."

"You watch out for the Folsoms, old man. They're as waspy as a pack of cur dogs." Cam looks fondly at Caintuck. "I ain't comfortable with you going in alone."

"You need anything, lad?" Caintuck grins. "Maybe a redheaded woman?"

"No, can't think of anything." Cam ignores the remark.

"Well, suit yourself young'un." Kicking the roan, the old man laughs and rides off, tossing a few words over his shoulder. "Don't worry none about the Folsoms. They sure ain't going to work up a lather on an old wore out skeleton like me."

"Just the same, you be careful." Cam watches as the calico shirt of the man disappears around the first switch back of the mountain trail.

Clucking to the team, Cam feels the tug on the wagon as the lead rope tightens then the string of horses start forward, following the wagon docilely. The two mules that belonged to Abe Johnson were traded already. The day before riding the palomino, Cam had been shoeing a horse at the livery when an old prospector came in wanting to buy mules to sell to the mining camps. After Johnson traded the mules to Caintuck, the prospector got what he wanted so Cam and Caintuck profited nicely from the sale.

The youngster looks over at the Steeldust stallion and nods, Caintuck knows horses and he acquired the best-blooded stallion found anywhere in the southwest. Well-muscled, a little over fifteen hands and clean-limbed, the horse is indeed a thing of beauty. Caintuck was gone almost a month, riding into Texas, almost to Indian Territory to purchase the stallion from a rancher he knew around Dallas. Smiling, he leans over and strokes the stallion's neck softly. The stud is the old man's pride and joy. The stallion will be the foundation for their horse ranch. A thing of beauty, Steeldust breeding runs through his veins, the best bloodlines a horse rancher could want. Cam can already picture the stallion running with his broodmares as free and wild as the blowing wind through the beautiful valley they were fixing to buy.

For five years, Cam rode with Caintuck, following him from town to town, riding bad horses, trading horses, or honing his riding skills while breaking the green colts Caintuck traded for. Looking up from time to time, from the rawhide reins he is plaiting as the team follows the well-marked road, Cam studies the flat, rough ground, the wagon is passing over. This part of Arizona is a dry and harsh land, but the air is fresh and sweet to his nose. Caintuck taught the youngster to live with the land, not fight it. Rain or shine, heat or cold, the old horse trader is always the same. He seems one with the land, enjoying it when he can, enduring it when the weather turned bad. Cam never heard the old trader complain about anything unless he ran out of something to wet his whistle or tobacco for his pipe. Cam has a sneaking suspicion that is what Caintuck's hurry to get into Garden City was all about. The last quart jar of homemade whiskey, Caintuck traded for from one of the locals, went bone dry many days before.

Cam smiles lightly, remembering the deal Caintuck made with the whiskey peddler they met on their travels through the countryside many months before. Ten jugs of pure homemade corn liquor would be theirs, all the old horse trader had to do was have Cam ride the edge off a small bay gelding while they made rounds to a few nearby ranchers. They shook hands all around then the whiskey disappeared into the wagon as Cam was saddling the bay. Pulling his hat down tight, Cam led the little horse away from the man's corral and stepped into the saddle. Nothing, not a jump; nothing. That old horse rode off as quiet as a sulled possum. The whiskey trader swore a blue streak until they were out of sight, saying he was cheated, but Cam rode the horse as agreed while they were in the vicinity. No one said anything about the horse having to buck. Caintuck laughed until he almost had a fit.

Patting on one of the whiskey jugs, he shook it a little and watched the bubbles the whiskey produced. "It's his fault. Any man afraid to get on his own horse should walk."

"He was taking the horse as a present for his woman back in the hills."

"That's even worse, swapping ten jugs of good coffin juice to impress a woman," Caintuck laughs. "That feller knows how to cook real whiskey, I'll give him that."

Cam becomes tired as he braids the leather reins, the serenity of the late afternoon and the easy motion of the wagon lulls the young rider into a sleepy daze. He is unaware of dust stirring up from several riders as they close in on him. Only the soft nickering of the stallion, as he senses the oncoming men, brings him wide-awake and alert. Instantly, Cam's dark eyes focus on the lathered horses as five riders whip their tired animals toward him. Slipping the tie down thong from his low-slung holster, Cam pulls the team up and waits for the horsemen to ride up. It is far too late to try to get out of sight, even if there was a place to go with so many horses. He can see the men watching him suspiciously as they slow down and come toward the wagon at an easy walk.

The five riders pull their worn out horses in, spreading out in a semi-circle in front of Cam. There is no doubt, these men are hard cases, outlaws that frequent this lonely backcountry and hide out in its harsh unsettled mountains. In front of him sits cold-blooded men, the kind of men that kill for little or no reason. They are hard men that don't need an excuse to kill, killers who show no mercy to the weak or helpless.

"Are you a horse trader, kid?" A little runt of a man sticks out his chin at the horses then answers his own question. "Yeah, reckon you are."

"Those horses broke to ride, mister?" Another rider speaks up before Cam can answer the first rider.

"I trade horses." Cam looks across at the big man who spoke to him. "They're all broke."

"What about that gray stud?" Another larger man with a lisp spits out, motioning at the Steeldust.

"What about him?" Cam studies the smaller man.

The biggest of the men pulls the forty-four pistol smoothly and points it casually as he thumbs back the heavy hammer. "We need horses, lad. Now we got nothing against you personally. Don't want to kill you, but we've no time for arguing or haggling with you so get yourself down off that wagon."

Cam stares into the big bore of the pistol and knows the man isn't bluffing. Climbing down from the wagon, he looks up at the man. "Well mister, if you put it that way, I do believe he is broke."

"Now then, that's better." The pistol slides smoothly back into its holster. "You got any ideas about that hog-leg you're carrying, forget it. These boys will cut you down before you get it out."

"Reckon I ain't got much choice." Cam clenches his jaw as he watches the men pull the saddles from their sweaty horses.

"You're a smart kid. You're right, you ain't."

"Are you planning on paying for the horses?" Cam addresses the big man who he figures is the leader of this bunch.

The outlaw leader smiles. "Shucks youngster, you're getting the best of the deal for your crow baits. Ours are all thoroughbreds, best horse-flesh in the country."

"Then why do you want mine?"

"You may be a smart kid, but you also got a smart mouth." The runt looks up, trying to look over the tall bay, he is unsaddling. "Ours are worn out, even you can see that."

Cam studies the long-legged horses. The man is telling the truth. They are all top-notch mounts, horses outlaws ride, animals that can outrun a posse that would pursue them. "They're good horses alright, but whose?"

A slender man squints his dead, grey eyes, as he looks up at Cam. "You got yourself a good eye for a horse kid, but just so you know, Jack Ketchum rides nothing but the best, and they ain't stolen."

Cam looks over at the big outlaw. Everybody in Arizona, Texas, and New Mexico heard of the outlaw. "Jack Ketchum!"

"You got yourself a big mouth, Giles."

"Don't take the stallion." Cam watches as the leader starts to saddle the gray.

"Why?"

"We need him, mister." Cam knows he is fixing to lose Caintuck's beloved and valuable animal as the one who seems to be the leader looks queerly at him. "Bad."

"So do I." The big man cinches his saddle up and looks down the trail as a cloud of dust starts to show itself. "I'm afraid, a lot worse than you do right now."

The smaller outlaw named Soapy, waves his pistol at Cam. "You just stand tight and don't make a move and you won't be hurt."

"Let's go Ketch, now." Giles speaks up as he watches the approaching riders. "That posse is getting too close for comfort."

"You boys lead the rest of them fresh horses for a ways until the posse gives up and turns back." Ketchum looks down at Cam. "The rest of your horses will be scattered somewhere in these hills, mister. You'll be able to round them up okay in a day or two."

"I thank you for that Ketchum. Ours are good animals too."

"Yes, they are."

"What about ours, Jack?" Soapy looks down disgusted at the worn out horses that they are fixing to leave behind. "These Thoroughbreds are the best we've ever had."

"Leave 'em. They're worn out and won't do that posse one bit of good." Ketchum looks at the sweaty horses. "You're right, they're good horseflesh."

"Yeah, a lot better than the hides we just traded for."

"True enough, but these horses are fresh with plenty of run left in them." Ketchum laughs, "I bet the posses' ain't."

"There's nothing wrong with our horses." Cam feels insulted the outlaws are insinuating they don't know horses. "They're all good mounts."

Giles jerks the horse he saddled cruelly, grinning down at Cam. "Sure hope that posse don't shoot you before you get a chance to wiggle your way out of this kid."

"Here, young man." Ketchum flips Cam a double eagle gold piece, then laughs as he turns the Steeldust and looks at the wagon. "We weren't expecting them to be after us so fast or follow us so long. It caused us to use up our horses on that long run out of New Mexico. You my boy were a sight for sore eyes, a mighty welcome sight."

"Thought you said they wouldn't follow us out of their jurisdiction and across the line." A tall, lean rider watches the approaching dust, rising over the trail.

"Well, now Cousin Len, even old Ketchum can be wrong now and again." The outlaw leader grins. "We better make tracks. Good luck, kid."

Cam watches the riders disappear down the narrow road. He looks down at the gold piece in his hand as several men ride up to him with their guns drawn and ready. Badges glitter in the early morning sun as the men close in on him.

"Who are you mister?"

"Cameron Mitchell." Cam looks into the cold eyes of the lawman. "Why?"

The sickening sound of a steel barrel hitting against Cam's head is heard as he is knocked backward, into the dirt. "Smart mouth, let's hang him now Sheriff and get after the others."

"Stop that, Harvey." Sheriff Andrew P Stark shakes his head and slowly dismounts. "We ain't got a tinker's chance of catching Ketchum and his bunch with them mounted on fresh horses. No sir, we'll never catch them now."

"There goes the bank's money," another rider swears. "I say we hang him for helping them."

Blood oozes from a large goose egg that starts to show on Cam's head as he stands shakily to his feet. "Hang me for what?"

"For helping Ketchum and his bunch rob the Elcho City Bank." The little deputy points his pistol at Cam. "They killed three men back in town, good friends of ours."

"I ain't helped anybody rob nothing."

"This proves different mister." One of the deputies holds out the double eagle Cam dropped into the dirt when he was hit. "Look Sheriff, here's a fresh minted gold piece just like the ones taken from the bank."

Cam leans wobbly against the wagon wheel and looks at the coin the deputy holds. "One of the riders gave it to me as a joke for taking my horses."

"That's a bunch of crap. Let's hang him Andy, save the county the trouble of a trial." The biggest deputy, Frog Coontz, takes down his lariat.

Taking the gold piece, Stark studies it for a second, then looks at Cam. "No, we'll take him into Garden City and lock him up, then let the judge do the deciding."

"To town!" Cam steps forward as the smaller deputy cocks his weapon. "What about my horses?"

"Now that's ripe mister, after you plan this little stunt with Ketchum, meeting him with relay horses so he can get away."

"You're a liar."

"Why you!" Harvey draws back his pistol for another swing, but doesn't reckon the speed of Cam's right hand, as the solid fist knocks him backward, onto the road.

"Now I recognize him, Andy." Another deputy speaks up and grins. "He's the young fellow we watched whip Emmett Folsom last summer over in Garden City when we picked up one of Ketchum's men from their jail." You remember the one Caintuck Waters took under his wing?"

"That's him alright. I remember that right hand and his face," another speaks up. "That doesn't mean he wasn't in on this little caper."

"I'll bet old Emmett remembers it too." One of the mounted deputies speaks up and laughs.

The smaller deputy, Harvey Clay, rolls to his feet, dabbing at his face. "I say we hang him now."

"I said we're taking him into Garden City and let Judge Leery hear his story." The Sheriff places the gold coin in his pocket. "We'll make sure Leery gets the full monte on this pigeon before we go on after this bunch. Let's head in."

"Tell us kid, did Ketchum pull this robbery and kill all those people because we hung his man last year for killing our liveryman?" Frog persists. "I ought to shoot you right now."

"You do Frog Coontz and I'll hang you myself right here and now." The Sheriff glares down at the little deputy, "Now, shut up."

Frog pales as he can see the cold look in Stark's eyes. "Shucks Andy, I was just trying to scare him into talking."

"You don't scare a man like this, Frog." One of the other deputies speaks up. "Not today or any day."

Caintuck sits outside the Garden City General Store, whittling on a short pine board while waiting for his order of supplies. The tired horses of the posse pass by where he sits, plodding down the street, then pulling up at the jail. Straightening in his chair, as he recognizes Cam and his wagon, the old horse trader closes his barlow knife and hurries across the broad street. Staring up at the wagon where Cam sits, Caintuck's eyes take in the large bump and bloody bruises on Cam's face and forehead before turning to where the sheriff is dismounting.

"What's the meaning of this Andy?"

"You men grab you some food, then saddle up some fresh horses and pick up Ketchum's trail." Stark climbs the steps onto the boardwalk with Cam in front of him. "I'll catch up with you soon as I see Sheriff Mason and get this gent locked up."

"I asked you a question, Sheriff Stark," Caintuck persists.

Ignoring the horse trader, Stark pushes Cam ahead of him, into the jail, with Caintuck dead on his heels. Inside, he turns to the two deputies sitting behind an old scarred up desk. Only seconds pass before another man, toting a badge, steps into the jail. "George Mason."

"Andy, what have you here." The fat sheriff shakes hands with Stark then looks Cam up and down, turning to Caintuck with a puzzled expression. "I know this boy."

"His name's Cam Mitchell."

Mason shakes his head. "I know that. Why is he here in my jail?"

"I believe he helped Jack Ketchum rob the Elcho Bank yesterday."

"Caintuck, ain't he your partner or something?"

"He is George and he hasn't helped anybody rob anything."

"I say he has." Andy Stark looks hard at Caintuck. "We caught him red-handed with Ketchum's used up horses."

Caintuck spits out the door. "Did you ask the boy what happened?"

"We asked him, alright. We got some fool story of his horses being stolen by Ketchum and his bunch."

"You didn't believe him, Andy?"

"Would you?"

Caintuck looks over at Sheriff Mason and shakes his head. "Dang fools, me and the boy just rode up from Hammer's spread this morning. There's no way we could have been anywhere near Elcho yesterday."

"Y'all had it planned, you old horse thief." Harvey Clay glares across at Caintuck.

"You want to step out into the street Harvey Clay, you little runt?" Caintuck taps his pistol butt and turns toward the door. "Bring that big mouth of yours with you, you yellow whelp."

"I'm a law officer. I can't be fighting with plain citizens," Clay mutters and backs down.

Caintuck looks over at Cam, ignoring the deputy's last comment. "What happened boy?"

"Like I told the sheriff here, Caintuck." Cam shrugs loose as a deputy pushes him toward the cell. "I was headed for Sand Wells, as you told me, when I ran smack-dab into Ketchum and his bunch. They swapped their worn out horses at gunpoint for our fresh mounts, then rode off."

"And?"

"Then this Sheriff and his brave deputies rode in, pistol-whipped me, and accused me of helping Ketchum." Cam stares at the cell. "They didn't want to hear my side of the story."

"Which one pistol-whipped you?"

Cam looks over at the shorter deputy. "I'll tend to that matter later."

"You ain't tending to nothing boy, but a necktie party." Clay steps forward with his pistol drawn again.

"Shut up, Deputy Clay." Sheriff Mason points at the cell. "Step inside that cell Mister Mitchell, now."

"Where's the Steeldust?" Caintuck watches as Cam is herded into a cell.

"I dunno, the gang took him with them. I don't know where." Cam shakes his head. "The big man, Ketchum, said he needed the stallion worse than we did."

Caintuck swears then turns on Stark. "Less than two hours after leaving this young man on the upper road, I arrived here in town, then you and your men come riding down the street."

"We ain't saying he robbed the bank." The small deputy grins. "We're saying he helped them killers get remounts and escape."

Caintuck looks over at the sheriff. "We've been on the road for a week, George Mason. We ain't seen or talked with anybody."

"You sure about that, Caintuck?"

"Both of you, George Mason and you, Andy Stark, have known me a long time. You know I don't lie. I'll testify to that in court." Caintuck shrugs. "You know dang well, I wouldn't be a party to robbing and killing."

Sheriff Mason stares across the room, then shakes his head. "Okay Caintuck, speak your piece. What are you saying happened?"

"Sounds simple enough to me, like the youngster here said, he ran into Ketchum by pure accident and our horses were stolen." Caintuck shrugs. "Wasn't a thing he could do about it. Believe me, if there was, he wouldn't have let them get away with that Steeldust stallion, as bad as we need him."

"You make it sound simple." Stark sits down tiredly in a swivel chair.

"It is Andy, plain as the nose on your face if you'd just wake up." Caintuck shakes his head. "Cam here ain't guilty of nothing but being in the wrong place at the wrong time. Ketchum and his bunch fought off the whole town of Elcho and killed three men in the process. You're thinking this youngster should have stood up to them alone without any warning."

Stark rubs his chin thoughtfully. "Maybe you're right, old man."

"Before today, I doubt he ever heard of Ketchum."

"Come on Stark, you ain't falling for that crap are you?" Clay and Frog, the deputies who stayed with Stark, speak up, as they turn red in the face.

"I told both of you to shut up."

"You through with me now, Sheriff?" Cam thinks Stark is convinced enough to turn him loose.

"Not yet, Mister Mitchell, I'll step over and have a talk with the local judge and let him decide." Stark looks over at Sheriff Mason. "Sheriff, you and Caintuck come with me."

"You boys stay with the prisoner until we get this hashed out." Mason nods at his deputies then pulls his hat from a peg near the door.

Before following the lawman, Caintuck watches as the little deputy walks close to the locked cell, staring at Cam. "He better be in one piece when we get back, Mister Clay."

"I'll baby-sit him real soft like."

"You better." Caintuck taps his pistol. "Or you'll answer to me and I won't be a plain ordinary citizen then."

Two hours later, after waiting for the judge to finish his supper in his quarters, Caintuck and the sheriff show him the gold piece. Then they give their separate versions of the happenings of the early morning. Agreeing with both men, the judge dismisses all charges against the prisoner for lack of evidence. Returning to the jail, Mason has one of his deputies bring Cam from his cell.

The Sheriff shoves Cam's pistol across the desk to him then nods. "You're free to go Mister Mitchell. I'm sorry about the roughing up you got."

"Does that door lead out back?" Cam nods at the back of the jail.

"It does."

"Good." Suddenly, Cam grabs the short Deputy Harvey Clay and slings him bodily into the door. Pulling the door open, he pushes the cringing man out into the back ally.

Knowing Cam and anticipating what is fixing to happen, Caintuck blocks the door as Stark, Mason, and the other deputy try to push their way out back where heavy blows are heard. "Boys, we'll just let them settle their own affairs."

Caintuck and Cam finish watering and feeding their horses, then walk over to the local café for supper. They both want to be on their way, but Ketchum took five of their best horses and ran off the other fifteen. They have to recover their horses.

Looking down at the plate full of potatoes and beefsteak, Caintuck shakes his head. "We've got to recover our horses before we pull out of these parts."

"They are a rough looking bunch." Cam knows Caintuck is fuming over the Steeldust. "They're just horses, not worth getting killed for."

"You really feel that way, Cam?"

"Peers to me, if we can round up our other horses, we'll only be down five."

"Without that stud, we can't start our horse ranch." Caintuck stares listlessly into his coffee cup. "I can't replace him."

"There are other stallions."

"Not like him, there ain't," Caintuck swears. "You can breed that Stud to a goat and get a real using horse. No sir, he's one of a kind and the only one with Steeldust breeding, I know of."

"You want him back that bad?"

"I aim to have that animal back, even if it kills me."

"Alright Caintuck, I'll get him back." Cam nods. "You ride out and pick up our other horses and I'll go after the stud."

"You can't go alone, Cam."

"You round up our horses. I'll bring him back to you."

"I can't let you go alone, boy," Caintuck protests. "You'll be up against too many."

"I'm going old man." Cam looks over his fork at Caintuck. "I'll bring him back to you."

"To us young'un, to us."

"After you get the horses, you rest your old bones and wet down your tonsils until I get back."

Sheriff Mason walks through the open door and approaches the table where the two men are finishing their meal. "You men mind if I join you?"

"Pick yourself a chair, Sheriff." Caintuck smiles for the first time today. "Take the load off your dogs."

"Thank you kindly, Caintuck."

"Are we in trouble again, Sheriff?" Cam looks at the older man as he takes a seat.

Waving the waiter off, Mason shakes his head. "No, just thought I'd let you know those horses Ketchum and his bunch swapped to you, are legally yours now."

"How's that?" Caintuck stops chewing, as he looks curiously at the Sheriff. "Who said?"

Mason smiles, laying a bill of sale on the table beside the old trader's plate. "Those ponies ain't hair branded or marked. There's been no report of any stolen horses matching them, so the judge made you out this bill of sale. They're yours, free and clear, to replace the stolen ones and for your imposition."

Caintuck picks up the papers and studies them a minute before placing them inside his shirt. "Well, now that's mighty generous of the judge. Thank him for us, George."

"I will." Mason looks across at Cam. "They're good horses. They may not replace the Steeldust stallion you've been talking about but they're mighty fine horses."

"You got any idea which direction Ketchum took after he stole our horses and rode out?"

Mason shakes his head. "Not yet lad, but Sheriff Stark and his deputies rode out this afternoon looking to pick up Ketchum's trail. They'll know something come morning, I 'spect."

"You didn't ride out with the posse, Sheriff?" Caintuck speaks absently as he swallows his coffee.

"Peers to me a waste of time. I figure by the time Andy and those boys catch up, they'll be across the state line and plumb out of my jurisdiction."

"That's it then, is Ketchum gonna get away with the money and killing those men?"

"I've sent out telegrams to the surrounding counties, but I doubt it'll do any good." Mason shakes his head. "Ketchum is a bad man. He leads a tough bunch and he's smart."

"He wasn't too smart, George. He took my horse and got me on his trail."

"Y'all going after the Steeldust, I reckon?"

"I aim to, come morning."

"Alone, just you and the youngster?"

"No Sheriff, just the youngster as you call him."

Mason smiles. "No offense Mister Mitchell, but compared to me, you are a youngster."

"No offense taken, Sheriff Mason."

"Ketchum's gang is a mighty rough bunch son. They killed three men in cold blood when they robbed the bank." Mason shakes his head. "Without help, you could be fixing to commit suicide."

"You're probably right about that Sheriff, but Caintuck has to stay behind and round up our horses, those boys scattered back in the hills." Cam smiles as he pushes back from the table. "I'll try my best to prove you wrong."

"Well Mitchell, I can only wish you luck. As I said, Ketchum and his bunch are probably out of my jurisdiction by now. Legally, I can't help you none."

Caintuck and Cam bed down in the corrals next to the horses for the night, but are up at the break of day. Mason shows up at the corrals, just as they are rolling up their bedrolls. He informs them, Ketchum and his men trailed off to the south, through Echo Canyon, heading for the Mexican border.

"Ketchum and his bunch ambushed Stark and his men ten miles or so from town. Two men were shot up pretty good, but they believe they got some lead in one of Ketchum's men before they got away. They just rode in and most are with the doctor now."

"Echo Canyon, that's mighty rough country down along the border," Caintuck swears. "Miles of Apaches, Mexicans, rattlesnakes, mountain lions, Gila monsters, and the men who ride the back trails.

"Yes it is, and just as I figured, way beyond my jurisdiction." Mason looks off to the south. "I figure Ketchum has a place down there somewhere in those mountains to lie low and lick his wounds."

"He probably does. He sure kept out of the law's hands for a long time now."

"Not too many lawmen or posse are willing to go too deep into that pest hole." Mason shrugs. "You should see how Stark's men looked when they came back, and they're mostly all good men with a gun."

"The Moore's place, the Rafter 5, is down there and they're respectable folks." Caintuck looks over at the sheriff. "At least that's the way I've always heard it."

Mason squints into the morning sun. "They are that, but old Angus Moore is probably rougher than any of those so called outlaws. Even the Apache learned to leave him alone, but one other thing keeps his place safe from men like Ketchum."

"What's that, Sheriff?" Cam is curious. He never met Angus Moore or been on his range.

"Angus lives by one rule and that is, he minds his own business."

"Live and let live, is that it?"

"You said it."

"Ketchum started this little party by stealing our horses. Now, I'll finish it."

"Mighty big job you've cut out for yourself, Mitchell."

"He's just a man, Sheriff."

"Yes, he is just a man, a man with a fast gun and a big reward on his head."

Caintuck pushes back his hat and grins. "How's old Harvey this morning? Did he ride out with Andy and the posse?"

"Sore, real sore." Mason shakes his head and grins. "No, he didn't ride out. He could barely see out of one eye and nothing out of the other, but he's moving about."

"He's lucky he can walk." Cam ties a leather thong around his blankets, remembering the pistol-whipping at the man's hands. "Caintuck, pick me out the best of them thoroughbred horses, Ketchum donated us, while I get a few supplies from the store."

"You really going, boy?" Caintuck shakes his head. "If we get our fifteen back and with these five horses of Ketchum's, we're ahead of the game."

"You said we had to have the Steeldust back, didn't you?"

"He ain't worth your life." Caintuck shakes his head. "We can't get our land down on the Pecos with you dead."

"Ain't he?" Cam nods and looks over to where the older men stand. "I want that ranch as bad as you do and I aim to have it. Now, it's a personal thing between me and Ketchum."

"How much money you figure you'll need?" Caintuck reaches in his pocket. "Most of our land money is in the bank in Gila."

"I've got enough. Just round up our loose horses and have them ready to go get our ranch soon as I get back." Cam smiles easily.

"You make it sound like a picnic you're heading out on." Mason frowns at the younger man.

"I'll be back." Cam starts toward town. "Get me a horse picked out, Caintuck.

"You wanna get some breakfast under your belt before you ride out?" Caintuck studies the retreating back.

"I'll grab me some crackers and a hunk of cheese at the store."

"That boy sure seems mighty set in his ways." Mason comments dryly as Cam walks away. "Mighty hardheaded young man."

"Don't sell that one short sheriff, he's pure poison with his fists or that forty-four he's toting once he gets his mind made up on something." Caintuck shakes out his blankets. "He's got cause. Andy Stark and his posse treated him rough and it was all Ketchum's doing."

"I'm inclined to believe you, Caintuck. I saw what was left of Emmett Folsom last year after they tangled." Mason laughs lightly. "Poor old Harvey's face this morning."

"Both of them had it coming."

Chapter 3

The powerful gelding Caintuck picked out is at least sixteen hands, deep chested, and clean-limbed. Cam checked the horse's shoes before riding away from Garden City and found they were on tight. Apparently, Ketchum and his men freshly reshod them before riding on to rob the Elcho Bank. After a few miles, Cam knows one thing about Ketchum, the man knows his horses as he has seldom ridden a better mount. It was only the day before the horse was ridden hard, but this morning he is fresh and ready to go. As the big gelding hits a running walk along the mountain road, Cam lets his eyes study the tracks that are plainly visible in the dirt. Many horses passed recently in both directions. Cam knows it was the posse following Ketchum and his men then they returned along the same path on their way back to Garden City with their wounded.

Shifting his gaze back along the mountain road, Cam ignores the tracks. Stark said his posse reported Ketchum heading for Echo Canyon so he figures that is where he will pick up the trail. Occasionally, he looks at the tracks and locates the larger print of the Steeldust, cutting deep into the soft trail. Cam's thoughts settle on the stallion. He knows Caintuck was right; they can never replace the studhorse, as they need him for their new ranch.

Cam shifts slightly in his saddle. He has ridden this trail, pushing horses with Caintuck, heading for the next town or some remote ranch on several occasions. Those days were free of danger, except for a rattlesnake or maybe getting bucked off and landing atop an unforgiving rock. No, today he has to be alert for anything moving, man or animal. Ketchum and his killer gang are somewhere ahead. Maybe they were already past Echo Canyon, which is twenty or so miles ahead. Cam knows they could have doubled back to throw the Posse off their trail and confuse whoever else is following them. He was caught napping and under their guns once, he didn't aim for it to happen again.

As the sun settles over the mountaintop, it feels good on his back as the day starts to warm. At midmorning, Cam notices the paw print of a large mountain cat that stopped to investigate the different smells along the road earlier this morning. Young colts are snatched from the many small herds of wild horses roaming these mountains and valleys. They are a main feast for the cougars roaming the wild uncharted reaches along the Mexican border of Arizona and New Mexico. Cam knows these cats are territorial, sometimes covering over five hundred miles around the boundaries of what they consider their territory. Willing to defend their marked territory, they check continually for any interlopers. The big cats are known to attack a man on horseback during a time of scarce game, drought, or if they are old or injured. As he passes, Cam studies the many outcroppings of rock along the road to make sure a cat isn't waiting, ready to spring on an unwary traveler. He knows it is unlikely a cat will attack, but there has been a drought in these parts, so he stays alert. The gelding's sense of smell will give him notice if a cat is lurking anywhere on the remote road.

It is almost noon as the sun starts to heat up enough to cause the gelding to work up a sweat. Reining in at a small spring fed trickle of water, he slips the bridle from the horse and lets the animal graze along the banks for almost an hour. He knows, a few miles ahead, where the road forks off to the west; Angus Moore has his remote, Rafter 5 M Ranch. He plans to ride in to determine if the rancher knows anything about Ketchum and his gang. He and Caintuck spent the night with Moore and his son last fall, swapping their younger horses for Moore's old and worn out ones with a little boot thrown in. Some ranchers back in these remote reaches are a little shady. Some are downright thieves and rustlers and are known to hide and protect the outlaw element riding the, almost inaccessible, mountain ranges. The grandson, Bob Moore is not an outlaw, nor is he the least shady. The man is just a hardworking cowboy, true to his brand. He came into these mountains many years ago to live with his grandfather and take over running the Rafter 5 from Angus Moore. Cam heard Caintuck say, on many occasions, that Angus and Bob Moore are as tough as they come, but they are also as honest as the day is long.

After a hard afternoon's ride, the low evening sun finds Cam riding in the front yard of the Rafter 5. Dusty, tired, and hungry, Cam reins up in front of the half rock and half log ranch house, causing several rangy lion hounds to come bellowing and growling from under the house. While the hounds circle the tired gelding, Cam watches the door of the ranch house swing open slowly, letting a stout built, middle-aged man, exit and walk across the porch.

"It's me Mister Moore, Cam Mitchell."

"Cam, it is you; light and rest your saddle son." Bob Moore kicks and hollers at the hounds, running them back under the porch. "Where's old Caintuck?"

"We've had trouble Mister Moore so he's back in Garden City." Cam dismounts and shakes hands with the Rancher.

"Let's see to your horse then you can tell me all about it if you wish." Moore motions toward the barn. "It's good to see you."

Cam pushes back from the long dinner table and smiles contentedly at Louise Moore, who sits across from him. "That was an amazing meal, Mrs. Moore."

The woman smiles, the deep blue eyes crinkling at the edges. "Men with good appetites are a real pleasure to cook for Cam."

"Thank you, ma'am." Cam looks across at the skinny, weather-beaten old cowboy sitting beside Bob Moore. "Cooking like yours makes a man have a good appetite."

"Yeah, especially when a man hasn't eaten all day, it makes a man's appetite even sharper," the old man pipes in sarcastically.

"Cam, I don't reckon you've ever met my granddad, Angus Moore." Moore nods at the older man. "Believe he was in bed with a broken leg last time you and Caintuck passed through."

"Well, I hope it mended alright." Cam smiles at the old man. "How'd you break your leg, Mister Moore?"

"I tried riding a young horse." The old man shakes his head. "The leg's fine, thank you."

"You're still riding broncs at your age, sir?" Cam is curious, as the old one has to be at least in his eighties.

"Sonny, I was busting broncs before you were hatched and probably will be when you're in a rocking chair." The hard-crusted old rancher grunts.

Cam grins. "Yes sir, I just bet you were, but aren't you a little old now for that line of work?"

"Old? Why you young squirt."

"Okay, Grandpa, eat your supper." Bob Moore can only shake his head at the feisty old man and grin. "You are too old for young horses, especially one like that black devil out there."

Only grumbling and the sound of a knife and fork, stabbing at his plate, can be heard from the old man as he turns his attention to his supper.

Angus Moore moved into these mountains long before the main band of Apaches quit warring on the white settlers. First, he panned and dug for gold, and later, after finding this small valley with its good grass and water, he drove cattle into the mountains and started the Rafter 5 brand. After the death of his son and the letter from the boy's mother arrived, Angus rode to Tucson and brought the boy back here to the Rafter 5, raising him here on the ranch. Bob Moore was waiting for him at the sheriff's office when he arrived in Tucson. Nothing was said of his mother or of the men who shot down and robbed his father, Jim Moore. Six months later by persons unknown, word spread around Garden City and other small towns, three men thought to be linked with Jim Moore's death, were mysteriously hung outside the wild town of Tombstone. Leastways, that was the way the paper wrote it up. Nothing more was ever seen or heard of the boy's mother. Everybody knew Angus Moore was a crusty, tight-lipped old pioneer, meaner than a mama grizzly bear with cubs and better off left alone. Law officers decided to let the matter drop, rather than ride back into the Apache infested mountains to question the rancher. Cam studies the weather bitten old face and knows trying to get anything out of Angus Moore about the loss of his horses or Ketchum would probably be useless.

Just recently, an uneasy truce with the Apache under Cochise has been made, even though a young warrior known as Geronimo, still raids the ranch on occasions. Angus hired the toughest cowhands he could find to work for the Rafter 5. It didn't take long for even the wily white hating warrior himself to keep clear of the ranch, unless it was just an occasional theft of a horse or cow. Unlike his hard-nosed old granddad, Bob Moore, let the small thefts go unpunished, as long as no one attacks or threatens the ranch. Never a night passes that a lookout isn't posted somewhere around the ranch, keeping a lookout for hostile warriors from the ranch house windows or the bunkhouse.

Cam smiles thoughtfully as he swallows the thick black coffee in front of him at the table. He remembers many a smoky campfire, sitting across from Caintuck, listening to the old buffalo hunter, now horse trader, tell tales of a younger Angus Moore whenever they passed through these mountains. The stories spoke of the hardness of the rancher, and few of the tales were pleasant.

"Now, off to the porch with all of you." The plump little Louise Moore stands up. "I know you've got important things to talk about and I've got dishes to do."

"You need help, ma'am?" Cam offers.

"No young man, but thank you," Louise looks at her two men and grins, "It's nice to have a gentleman offer."

The hounds sniff and mill about the plank porch as the three men find seats and lean back against the walls of the house. Cam looks across the yard where several cowhands play a game of horseshoes beside the log bunkhouse.

"I appreciate the supper and you taking care of me and my horse for the night, Mister Moore."

"Old Caintuck has been coming through here trading horses and hunting since before you were born. He's always been welcome." Angus looks down at the hounds. "If you're half the friend he's been, young man, you're welcome the same."

"Thank you, I appreciate the hospitality." Cam pets one of the pups. "You've got some good-looking pot lickers here."

"They earn their keep up here for sure. The big cats in these mountains would bring down a lot of beef if I didn't have them." Bob Moore pushes one of the pups away from him as it tries to get in his lap. "Louise spoils them rotten when they're little, letting them sit in her lap."

"She's a sweet woman."

"Yes, she is," Angus growls. "She'd be even better if she'd leave my dogs to be dogs."

"You've got a beautiful ranch here. With a woman like her beside you, it's got to be a great place to live."

Bob Moore nods, then changes the subject. "Tell me the trouble you spoke of Cam."

Cam quickly tells of the robbery and killings in Elcho City and the loss of Caintuck's horses, especially the Steeldust stud. "That's why I'm here, Mister Moore."

"Do me a favor Cam; just call me Bob."

"Alright, Bob it is."

"Now, what do you want us to do for you?" Angus Moore coaxes a scarred up hound to him. "You need petting or something."

Cam looks to where the old man sits, smoking on his corncob pipe and examining the cuts on the hound's head. "I'm looking for Jack Ketchum. I just wondered if you might know where he might be holed up is all."

Only a glance comes from the old rancher's faded blue eyes as the words are spoken. "Go home young man, while you can."

Cam pulls at a pup's ears and nods. "Nope, can't do that Mister Moore."

"Can't or won't," the gravelly old voice sounds again. "There's a difference, boy."

"Won't. Ketchum stole five of our horses and rode off with them." Cam stands up and walks to the edge of the porch frowning. "He took one very valuable studhorse and got me pistol-whipped pretty bad to boot. No sir, Mister Moore, I ain't going anywhere but straight into these mountains after him."

"That hurt your pride, did it?" Angus grunts then laughs. "Better your pride boy than your hide."

"I understand why Ketchum took our horses. If I were a thief and killer with a posse chasing me, I probably would have done the same. Make no mistake, Mister Moore, I aim to get that stud back, come hell or high water."

"Well, you try it youngster and you're liable to catch hell and high water both," Angus quips sarcastically.

"We saw the horse," Bob Moore speaks up. "He's sure something all right."

"Then Ketchum was here?"

"He was and we patched up one of his men and Ketchum rode on."

"Mountain lions are pretty tough customers, youngster. Five or six full-grown hounds can't whip one, kinda like Ketchum," the old man speaks up, looking squarely at Cam. "One pup sure ain't gonna whip him."

"Reckon that depends on how much grit the pup has in him, don't it?" Cam can sense the old man's contempt of his youth. "Do you know which way he rode out?"

"Same way you rode in probably then turned toward the border at the cross trails down below." Moore can see the fire in Cam's eyes. "Don't pay attention to Gramps."

"Was Ketchum's man hurt bad?"

"Bad enough; I figure too bad to be riding far."

"Then he is close or their hideout is close." Cam rubs the pup absently.

"Wouldn't count on it, bub. You best ride back out of these mountains while you can." Smoke rolls from the old man's mouth. "Like I said, that Steeldust won't do you much good if you're dead."

"No disrespect, Mister Moore, but I've come a long way after that horse and I ain't leaving without him, and right now, I feel very much alive."

"Your funeral, bub." The old man stretches. "Well, it's bedtime for these old bones."

Moore and Cam say goodnight then watch as the old rancher goes inside. "He's survived these mountains by using one motto."

"What's that, Bob?"

"If it doesn't concern the Rafter 5, we mind our own business."

"I understand your position, trying to run a ranch alone, way out here among the Apache and the outlaws." Cam stands and looks toward the bunkhouse. "Don't blame you one bit."

Moore looks off in the same direction. "I'd be kinda closed mouth over there, if I were you."

"Ketchum has friends, huh?"

"Money buys loyalties, sometimes even from honest men." Moore nods. "For the most part, they're loyal to the Rafter 5, but there could be one or two that ain't."

Cam shrugs. "I never knew a truly honest man that would take stolen money or side with a killer like Ketchum."

"Ketchum is a killer, but he hasn't killed here." Moore nods. "You know he used to be a fair hand at cowboying."

"I've met Mister Ketchum and he is a likable sort, but I aim to get that stud back if I have to walk over the man's grave."

"Take breakfast with us before you ride out." Moore stands up. "Find you a bed over at the bunkhouse for tonight."

"Thank you, I'll check on my horse first, then turn in."

"Hey, bub." Cam starts to leave, then turns to where Angus Moore reappears in the doorway and calls to him. "You want some information? Well, I have a horse out in the corral that needs breaking. You ride him before you ride out and you'll get information, anything you want to know."

"What if I don't ride him?"

"Then I'll figure you're yeller and you can just tuck your tail and get back down the trail the way you came in."

"I see, Mister Moore." Cam grins. The old rancher doesn't leave him much room; either ride the black or just ride. "I expect it was the horse that broke your leg."

Angus cusses under his breath and disappears back inside the house without answering. Bob Moore steps up beside Cam. "It's the same horse alright, twelve hundred pounds of pure dynamite."

"Pretty rank colt, huh?"

"I've never seen anything that can buck like him. Powerful, full of pure meanness and hate, old Thunder can sunfish and turn upside down on you in a blink." Moore nods. "The horse is downright dangerous and hurt many a man here, but Granddad raised him and won't let me get rid of him. I'd dang sure shoot him if he was mine, but he doesn't belong to me."

"He sounds rough."

"He's got a good bloodline in his lineage, foaled out of one of our finest mares." Moore grows serious. "The old man tried to ride him after he hurt two of our best bronc riders and put them in bed."

"Y'all let him ride something like that?" Cam is amazed.

"We were out on the range and didn't know a thing about it. Only he and Louise were here at the ranch." Moore shakes his head. "She found him outside the corral where that colt deposited him."

"If I'm here in the morning, I'll try him on for size." Cam nods. "Your old man didn't give me much choice in the matter, if I'm to get any information."

"Caintuck said you were good. His bragging on you got under Granddad's skin, I think." Moore grins. "I figure you're good alright, but if I were you, I'd ride on before daybreak. This is one animal that won't be ridden."

"I'll sleep on it tonight."

After checking on his gelding, Cam crosses to the Rafter 5 Bunkhouse, finding it lit up by two coal oil lamps. One of the lamps is above a poker table, shining light on a table where four men are playing cards. Cam notices they use beans for money; some call them cowboy gold. Any old-timer riding the grub line would tell you if you were starving in the middle of a snowstorm, beans come in a lot handier than money. Every eye in the room turns to the newcomer, sizing him up as he tosses his bedroll on the end of an empty bunk.

"Evening, boys."

Heads nod, but few speak as he makes his way to where a well-used coffeepot sits steaming atop the wood stove. Pouring himself a cup of the black liquid, he pulls out a seat next to the poker players and sits down.

"You're the young feller that rode in here with Caintuck last fall, ain't you?" An older rider speaks up without taking his attention from the game. "I remember you."

"I'm him alright."

"You wanna play?"

"No sir, can't afford the beans."

A grin comes from the rider as he shuffles the well-used cards. "Don't blame you. These fellows are kinda shady."

"Deal Kirby and shut up," a rough bearded, middle-aged man, with his black hat pulled low so Cam couldn't see his face.

"Huh, oh must have struck a nerve." The friendly cowboy grins and nods at Cam. "Man's sure in a hurry to lose his beans."

Cam studies the gruff speaker for several seconds as he tries to place what seems like a familiar voice. He then averts his attention to a slender figure, just a boy, lying in a bunk close to the stove.

"Howdy." Cam can see the paleness of the man's face. "Feeling poorly?"

"He's fine." The gruff poker player at the table raises his face, cutting his hard eyes at Cam. "Leave him be."

"Just being friendly; no harm intended."

Cam can see the white bandage that crosses the sick man's chest and what looks like bloodstains in the dimness. The darkness and shadows of the bunkhouse keep him from being certain. Rising, Cam walks back to his bunk and pulls off his boots and gun belt. Riding the bad horse, come morning, crossed his mind and was dismissed, but now, maybe he would give it a shot. If the stains are blood on the man across from him and he is wounded, it was probably a gunshot wound. If that's so, then it could be the outlaw the Stark posse got lead into when Ketchum ambushed them. The outlaw leader is known for his loyalty to his men. The gruff poker player is probably another of Ketchum's men, left behind to watch over the wounded one. Maybe riding the horse, come morning, would be a good excuse for staying longer at the Rafter 5, so he could nose around a little.

Rolling out his bedroll, Cam lays back and stares at the rafters crossing the shingle roof. The poker players look his way several times, then turn their attention back on the game. Cam pulls his hat across his face and closes his eyes.

The aroma of boiling coffee and frying bacon as he nears the ranch house makes his stomach growl with hunger. Louise meets him on the front porch and points out the washstand before ushering him inside the warm kitchen.

"My mama taught her young'uns, cleanliness is next to Godliness." The little woman smiles at him. "Wash behind your ears."

"Yes, ma'am," Cam laughs aloud. "You're sure up early, Miss Louise."

"My mama also taught her young'uns, the early bird always gets the worm. Now, young man, get yourself to the breakfast table." The heavyset woman smiles and ushers him into the warm kitchen.

"Don't know about the worm, but I'll surely take some breakfast," Cam laughs as Bob Moore and his granddad enter the door.

"Well, young feller, you're still here." Angus pulls out his chair. "Reckon you decided to ride old Thunder this morning."

"After a good breakfast to weigh me down, I can't lose."

"Well, I always heard a man gets his last meal before hanging," Angus snickers.

"Don't take it wrong, but I hoped you'd be long gone, Cam." Bob Moore takes his seat. "Pull up a chair."

Angus slaps his leg and laughs. "Oh, he's gonna be long gone when that bronc gets through with him."

Cam knows his pockets are as empty as a dried up well, if he wants to wager anything, but he has to dig at the old rancher some. "You pretty sure of that, Mister Moore?"

"I'm sure enough to bet on that horse, sonny."

"How sure are you, sir?"

"A hundred dollars, if that ain't too rich for your pockets?" Angus looks across the table, never blinking an eye. "You got the sand to bet a hundred, lad?"

"Now Granddad, you know you're putting Cam in the line of getting hurt," Moore speaks up. "Besides, cowhands don't normally carry much money around with them."

"No, I ain't. He could have ridden out before breakfast. If he's yeller then he should have been long gone this morning," Angus blusters. "I ain't holding a gun on the youngster, am I?"

Cam picks up his coffee cup and nods at the old rancher. "You've got a bet Mister Moore, but remember, you promised me some information on the Steeldust too."

"Good, good. I've been needing a new pair of boots for a spell now." Angus nods sharply. "You got a hundred, boy?"

"Maybe I do, but I doubt I'll need it."

"You're awfully sure of yourself," the old man snorts. "You ain't even laid eyes on your opponent yet."

"He's just a horse with four legs, ain't he?"

"He's a horse alright," Angus laughs a quick yip then nods. "For a fact, sonny boy, for a fact."

Bob Moore didn't overstate the size and power of the black horse that watches warily as they approach the round corral where he stands hipshot. Coal black, he stands a good sixteen hands high, deep of girth, broad hipped, and powerful. A wide white blaze runs the length and breadth of his broad head. The animal could be an outlaw, but he is a magnificent piece of horseflesh. The only flaw Cam can see in the horse, if one wanted to call it a flaw, is the one glass eye that stands out like a bright new penny. He has never liked a white-eyed horse. He was told they couldn't see well on the night of a full moon. Cam doesn't know that for a fact, as he has never ridden one, but that's what the old-timers swore by. It was similar to a horse with four stocking feet. Old-timers said to leave them be, but he found out that was just an old wives' tale. It doesn't matter today since he isn't riding the horse's eye. The black definitely has one glass eye and he has it pegged, dead center on the men looking at him and it is broad daylight. He doesn't figure the animal will have one bit of trouble seeing him.

The bunkhouse door swings open with a bang, as the Rafter 5 Cowhands hurry from their breakfast after the old cook Nellie, spots the Moore's and the stranger looking over the black. They heard Caintuck brag on this youngster's riding ability last year when they were here and they heard tales of him in the surrounding towns. Figuring what is fixing to happen, they sure aren't about to miss the show, not one second of it. Almost every man on the Rafter 5, except the cook has tried to ride old Thunder. The black is an outlaw and powerful. Not one man has gotten himself set in the saddle when the horse dumped them.

"Dang, that youngster is dumber than I figured, if he aims to try old Thunder." The friendly poker player from the night before leads the riders at a quick walk toward the corral. "Any of you boys got any loose money you want to wager on the youngster?"

Not a word comes from the watchers as Bob Moore looks uneasily at the horse then over at Cam. "Take my advice and ride out. The black is loco and won't be ridden."

"I probably should, but I'd be the laughingstock of the range if I did." Cam grins as he studies the big animal. "Yep, I probably should."

"Yes, you should, bub." Angus grins, believing Cam to be backing down. "You might be the laughingstock, don't know about that, but at least you'd be in one piece and alive laughing."

"A man with no pride ain't alive, is he?" Cam looks over at the expectant faces. "No, sir, Mister Moore, I've come too far now to back out."

"Well, it's your funeral son, good luck." Moore motions at the rider named Kirby then at the horse. "Get a saddle on him, Kirby."

"If you don't mind Kirby, I'll saddle him myself."

"Alone?"

"Yes sir, alone."

"Alright, it's your party." Cam can tell the rider seems relieved.

Cam turns to where Angus is sitting. "I aim to ride your horse, Mister Moore, but my way. Is it agreed?"

"Long as he ain't tied down sonny, you ride him any way you want." The old rancher laughs lightly, then grins over to where the other men wait expectantly. "Better use some mighty powerful medicine, is all I've got to say."

"It doesn't take medicine, just good balance, and a little know how."

Picking out a good lariat from the corral posts, Cam waits as Kirby opens the gate and then walks through. He hardly steps inside the gate when the black explodes and charges at him with his ears laid flat and his mouth open. Clearing the pole corral, Cam lands outside the enclosure as the horse slams into the poles, trying to reach him.

"You can't ride him from this side, sonny," Angus roars, laughing as he slaps his leg. "That ain't fair."

Kirby shakes his head as Cam nods toward the gate. "It normally takes about three of us to saddle that killer."

"Just work the gate, I'll manage."

"You got anybody you want us to send your remains to?" The old rancher is having himself a time. "What's left of them?"

"Grandpa, that's enough," Bob Moore speaks up, irritated, thinking Angus is just trying to get Cam hurt.

Cam hesitates at the gate and looks at Kirby. "Tell me, how did that old man get a saddle on the black alone?"

"He didn't. He outfoxed us and told us to saddle the horse and leave him tied until we got in off the range." Kirby grins. "He told us it'd help take the edge of the colt fighting it."

"Then when you left, he tried his luck, huh?"

"That he did." Kirby nods. "I'll give you a piece of advice; when you and him part company in there, and you will, you better be running when you hit the ground or he'll paw you into next week."

"Thank you, Mister Kirby, I'll try to remember your advice."

Cam steps through the gate again, but this time he has his loop ready when the horse charges. Climbing nimbly up the corral pole, he swings the rope and lets it go, catching the turning horse by the left hind leg. Quickly dallying the rope around the bottom of a heavy upright post, he pulls his slack and jerks the fighting black's leg out behind him. Racing down outside the corral, he grabs another coiled rope and races to the front of the lunging horse. Pulling hard on the rope, holding his hind leg, the black doesn't try to back up as another loop settles around his neck. Taking slack from the rope, Cam circles the snubbing post in the center of the breaking pen and snubs the horse tight. Stretched out in the way he is, old Thunder is caught tight. He can't bite, kick or jump without throwing himself. Cam waits as the horse settles down. One thing is sure; the animal isn't a complete idiot, as he doesn't try to fight the ropes holding him.

"You boys got a saddle I could borrow?" Cam looks over at the shocked faces.

"We got one." The gate swings open as another hand, hurries in with a high backed, heavily scarred rig and a hackamore.

"You watch him, mister. He'll roll on you quick as a cat." Kirby gives his advice as he is working the gate.

"Thank you, just turn him loose when I get aboard."

Only a deep moaning grunt comes from the black's throat as Cam positions the saddle and pulls the cinch tight. Letting the horse blow a few times, he takes up a little more slack then finishes tying the girt. He tries several times with the hackamore. Cam has to keep away from the snapping teeth as he places the rope bridle on the enraged horse.

"Well old son, I reckon we're ready, at least I am." Cam pats the already sweaty neck. "Turn him loose and clear out when I get aboard."

"Don't you worry about me, mister. I'll be outta here before that rope hits the ground."

Pulling his hat down tight, Cam takes up the plaited hackamore reins and in one fluid motion, is in the saddle. Nodding as the rope drops, he jerks the loop from the black's neck, freeing his head. The back rope will be kicked loose as soon as the horse knows he is free. Letting his body relax, waiting for the explosion, he knows is coming when the horse feels the ropes loosen, Cam takes a deep seat and a firm hold on the hackamore reins. He can feel the power beneath him. With the sudden release of the ropes, the black launches himself forward, then just as quickly, he rolls, throwing himself into the air and over backward, intent on landing atop the man on his back. The sudden impact of the sandy corral, as the black lands atop the empty saddle, causes the horse to be addled as his head slams hard into the dirt. Temporarily stunned from the hard lick, the horse starts to his feet when the hard boot heel of the rider lands twice against his tender ear.

Scrambling to his feet shakily, the horse is not finished. He is still full of fight. He feels the man again on his back and ducks his head, bawling and bucking across the corral. Cam has been on bad horses before, but none can compare to this black. A loose stirrup catches him in the mouth as the horse rolls, causing his lip to bleed freely, dripping blood down the front of his shirt. Again, the Black sunfishes sideways, but this time, he doesn't straighten himself, but lands with a hard thud on the ground. Cam kicks loose again, from the saddle and kicks the horse hard on an exposed ear until the black regains his feet. Suddenly, as the horse bucks to the left, the head snakes back, grabbing at the rider's leg, only to be met by a hard kick to his tender nose.

The black screams and bawls in rage as he bucks. Never has he had a man on his back he couldn't dislodge, one way or the other. He finds the ground a rough place to be as the human kicks away at his tender ears and nose when he is down. Bucking along the pole corral, the horse lunges hard into the poles, trying to drag the rider from his back. With a last surge of power and fury, the black launches himself into the poles, as the watching riders stare aghast as the horse paws himself clean through the corral, knocking the broken and splintered poles to the ground.

Stumbling to his knees, the black regains his footing outside the broken corral then again, starts bucking across the flatland, leading down the valley. Cam is tired beyond belief, but he can also feel the ebbing strength of the fighting horse as well. He knows as soon as the black bucks across the small valley and tries to run, the last of his strength will be gone. The horse is finished; beaten. Cam doesn't like doing a good horse this way, but the black is an outlaw, a fighter that only knows to fight. Maybe now, with a lot of work and a strong firm hand, he would make a good horse.

Out of sight of the ranch buildings, the horse slows, barely crow hopping across the grassland, until at last, Cam pulls him in a circle and to a stop. Stepping warily to the ground, he loosens the cinch, letting the hard blowing horse catch his air. Only once did the black try to nip at him and then a sharp blow to the tender nose, changes his mind. Looking down at his bloody shirt, Cam pats the sweaty neck and grins.

"You're something old feller, but you're dead game, I have to give you that."

Pulling the cinch back tight, Cam dodges a cow-kick as he steps into the saddle and starts back toward the Rafter 5. The black is exhausted from the long fight. Cam's arms and leg muscles feel like noodles; both have been through a war. Cam doesn't know who looks worse, the sweat stained horse or himself, all blood splattered and disheveled.

"Here they come, Boss." Kirby points down the valley from what remains of the corral fence as Cam and the black come slowly into sight. "He looks a little beat up, but he's riding that horse."

"Well Granddad, reckon there went your new boots," Bob Moore laughs and walks a few steps toward Cam and the oncoming black. "I'll say this, that boy is a sure enough bronc rider."

Only a slight grin comes from the old rancher as he mutters. "Well Caintuck, reckon you weren't lying about the boy being tough."

Cam brings the black back to the corrals in a slow walk, giving him time to cool out. Stepping down from the saddle, he still keeps a close watch on the horse's teeth. Handing the reins to Kirby, he smiles as the cowhand nods.

"Cool him out for me, would you, Mister Kirby?" Cam hands him the braided reins of the hackamore. "Watch him, as I believe he's half alligator the way he bites."

"Sure thing, Cam." Kirby leads the black warily toward the barn. "That was some ride, I'll tell you."

"I agree, Cam Mitchell that was some ride." Bob Moore extends his hand. "I never saw the likes in my whole born days."

"That is some horse." Cam looks to where the horse is led away. "I need a drink."

Angus Moore walks up in front of the two and nods. "I believe I owe you some money young man and an apology."

"No, sir, you don't owe me a thing." Cam looks at the old rancher. "If I lost that bet, I couldn't have paid off on it. I'm broke."

The confession brings a smile, then a laugh from Angus. "Well, I'll be, sounds just like old Caintuck."

Cam looks around for the rough talking rider who sat in on the poker game last night. He didn't see him around the corral and he is curious. With all the noise and dust, any cowman in Arizona would have been out watching the show. In any community in the west, an outlaw horse always draws a crowd whenever someone tries their luck riding him. A bad horse is almost as notorious as a bad outlaw. People are drawn to them like bees to honey. Cam is curious why the man didn't make an appearance this morning.

Moore notices Cam is studying the bunkhouse and the other riders. "I'm afraid they're gone already, Cam."

"When did they pull out?"

"Right after you came to the house for breakfast." Moore offers Cam a dipper of water. "Nellie came and told me Len Fox was sure in a hurry to leave."

Angus steps closer and looks up into Cam's face. "I made a deal with you, Mister Mitchell and I always keep my word. I didn't think you were man enough to take your horses back from Ketchum, but now I'd have to bet on you, young man."

"Thank you, Mister Moore." Cam nods. "I aim to try my best."

"Here's your money, no arguing." Angus hands over a fistful of gold coins. "You'll find Ketchum and your horse due east of here, maybe ten miles in what looks like a box canyon."

"But it ain't really a dead end canyon?"

"Nope, just looks that way." Angus shakes his head. "There will be a stand of mountain cedar hiding the mouth of the canyon where the main trail narrows. Be careful from there on in. Ketchum always keeps a guard at the base of the canyon and it's a rough trail down."

"There's another way out of it?"

"Straight through, the trail is worse than rough and barely passable." Angus looks off toward the far mountains. "I led my burros through there many a day, but mind you; don't try that pass in the dark. It ain't fit passage for a horse."

"I'll be pulling out soon as I get saddled."

Moore nods. "I'll have Miss Louise fix you up a poke of food."

"Thank you." Cam nods. "I appreciate that."

The old Rancher and Cam walk together toward the barn where the bay is stalled. "You be careful out there young man and come back to us."

"I'll be careful, Mister Moore."

"When you get back, I want you to have the black."

"Why, with a little work, he'll make the Rafter 5 a good using horse now."

"Sure he will, but you couldn't melt and pour any of these cowhands here on Thunder if you tried," Angus laughs. "If you hadn't come along and rode him, he'd have never been ridden; either been turned out or shot. No, he's yours and you're welcome to him."

"Well, thank you, sir."

Angus watches as Cam saddles up the bay and shakes hands. "Hear me now; up there you shoot first and ask questions later."

"Yes, sir."

"I don't think that wounded kid can make it back to Ketchum's hideout. He's shot up pretty bad." Angus looks up at the mounted man. "Watch the trail, your back and the ridges. They could be waiting to ambush you."

Bob Moore walks up and hands Cam a sack full of food. "Ride easy, Cam Mitchell."

"I'll be seeing you, boys." Cam turns the thoroughbred gelding.

"Youngster, don't forget the Apache. They sure ain't forgotten about white folks." Angus Moore looks off toward the far mountain pass. "A lone man is easy pickings for them."

Watching the tall man ride away, Bob Moore shakes his head. "I don't think so Granddad; there's one young man that won't ever be easy pickings for anyone again."

Chapter 4

Cam trails east from the ranch, carefully following the directions Angus Moore had given him as he rides away from the Rafter 5. The trail shows tracks of both cattle and loose horses, but it also plainly shows where two shod horses crossed the sandy trail just this morning. The tracks are fresh, not an ounce of dirt or a leaf has blown into the deep tracks. The trail is plain for a tracker to read. One horse is led as it follows almost in the tracks of the other horse. Cam figures the front horse carries the gruff one from last night's poker game who Angus Moore identified as Len Fox, a cousin of Jack Ketchum. Cam doesn't remember the face of the gruff man from the poker game. He does remember Ketchum mentioned the name, Len Fox, the day they had taken the horses and the Steeldust from him near Garden City. The other horse, carries the wounded man who Angus said is Jeremy Jackson, a youngster from one of the smaller ranches, deeper down in the Guadalupes. Apparently, the younger man is too weak to handle the horse himself so he is being led. Bob Moore assured Cam the young man is basically a good lad who fell in with a bad bunch and got on a bad track.

Pulling the bay in, Cam dismounts and touches the ground where a red spot shows. His fingers come up sticky and he knows it is blood. Obviously the wound has broken open and the younger outlaw is bleeding profusely. Even one drop of blood on the ground shows the wound is bleeding bad as it has to run all the way down the wounded man's body and leg then fall to the ground. The man cannot ride far before he bleeds to death. Cam believes like Angus, down the trail there could be an ambush waiting for him; there has to be. Mounting, he pushes the horse slowly along the treacherous terrain, letting his eyes roam the underbrush ahead for danger. This country is rough, strewn with fallen rocks from up high that rolled down, into the trail. It holds heavy underbrush that could hide a man and his horse, and several switchbacks that temporarily hide a man from the trail where an unseen enemy can hide and shoot from. Where, he does not know, but some-where ahead, the wounded man will be down and if he is alive and able, he could be waiting with a rifle.

About two miles now, the hair on Cam's neck stands on end. He can't see anything, but he senses trouble as if someone is watching him. Dismounting, he ties the gelding and scouts the trail ahead on foot. Finding nothing, he returns to the horse and leads him forward a few hundred yards then reties him. Using caution and moving slow is time consuming, but at least he is alive and hasn't given anyone a clear shot at him. Kneeling beside a small cedar tree, Cam studies the open ground ahead, which he will have to cross. Suddenly, his eyes spot what he has been looking for. Just a few yards ahead past the clearing, he can see the sun shining on what looks like a rifle barrel. Circling silently along the edge of the clearing, Cam eases his way forward, stopping every few feet to study and survey the terrain.

Finally, he finds what he is looking for. He can see the man's body lying propped against a small tree, his rifle resting across his lap. Cam knows the rifle's position is what gave the man's location away. Moving silently near the waiting man, he stands up slowly, his rifle pointing at the blood soaked body.

"You alive, young feller?" Cam moves in cautiously.

"Barely, mister. Who are you?" The voice is weak, barely a whisper.

"Cam Mitchell."

"You're the man who came in the bunkhouse last night." The youngster stiffens in pain. "Fox said you'd be along. He said you'd probably finish me off if I were still alive and didn't get you first."

"He said that, did he?" Cam looks into the pain racked face of the wounded man from bunkhouse of the Rafter 5. "He left you here alone, hurt like you are?"

Only the blond hair moves as the youngster nod, his voice almost too weak to speak. "Yeah, he couldn't wait to scoot out of here."

Studying the nearby ground, Cam turns to examine the wound. "Where's your horse?"

"Len took him. I reckon he didn't figure I'd be needing him. You got a drink of water, mister?" The young man moans. "Man, I hurt bad, and I'm so dry."

"I'll get you a drink. It's on my horse."

Only a nod comes from the young boy as Cam quickly retraces his steps back to the bay gelding. Quickly leading the horse back to the youngster, he takes down his canteen and puts the water to his lips. The wounded boy watches weakly as Cam removes the bloody bandage and examines the wound. Wetting a small cloth, he wipes the crusted blood away and cleans the wound.

"It's bad, ain't it mister?"

"Yes, I won't lie to you, it's bad." Cam nods. "I sure ain't no doctor."

"I'm gonna die ain't I?" The young man's eyes study Cam's face. "You can tell the truth, mister, it won't matter much now. I deserve exactly what I got."

"Maybe not; you're young and strong." Cam shakes his head. "If I can stop the bleeding and if fever or infection doesn't set in, the bullet went clear through. Hopefully it didn't hit anything vital."

"I told Len to leave me back at the Rafter 5, but he wouldn't do it." The blue eyes of the youngster look away. "Now, he's up and killed me for sure."

"You reap what you sow, young feller. Running with murderers and robbers does have its consequences."

"I ain't killed nobody."

"What about Elcho?"

"I didn't fire a bullet there. I only held the horses."

"Same difference; I believe the law calls it guilt by association." Cam softly dabs at the wound. "If you run with a wolf pack, you're labeled a wolf."

"My name's Jeremy, Jeremy Jackson." The face makes a painful frown as the youngster tries to sit up. "My folks live down in Jackson Basin."

"Lie back and save your strength now." Cam pushes the slender frame back then dabs at the wound. "I'll try to get you fixed up."

"You're wasting your time. I'm a dead man."

"You wanna die, youngster?"

"No sir, I don't."

"Then buck up and want to live."

Cam knows it is dangerous to build a fire, but if the wounded man is to live, he needs to keep warm. Here in the mountains, the temperature can drop forty degrees overnight and Jackson is wracked with fever already. Cam thinks about trying to get the man back to the Rafter 5, but he knows it would be useless. The young outlaw would be dead in less than a mile if he tries to put him on a horse. He doesn't even dare try to move the youngster to a safer position. Any movement at all will open the wound again, start the bleeding and no doubt kill him. The wounded man has bled profusely. He cannot spare another drop of blood and survive.

Seeing Jackson is awake, Cam speaks quietly to the man. "Do you know of any water near here?"

Looking about, the head shakes. "I don't even know where we're at."

"I've used too much of our water and you're gonna need water to cool that fever." Cam picks up his rifle. "I'm gonna scout around a little."

"You ain't gonna leave me, are you?" Jeremy's voice is fearful. "You'll be back?"

"I'll be back, don't fret yourself." Cam pulls the blankets higher on the wounded man. "I wouldn't leave my blankets, now would I?"

Cam knows there is no water behind him for several miles, so he turns to the east, following the tracks of Len Fox across the lower valley. The trail slowly slopes off, downhill. Cam is hoping, somewhere below he will cross a small stream. He has no choice as he has to find water somewhere. The boy will not last through the night without water to lower his fever and quench his thirst. He also needs water to make him some kind of broth.

Hardly a mile passes before the gelding's ears prick and Cam can see the sun shining off the water, just ahead. Smiling in relief, he knows, maybe Jackson's life has been spared.

Filling his only canteen, Cam listens as the horse noisily guzzles his fill of water. Pulling the satisfied gelding back from the water, Cam tightens his cinch, mounts and starts back toward the wounded man. Cam has himself a real dilemma. If he holds up and nurses the boy back to health, he could possibly lose Ketchum and the Steeldust. However, if he rides on and leaves the wounded Jackson alone, the youngster will surely die. He can ride back to the Rafter 5 for help, but he doesn't want to leave the defenseless youngster alone in his condition against man or animal. No, although the boy is an outlaw, he's still an injured man, unable to defend himself. Cam will not leave any helpless critter alone out here in this desolate country.

Three days have passed since Cam first found the youngster. He knows Len Fox easily reached Ketchum's hideout by now and could, at this moment, be leading the outlaw chief back to where he left young Jackson. Jeremy Jackson is young, his body strong. In the three days the wound has begun to heal. At least it has scabbed over, and the high fevers and shakes have finally diminished. Tonight, for the first time as the sun sets, the youngster stares into the campfire talking quietly with Cam.

"I'm much stronger now, Cam. You need to ride on." Jackson looks off, across the valley. "I figure Fox will ride in any minute."

"You're stronger alright, but you can't fend for yourself yet." Cam shakes his head. "Can't cook for yourself or get wood for the fire."

"It's too dangerous for you to stay here with me. They could be coming in any minute," Jeremy protests. "I'm surprised they're not here already."

"It'll be good if they come. That'll save me from having to go to them." Cam smiles, "I'll stick around for a spell yet."

"Len Fox is a bad one, a dangerous killer, and fast with a gun." Jackson frowns. "The only man I've ever seen faster is Jack Ketchum himself."

"I'm not leaving, Jackson." Cam looks into the small blaze. "I don't know Len Fox. My beef is with Ketchum."

"They're Cousins, so I've heard the others say."

"Don't matter none who he is."

"You saved my life. I owe you now."

"No, you owe me nothing."

"My folks have a ranch across the mountains." Jackson points south. "We could give it a try."

Cam looks the direction the bony finger points, then pulls back the blanket and examines the wound. "You wouldn't make it a mile."

"I'll make it. Don't be a fool," Jackson frowns. "You don't stand a chance here alone. Ketchum has many more men, just as mean as Fox, back at his hideout near the border."

"Is that how he stays on the run?" Cam places the blanket lightly across the youngster. "Just crosses the border when things get too hot on this side."

"That's what Fox told me." Jeremy nods. "He says Ketchum pays off the Rurales down in Mexico for them to turn a blind eye."

"He's got a neat set up down here."

"Are you telling me you never heard of Jack Ketchum before?" Jeremy shakes his head. "Everybody in these parts has heard of Ketchum."

"I heard of him, but nothing much. At least I didn't take much interest in him until he stole our horses."

"Fox said they swapped you even."

"Fox lied." Cam pours them both some coffee. "They stole my horses, they didn't swap for them. A trade takes two parties agreeing and I sure wouldn't have swapped that Steeldust stud for every horse he had."

Angus Moore watched as Cam rode out of the ranch yard, heading east in a high lope. After the ride he made on the outlaw horse Thunder, Angus grudgingly has grown to respect the young man. He saw a lot of himself in his younger days.

"There goes a lot of man, Granddad."

"Maybe we should go help him," Angus muses softly. "He's a good young man, too good to get killed over a horse."

Bob Moore shakes his head. "No, sir. You know we've survived out here alone for years by minding our own business and staying to ourselves. It was your law back then and we're gonna keep it that way now."

"You know Ketchum has been running loose around here, robbing and killing for far too long." Angus shakes his head. "You know it as well as I do."

"Like you said, for several years, it's none of our business." Bob Moore shakes his head. "If the lowlanders want him that bad, why don't they send their lawmen up here to get rid of Ketchum and his gang?"

Angus nods slowly. "I reckon you're right, but I like that boy and don't want anything to happen to him."

"You know I'm right, Granddad. All we can do for now is, wish him luck." Bob Moore nods. "I've got a hunch, maybe Ketchum and his bunch will be the ones needing help before this is finished."

"I hope you're right, Grandson."

Jack Ketchum pulls on his smoke and stares across the scarred table at Len Fox, his second in command and his blood cousin. They have ridden together since leaving Texas, two jumps ahead of the Rangers, and landing here in the wilds of the Mogollon Mountains, bordering Arizona, New Mexico, and Old Mexico. Ketchum is smart. He knows the law is growing stronger as the country becomes more civilized and populated. The gang never struck in the same territory twice and never used the same escape route home. The one mistake he made was, not killing the young man they encountered when they found him leading the string of horses, days ago. Yes, it was a mistake leaving someone behind alive to identify the gang and worse still to misjudge someone who would follow determinedly after them. He looks out the window where the Steeldust stands hipshot under the shade of a tall cedar. He doesn't blame the young man as the horse is one of a kind. He has to admire Cam Mitchell for his courage, if he is the one following his gang into the wilds of these mountains as the rider from the Rafter 5 that Len Fox reported.

"Was the Jackson kid dead when you left him behind?"

"Practically, he lost a lot of blood." Fox shrugs. "I couldn't wait for him to go under."

"Why didn't you leave him with Angus Moore at the Rafter 5?"

"I was afraid to leave him behind to talk." Fox lights his smoke. "We should have killed Mitchell. I can feel it. He's gonna be bad trouble."

"Think so, huh Len?" Ketchum swears. "You should have killed the Jackson brat too."

"Then we'd have old man Jackson on our tail."

"These mountains hide many stories." Ketchum looks out the open door. "He would never have known what happened to the kid."

Fox blows smoke across the table. "Yeah, they do, but they've also got eyes and ears everywhere. The Rafter 5 bunch knows he was with me and alive when we rode out."

"You think old man Jackson would have come looking for the boy?"

"The kid is his grandson. I know he would be out looking." Fox nods. "He's a rough old goat, mean as they come."

"This Mitchell, he makes you nervous too?"

"He's a cool one, walked in that bunkhouse and didn't bat an eye, even though he knew the Jackson kid got shot by the posse from Elcho. I figure he knew I was with the gang too."

"You think he recognized you when we took his horses?"

"Nah, he was too busy watching that studhorse." Fox shakes his head. "I kept my face in the shadows so he couldn't see it."

"I can't blame him for watching the stallion."

"Why don't you just give him that animal back and get him off our trail?" Fox looks at Ketchum. "We don't need this problem, Cousin."

"No, I ain't about to let a snot nosed kid get the best of me."

"Pride goes before the fall Jack." Fox shrugs. "At least, that's what I've heard a time or two."

"He ain't getting that horse back, unless it's over my dead body."

"Are we going back after the kid?"

"You are. Bring the kid in or make sure he's dead. I don't care which." Ketchum stands up. "Me and the boys have business across the border."

"You're raiding without me?" Fox can't believe his ears.

"I am." Ketchum nods. "You made this problem, now clean it up. We'll meet back here."

"I'll ride in the morning."

"You'll ride right now." Ketchum looks hard at the big man. "We can't afford to let Jackson run his mouth and give away our hideout's location to Mitchell. Take Miles and Soapy with you."

"Alright Jack, I'm riding."

"Len." Ketchum stops Fox. "Don't sell this young man Mitchell short. There's something about him, something about his eyes."

"I won't." Fox stands up and stares out the small window. "Maybe he'll come calling and we won't have him to worry about him anymore."

"Be careful, Cousin, I'd hate to lose my good right arm,"

Fox laughs. "Just you make sure you save some loot for me."

"You're part will be here as always."

Cam pours the steaming coffee and looks across the campfire to where Jeremy Jackson sits upright against a log, padded with Cam's saddle blankets. The color has returned to the youngsters face and he is now able to move into a sitting position. It's been five days now since he found Jackson, plenty time enough for Len Fox to ride to wherever their hideout is and ride back. Staying alert, with little or no rest, it's been several days since he let himself fall into a dead sleep. He can't afford the luxury. There is no way of knowing when or if Ketchum or Fox will come riding in.

"You think you can ride, Jeremy?"

The blue eyes lock onto Cam's face and nod. "I told you Mitchell, I could have ridden out two days ago."

"Alright then, I'll take you home today."

"You aiming at giving up on getting your horses back?"

"Nope, I'll get them."

"Then you must be getting the same feeling I am?"

"What would that be?"

"We're fixing to have company." Jackson looks out, across the valley. "I can feel them out there."

Cam can't help liking the boy. Anyone would like his outgoing ways and good manners. "Maybe."

"It'll be good to see grandpa and the folks." Jeremy smiles over at Cam. "For a while there, I had my doubts."

"Me too," Cam smiles. "Let's see what you're made of."

Leading the gelding east, down the sloping mountain trail, Cam is forced to head in the direction Ketchum would be coming from. The trail turns south, toward the border and Echo Canyon, is at least another mile down the trail. There, it flattens out in a valley just as the trail coming up from Jackson Basin intersects it, coming in from the south. Jackson sits straight in the saddle showing little sign of pain or discomfort. He watches the trail ahead, worrying they will run into Ketchum before they reach the cut off.

"If we can reach the cut off ahead of them, we may have a chance, providing they come this way, looking for us." Jackson mumbles.

"We may be worrying for no reason."

"Could be," Jeremy nods. "Ketchum is smart and unpredictable. That's why he hasn't been caught."

"How far you reckon it is to the cut off?"

"We're almost there now."

Mountain grass grows knee high on their horse, rough grass that is already brown and dry but the gelding enjoys what nibbles he can grab from time to time. Not green and tasty like the lower grasses of the flat valleys. The brown grass has the nutrients, making it fattening for horses, cattle, and wildlife roaming the mountains. Cactus, small and large, dot the landscape, with cedar trees, a few pinion trees, and scrub brush of every description.

"You see that jagged peak ahead? The south trail from the ranch comes in right there." Jeremy points out the landmark peak. "When you get to the fork, we'll stop so you can wipe out our tracks turning off."

Cam nods, then stops the gelding as he surveys the flat canyon crossing. He can see the turn off just ahead as it intersects the larger trail. Not a sound comes to his ears and the gelding doesn't portray any signs that he senses any other horses ahead.

"I think it's clear." Cam starts forward.

"We'll know soon enough, I reckon."

"You reach for that rifle and I'll blow you into next week." Cam nods at the rifle butt sticking from the boot.

"Trusting galoot ain't you."

Cam's eyes focus on the trail ahead. "I learned one thing, if I never learn anything else."

"Oh yeah, well, what's that." Jackson grins his likable grin.

"A skunk doesn't change his spots."

"I may have made a wrong decision, but I sure ain't no skunk."

"You ain't proven that yet."

"You want me to turn around so you can see my back?" Jackson laughs lightly.

Both men let out a sigh of relief as they turn onto the southern trail without seeing any of Ketchum's gang. Quickly pulling a broom-full of sagebrush, Cam sweeps the trail clean where they turned off. Handing Jackson the half-full canteen, he waits while the youngster takes a long pull then replaces the cap. Not wanting to take the wounded youngster from the horse, he leaves him sitting in the saddle. He slips back to the trail intersection for one final look before rejoining the youngster and taking the trail to the South.

"Let's go."

"You see anything?"

"Nothing, nary a sign."

"Good," Jeremy smiles. "You had at least a mile view down that trail so we'll have some lead on them if they study our tracks real hard and see where you wiped them out back there."

"You still figure they're coming back for you?"

"Oh, they're coming alright, not to help me, but to make sure I'm pushing up Cactus," Jeremy frowns. "More likely for you, Cam. Fox is smart; he knows you're coming and he doesn't want you on his back."

"Then why did they keep you alive and bring you back with them to the Rafter 5?"

"That's Ketchum's way. He takes care of his men and never leaves one behind or in jail." Jeremy tries to ease himself in the saddle. "Keeps them loyal, but now with you hunting the gang, they'll kill me to keep my mouth shut permanent."

"Why, what would you be able to tell me about them?"

"Their hideout location, down below, for one thing."

"The Moore's already told me that."

"Ketchum doesn't know that." Jeremy shakes his head. "The Moores have always had tight mouths."

"Not this time," Cam smiles. "You might say they talked because of a pair of boots."

"What?"

The rough rock and gravel trail leading across the mountains go up and down hills, turn back and forth around switchbacks then suddenly level out into a grassy valley. Jeremy Jackson is exhausted and starts to feel pain in the wound from the hard riding rough trails.

"You need to rest?"

"No, we're almost home. Let's keep moving." Jackson points to the southwest. "We'll cross the river west of here, two miles."

"Then how far?"

"Half day at most, the way we're traveling."

Jackson is hurting, but he is nearing his home range. He doesn't want to stop and rest. Only the river and one more small range of mountains leading into what folks call Jackson Basin, lie between them and a warm meal and a real bed. Keeping himself upright, by holding onto the saddle horn, he grimaces but says nothing. He can see Cam is limping slightly. The rough gravel trail and the high heel riding boots he wears are enough to make anyone limp.

"The river is just ahead. Let's stop there and rest the horse."

"Are you hurting?"

Jackson nods his head. "Yeah, I am. I feel light-headed again and the horse's feet need soaking in the river."

"The horse?" Cam shakes his head. He knows the youngster has seen him limping and is giving him some good advice about his own feet. "Okay, we'll stop a few minutes."

The small river is shallow, but the water coming down from the mountains and running over the rocky bottom is so clear you can see fish swimming along its bottom. To Cam's delight, as he puts his sore feet into the water, he finds it ice cold. Jackson lies resting against a large boulder, watching as Cam soaks leisurely in the river.

"Feels good, don't it?"

"Yep, it does."

"Try swimming in it, that'll wake you up."

"I imagine." Cam looks over at the youngster. "You want me to help you down here?"

"No, I'm doing fine right here where I'm at."

Leaning back against the boulder, Jeremy closes his eyes and tries to forget the pain throbbing in his shoulder. Feeling the pull on the bandage, he looks up to see Cam examining the wound. He didn't even hear the man walk over to him.

"Did I fall asleep?"

"About an hour now."

Jeremy smiles and nods, then as his eyes focus behind Cam and on their back trail, he stiffens. He blinks the sleep from his eyes as three riders come slowly along their trail, moving straight toward them.

"It's Len Fox," Jeremy straightens up slowly. "That's him, the big man in the lead. I can tell even from this distance. Get me a gun, Cam."

Limping slowly across the river gravel, Cam quickly pulls on his socks and boots and checks the loads his pistol. The three riders halt almost thirty yards away, sitting their horses out on the flats, waiting for something. Cam walks back where Jeremy sits, but stops a few yards away from the injured boy.

"What are you doing?" Jeremy hisses across the space separating them. "Get us safe behind some rocks for Pete's sake and get me that rifle."

"Why?"

"Why? Those boys are fixing to fill us full of holes, that's why." Jeremy tries to rise. "Are you plumb loco?"

The man on the black horse walks his horse out in front of the other two riders and dismounts slowly, dropping his reins to the ground. Walking in slow, measured strides, he advances toward Cam and Jeremy. Stopping forty feet from where Cam waits, he smiles smugly, then pulls the makings from his pocket. The cold eyes never leave the two men as he deftly rolls his smoke and lights it.

"You should have stayed back in Garden City trading horses, pilgrim." The words are cold and gruff, just like back in the bunkhouse, "Instead of sticking your nose where it don't belong."

"It's a bad habit of mine, I reckon." Cam watches the man's eyes closely. "Horse thieves always make my nose itch."

"Traded with you, the way I remember it."

"Wrong there mister, the way I remember it, Ketchum stole the horses flat out." Cam's face goes hard. "I don't remember seeing you with Ketchum that day, though."

"I was there alright, just like I'm here today."

"You left a wounded kid to die, Fox."

"How much did the kid tell you?" Fox turns his eyes on Jeremy briefly, then just as quickly, they settle back on Cam.

Cam ignores the question. Instead, he studies the three horses the men ride and nods toward them. "I believe the black you're riding and the other two horses your friends are on, belong to me."

"Do say," Fox grins, pulling on his smoke. "I believe that's my saddle on him."

"I do say," Cam smiles coldly himself. "I aim to have them back, plus the Steeldust stud."

"Then stop your yapping and take them, why don't you?" Fox grins evilly. "If you're man enough, that is."

"I'm fixing to," Cam shifts slightly. "You won't be needing horses where you're heading, big mouth."

"You talk tough for a horse trader." Fox blows smoke from his sneering lips, then pulls the smoke from his mouth, flipping it aside. "It's your call, boy. Let's see if you've got the stomach for it."

The canyon walls along the valley floor echo with the heavy boom of the revolvers as both pistols speak several times. The other two Ketchum riders reach for their pistols as they watch in disbelief as Fox sinks slowly to the ground.

"I wouldn't if I were you, boys." Cam turns his pistol on them. "Even at this range, you're dead men."

Relaxing, the men drop their hands to their sides. "You got us, mister."

"Toss your weapons, then ride over here and see if he's dead."

Jeremy sits against the boulder staring in complete shock. It is well known, next to Jack Ketchum, Len Fox is the fastest gun in the territory. He had proven it against many a man that carried big reputations across the territories. Fox was fast, a known killer and here, an unknown youngster has outdrawn him, hands down. He put two slugs into Fox's chest in what seemed less than a second. Jeremy saw the dust fly from Fox's shirt each time the bullets struck him. Talk of this will surely spread quickly across the mountains, making Cam a marked man for every gunman in the southwest. Jeremy is curious what will happen when Ketchum and Mitchell meet, and they will as soon as the outlaw hears Fox was killed. Everyone in the gang knows Fox and Ketchum are first cousins from a tight Kentucky family.

"Old Len's past help, mister."

"You little man, lead those horses over here."

"You ain't gonna leave us out here afoot are you?"

"Get your boots off and those gun belts off." Cam turns the pistol on the men as they hesitate, then watch as the pistol convinces them to remove their boots.

"Mister, we can't walk on this ground a mile before we'll be crippled."

"You know, y'all do a lot of whining for the line of work you're in."

The taller of the two outlaws glares across at Cam, but speaks to his partner, "Shut up Miles. Don't beg him."

"I ain't begging Soapy, but I sure don't want to be left out here without our boots or gun."

Cam examines the black horse Fox took from him back on the trail near Garden City. "At least you have taken good care of my horses."

"Yeah, we have, now how about giving us a break and let us go."

"I'm letting you go. Count yourself lucky that you're still alive." Cam leads the three horses over to where Jeremy is lying. "How long you stay that way depends on how fast you boys can run."

"Out here, unarmed and barefoot, you're not alive, mister. You're as good as dead," the one called Miles moans. "Have a heart, mister. At least leave us our boots and a gun."

"You boys get over there and help young Jackson on that bay gelding and if I were you, I wouldn't try anything funny."

"I don't need any help from that pair." Jeremy pulls himself up slowly and then starts for the horse, pushing the men's hands away as they try to help him mount.

Turning, the men shrug their shoulders. "We tried to help him."

"We're riding out. You men tell Ketchum, when you see him, I'll be coming after the Steeldust." Cam mounts the black horse. "I aim to kill him."

"You ain't aiming to leave us out here helpless?" Miles pleads. "Man, this is Apache country. After the noise of those shots, they're probably watching us right now."

After tying the boots and gun belts of the two men onto the spare horses, Cam takes the reins of Jeremy's bay and the other two horses and clucks to the black.

"Please, mister, don't leave us afoot." The taller outlaw speaks up.

"You told me not to beg, Soapy."

"It ain't begging. Have you ever seen what a man looks like after the Apache gets through with him?" Soapy is afraid. "Well, I have and it ain't pretty."

Cam turns in his saddle and looks at Jeremy. "What do you think, Mister Jackson?'

"Leave 'em to fry, they left me."

"You're getting hard."

"Yeah, you know getting shot and left to die has a way of making you that way."

"We didn't leave you to die, boy. We took you to the Rafter 5."

Cam clucks to the black and rides about fifty feet before stopping and turning the gelding. "I'm gonna let you boys borrow my horses. Your guns and boots will be on the saddles. They'll be about a quarter mile down the trail."

Both men are relieved. "We're thanking you, Mitchell."

"Don't, I wouldn't leave a dog to die." Cam looks hard at the men. "You hear me good; when I get back to the Rafter 5, my horses better be there and that includes the Steeldust."

"They'll be there."

"They better be, all of them or I'm coming after you and Ketchum. This time you won't need horses or guns again."

"We hear you, these horses will be at the Rafter 5, but we can't speak for Ketchum or the Steeldust, 'cause we won't be seeing him. We're through in these parts for good."

"You're learning, fat man." Cam kicks the black. "You're too soft for this line of work and I'll guarantee the next time we meet, I'll kill you on sight."

The two outlaws, Miles and Soapy, start walking down the trail, following the horses. "We're lucky to be alive, Miles. That's one hard man."

"He's a hard one, the coldest eyes, I have ever seen on a man." The shorter man nods. "Maybe the fastest gun too."

"Ketchum should never have taken his horses."

"Shucks, he seemed like an innocent, harmless youngster back there, sitting on that wagon."

"Tell poor old Fox that. He sure wasn't innocent today." Both men look back to where Fox's body lies.

Miles points ahead, to a lone mountain pine where their horses wait. "There they are, just where he said they'd be."

"You think Ketchum can beat Mitchell in a stand up fight?"

The two limp across the gravel road, trying to hurry as they watch the broad valley they are crossing. "It'll be a toss-up for sure. Ketchum is faster than Fox when they practiced, and Mitchell didn't beat him by much."

"If any, except he put them where they counted." Soapy pulls a sticker from his foot. "I thought Fox might have got one in Mitchell."

"He didn't let on."

"He wouldn't, he's too proud."

"I would. I ain't proud. I've been shot three times." Miles wipes his foot free of gravel. "Burns like the devil when hot lead hits you. No sir, this hoss ain't proud."

Soapy limps up to the horses and thanks his lucky stars. "Nothing ever looked as good as you, old horse."

"You know Miles, we're still young men and we use to be good cowhands."

"So?" Miles looks over at his partner. "What are you getting at Soapy?"

"Let's get out of this country, this line of work, and go back to honest work for a living."

"You're kidding, ain't you?"

"No, we'll drop these horses off at the Rafter 5, buy us some more from old Angus Moore then let's get out of these mountains for good." Soapy pulls the boots slowly over his sore feet. "We've got a good stake from that last job and we need a change in occupation, a healthier change."

Miles pulls his boots on and studies the trail Cam and Jeremy had ridden down. "We almost bought it today for sure; maybe you're right."

"Now this doesn't mean we've lost our nerve, we've just gotten a lot smarter, real quick like."

"Yeah, I reckon we learned a whole lot in one afternoon." Miles settles happily in the saddle. "Mitchell might be young, but he teaches a good lesson. Man, this saddle never felt so good."

Chapter 5

Cam gets his first look at Jackson Basin from a ridge far above the large valley, which reminds folks of a washbasin giving it the name. Jeremy's grandfather, old Spade Jackson, first came into these mountains years ago with Angus Moore, prospecting for gold. They hunted and panned for the precious metal all through this part of the state until both finally decided to start ranching. The partners separated on good terms, splitting what little gold they found in the small washes and streams. Both men wanted the valley they discovered on their travels throughout the Mogollons, the same valley where the Rafter 5 now sits. After several long arguments, both men decided to settle the ownership of the valley by the flip of a coin. Subsequently, a gold coin was flipped, deciding the fate of the valley and Spade Jackson lost. Taking his share of the gold, the prospector, after shaking hands with his longtime partner, headed south. He became a rancher, settling in what is now known as Jackson Basin.

Living right in the backyard of the savage Apache, had people living closer to the populated towns wondering how the older Jackson survived the savages and the Mexican bandits. Angus Moore knows as they both discussed the Apache on several occasions before going their separate ways. Both men wandered the mountains for years. They knew the Apache and most Apaches from all tribes respected them. The red warriors knew the prospectors would fight and they were good shots.

Both prospectors and Indians respected the other and if possible, both sides stayed clear of each other. Not all hostilities ceased as both ranches were raided from time to time by the wilder Apache warriors, but nothing serious.

From the high ridge Cam studies the ranch buildings and notes several smaller houses surrounding the large ranch house. "Looks like a fort down there."

Jeremy nods. "It is; every house has bulletproof walls, foot thick shutters and rifle slots with a rifle for every slot."

"What are y'all worried about, Apaches?"

"Mexicans, mostly."

"Mexicans?"

"More dangerous than Apaches and better armed," Jeremy nods. "Mexicans cross the mountains from Mexico are mostly cutthroats and banditos. I'd rather trust a rattlesnake."

"How many people are down there guarding the place?"

"Gramps had six sons and two daughters, now they all got kids." Jeremy shrugs. "Maybe fifty all told."

"All of them Jacksons?"

"Not all, we got a few hired hands," Jeremy grins proudly, "but most are Jacksons."

"Tell me, Jeremy, why did you go off and join with Ketchum?" Cam studies the far-off ranch. "It peers to me like you had a good set up here in the Basin."

"I did for a fact," Jeremy shrugs. "Stupidity; Ketchum rode through one day and I was being a stupid kid, listened to his romantic bull. Gramps tried to talk me out of leaving, but like I said, I was stupid."

"Ketchum just comes and goes back in the mountains without anyone saying anything?"

"Up here in the mountains, it's healthier for all concerned to live and let live." Jeremy looks off, toward the lower ranch buildings. "Grandpa figures if whites go to fighting against each other, it gives the Apache and Mexicans the edge."

Cam lifts his reins and starts to turn. "Well, Jeremy, you can make it the rest of the way, I reckon. This is where I leave you."

"No, you're riding in with me."

"Why?"

Jeremy smiles, "Several reasons; I'm still mighty weak. I might not make it by myself and all your work would be wasted. Second, you need a good meal and a bed, but mostly, you need that hole in your side patched up and we do have a good doctor down there."

Cam blinks as he had no idea Jeremy knew he had taken a slug from Fox. "It's nothing, just a scratch."

"Maybe, maybe not," Jeremy kicks the bay. "Sides, I need this good horse to ride on into the ranch and you'll probably want to take him home with you, now lead out."

Cam shrugs, his side does need looking after before it becomes infected. Kicking the horse, he follows Jeremy down the small path leading onto the valley floor where the Jackson Ranch is far out in the lower distant valley.

Jackson Basin is a hubbub of activity. Men surround the dusty corrals where several head of cattle mill. Others work some horses in a nearby corral while up by the house, several women stand around the steaming wash pots, washing clothes as children run pell-mell every-where around the ranch houses, yelling and screaming. All activity stops instantly. Even the children quit hollering as the two dusty riders are spotted riding slowly toward the ranch buildings. Men grab the long guns as the women round up the children, hurrying them inside. Cam nods as no army could react better when danger presents itself.

"They're on their toes, for sure."

"Gramps runs a rough crew." Jeremy watches the gathering men as they hide behind every conceivable shelter. "He has to because you never know who'll come calling at any time out here."

"Sounds like Angus Moore." Cam watches the nearing buildings. "Rough."

Jeremy laughs, then waves toward the corral. "They're cut out of the same cloth so I've been told."

Recognizing Jeremy, all the men rush forward and surround the horses, grabbing at the youngster's legs. An old man, almost the image of Angus Moore, pushes through the crowd and looks up at the boy. Staring up at his grandson then over at Cam for a moment, the old man smiles and nods slightly before motioning toward the house. Several of the riders start to pull Jeremy playfully from the saddle.

"You boys be careful with him. He's got a hole in his shoulder."

All movement stops as hard eyes turn on Cam and several hands go quickly to their pistols. "Who shot him?"

Looking down calmly, into the face of a big, redheaded man, who is glaring up at him, Cam looks over where Jeremy slumps painfully in the saddle of the bay horse. "Tell this gentleman who shot you, Jeremy."

"It wasn't him, Red Hacker. This is the man that saved my life, for a fact."

"Then who was it, Nephew? Tell us and we'll have him skinned and boiled before breakfast." Gage Jackson pushes forward.

"Well folks, I'll tell you if you have to know, it was a posse from Elcho City," Jeremy admits weakly.

"What?" The word of shock comes from several mouths as the gathered men stare in disbelief at the youngster.

"Bring my grandson into the house. We'll speak of this later," Spade Jackson speaks, returning to the porch, cutting off the questions then turns into the house. "Be careful with him."

"Cam's been shot too, Gramps."

The old man turns around slowly and stares at Cam. "Did the Posse shoot you too? Take him to the bunkhouse."

"Then I'll go to the bunkhouse with him. This man saved my life." Jeremy shoves the hands holding him roughly away as he tries to straighten up. "I owe him."

The elder Jackson looks at the boy then nods slowly. "Alright, bring both of them inside."

Both Jeremy and Cam are ushered into a small bedroom just off the kitchen that contains two bunks. An old woman with deep lines embedded in her aged face, turns back the blankets and starts helping Jeremy off with his boots and outer garments.

"You need a bath, Grandson." The old nose wrinkles from the smell. "You stink."

"Both of us do, we ain't been near a tub in a week or better, but it ain't catching." Jeremy speaks to the woman.

"You ever hear of a creek or pond water?" The old woman shakes her head in disgust. "It wouldn't have hurt either of you none."

"Amen to that." Cam's eyes follow the old woman as she leaves the room. "Your grandmother?"

"No, she's my great-aunt, grandfather's sister," Jeremy grins. "Grandma Jackson is dead."

"What about your folks?" Cam is curious. He hasn't seen anybody come forward like they were parents.

"Both are dead, killed in a Mexican raid when I was just a tad."

"Sorry."

"It's okay, I don't remember them." Jeremy shrugs as the door squeaks open. "Huh uh, the sawbones is here."

Cam's jaw falls open as the prettiest woman he has ever seen in his life, walks through the door. Tall, sandy blonde with freckles sprinkled across her nose and the bluest eyes, he has ever seen. The woman is a picture of beauty and grace.

"This is my cousin, Trish Jackson." Jeremy grins as he notices the look of awe on Cam's face. "Trish, this is Cam Mitchell, the man that saved my life."

Cam is stricken almost deaf and dumb. He can't speak for the life of him. "Well, which of you are hurt the worst?"

"He is, Cousin." Jeremy is enjoying Cam's shock and loss of words. This is the first time since they met that something unsettles the young man, leaving him practically speechless. "More ways than one, since you arrived."

"Alright Mister Mitchell, let's get that vest and shirt off." The young woman moves close and starts unbuttoning his vest.

"What?"

Jeremy laughs, "She can't treat you with your shirt on, hoss."

"Come on now." Trish starts removing Cam's vest and unbuttons his shirt. "You see, Mister Mitchell, I'm what passes as a doctor around these parts. I have several sisters, brothers, and many uncles. I assure you, sir, I've seen many a bare chested man."

"Not mine, you haven't."

"No, but I'm fixing to, now quit squirming around and sit still." A firm grip holds his shoulder as she looks at the wound in his side.

"It's only a scratch," Cam tries to protest.

Trish stares in awe as she removes the bloody shirt, exposing the heavily muscled chest and flat stomach of her patient. Cam notices her face blushing as she finishes removing his shirt, crusted with dried blood and stuck to the wound. Dabbing wet swabs to soften the hard crust, she can feel the solid muscle that ripples across his sides and chest. She swallows hard. She didn't lie to the man about seeing many a bare chest of men. However, she has never seen a physical specimen that compares with the man sitting on the side of the bed in front of her.

Examining the wound, she finds it much worse than a scratch. She can't believe Cam can sit completely still, without flinching, as she cleans and probes at the ugly gash, before wrapping it with a clean tight bandage. Recovering her composure, she smiles inwardly so he can't see her. It tickles her that he is more concerned with being half naked in front of her than by the pain of the wound. She wonders, what he would do if he was shot in the leg and she needed to remove his pants? Tying the bandage, she studies her work for a moment, then picks up her bag and turns to where Jeremy is lying.

"Now Cousin, let's see what you've gotten yourself into."

"It's only a scratch," Jeremy jokes. "Is Cam gonna live?"

"Uh huh, I've heard that one before. Trish looks back where Cam is examining his bloody shirt. "We'll get you a new shirt, Mister Mitchell, and yes, Jeremy will probably live a long life if he quits getting himself shot."

"Thank you, ma'am."

"Miss, if you don't mind."

"Yes, ma'am."

Buttoning the clean shirt the old woman brought him, Cam sits on the other bunk and waits as she ushers Jeremy into bed and covers him up. Nodding at the unhappy patient, he follows the old lady from the room to the adjoining dining area where Spade Jackson stands leaning against the stone fireplace, puffing on his pipe.

"How's my grandson?" The old prospector is grouchy. He doesn't mince words getting acquainted.

"Mister Mitchell did an excellent job taking care of Jeremy." Trish speaks up from the nearby kitchen.

"For that sir, we are in your debt." Jackson looks over at the tall young man. "What can we do to repay you?"

Cam watches the girl as she exits the room. "The shirt's enough. I'll be riding out as soon as I get my horses."

"Your horses are pert near used up. A day or two of rest won't hurt them any and it might just help you too." Spade rolls himself a smoke. "You and the horses both are all gaunt. It looks like you been rode hard and put up wet."

"It's been a lean week with little food for me or the boy." Cam looks again at the door where Trish disappeared. "Alright Mister Jackson, I'll stay a couple days, if I won't be any trouble."

"Sit down, sir, sit down." Spade nods to a kitchen chair. "Did you pass by the Rafter 5 on your way here, by any chance?"

"I did." Cam thanks the old lady as she places a cup and saucer of hot coffee before him.

"How was everyone there?"

Cam's eyes roam the well lived-in room where a pick and shovel hang over the fireplace, a reminder of Spade's past. "They all seemed just fine."

"That's good," Spade nods. "If you get back that way, tell Angus I said hello."

"I'll do that for sure."

"You want a shot of tarantula juice in your coffee young man," Spade grins. "It'll wake you up."

"What's that?" Cam has never heard of tarantula juice.

"Whiskey boy, whiskey," Spade laughs, as he pulls a jug from behind the woodpile.

Cam shakes his head. "Never heard it called that, but I reckon not."

"Not a drinking man, huh?"

"No, sir. I never got the taste for it." Cam nods. "My partner wouldn't refuse you though if he was here."

"You mean Caintuck Waters, don't you?"

"That's him alright."

Thinking of whiskey, partners and Angus Moore, the old man

suddenly laughs then shakes his head. "Old Angus, well he was sure enough young back then, but he had to be the worst gold prospector I ever knew, but he did like his whiskey."

"I thought y'all split up enough gold to get set up here in the mountains?" Cam is curious. "Looks like both of you are well set."

"We did, but I did all the finding. He just done the digging and drinking."

"Sounds like you got the best of the deal."

Spade shakes his head as he thought back to those long ago days. "Yeah, I reckon I did at that, except for the valley where he is now. That was a mighty pretty piece of land."

"Still is."

"I 'spect so. I ain't been down that way in nearly ten years now."

Cam can feel the sadness in the old voice. "You should saddle up and go pay Angus a visit. He'd like that Mister Jackson."

"Maybe I will one of these days." Spade drifts away for a second. "Someday never seems to come, just too much left to do around here."

The evening supper bell rings out its beckoning call across the large ranch as supper is arranged across the long table. After considerable yelling and hollering from Jeremy, he is finally allowed to come from the bedroom to eat at the supper table with the rest of the family. Trish frowns as he walks to the table. She doesn't want him up at all, but he is bound and determined to eat at the table and not in bed like a helpless cripple.

"You bust that shoulder open and you are on your own." She shakes her head at him.

"I rode all the way here from outside Garden City, where they shot me and that didn't kill me." Jeremy eases slowly into his chair. "So, I doubt this chair is gonna kill me either."

Cam glances sideways, snatching glimpses of the girl as she and the other women bring more platters of food and place them on the table. With this many mouths to feed, the women and children eat last, leaving room at the table for the men. At least twenty riders, sons and grand-sons, plus Spade Jackson, sit around the table as Trish leans over him to pour coffee. He can smell the fragrance of the soap she uses. He can't help himself, his eyes are drawn to her like a magnet, but he sure doesn't want any of the other men catching him in the act of staring at her. Jeremy smiles as he doesn't miss the looks and he can tell Cam is smitten with the girl, especially the way he blushes when she brushes up against him.

"You gonna stick awhile, Cam?" Jeremy questions.

Nodding slowly, make the black locks of hair fall forward on his face. "Couple days, maybe. Your grandpa said my horses are pretty jaded."

"They are mister, but they're sure fine horseflesh," a younger man speaks up. "That bay thoroughbred is as good as I have ever seen."

"The boss said you rode in from the Rafter 5 before coming here." The big redhead from the yard speaks up. "Is that so?"

"Maybe I did." Cam instinctively doesn't like the rough, ruddy faced rider.

"You didn't happen to see that big black horse they call Thunder when you were there?"

Cam nods, "I seen him."

"Is he really as much horse as the Rafter 5 riders have been bragging about over at Gila Town?"

"Well, now, I don't know what they're saying, but he's definitely a lot of horseflesh for sure."

"Hear tell, old Bob Moore is gonna take him all the way to Santa Rita to this year's Fourth of July Celebration to buck him out."

"You don't say," Spade Jackson speaks up. "Then he must be quite a horse."

"Yes sir, old Bob is putting up a hundred dollars to anyone who can ride him for thirty seconds." Red Hacker laughs, "All it costs to try is ten."

"Sounds like a profitable venture if a man can stick with him."

"I'll stick, you can bet on it." The redhead brags loudly as he looks over where Trish is pouring coffee.

Spade nods as he pushes back from the table and lights his pipe. "Well, I like a man with confidence."

Trish looks about the table as all the men finish their meal. "You men git yourselves gone, let the women and kids sit down."

"Thank you, miss," Cam's eyes stare into hers, "For everything, including this scrumptious meal."

"You're welcome, Mister Mitchell." She smiles, her beautiful lips separating, showing off her pearly white teeth. "We owe you a lot more. Thank you, sir."

Leaving the kitchen, Cam notices the men, gathering along the front porch, start to take more interest in him, but don't speak as freely with him as they did at the table. He doesn't notice Jeremy outside, sitting in a chair, talking with them. He stays inside speaking with Trish, while Spade shows him what a poke of real gold nuggets and dust look like. He heard of gold in the Mogollons, but he has never actually seen any. Several times he attempted to pan the small creeks that he and Caintuck camped beside, but to no avail. Nothing like gold materialized in his pan. Finally, he gave up, figuring it a waste of time.

Jeremy says you killed Len Fox in a straight up shoot out." Red Hacker fires up a smoke, looking over at Cam as he steps down from the porch. "Says that's how you got winged."

Cam looks over where Trish has walked outside and is standing beside Jeremy then averts his attention to the sinking sun. "Reckon it's past my bedtime."

"I asked you a question, raw hider."

"I heard you plain enough." Cam turns slightly, facing the big man. "Goodnight."

Spade Jackson, who followed Cam from the kitchen, looks over at Jeremy and frowns. "If you're so talkative about this man, Jeremy, why don't you keep talking and tell us all how you happened to get shot by a posse."

"I guess, Granddad, I didn't duck fast enough."

"Don't get cute with me, boy. I'll tan your hide, wounded or not," the old man bristles. "How did you get shot?"

"Sorry, Grandpa."

"Spill it, what happened?"

"I was wrangling horses for Jack Ketchum and Len Fox when a posse rode up behind us and started spraying lead everywhere." Jeremy looks down at the ground, embarrassed. "We made camp thinking we lost them, when suddenly, everything broke loose and I caught one in the shoulder."

"You were riding with Jack Ketchum, the outlaw, after me talking to you a month back?" Spade looks hard at Jeremy. "Why, boy?"

"Yes, sir, I reckon there's only one Jack Ketchum in these parts." Jeremy nods. "Reckon I didn't listen good enough."

"You've been riding with that wild bunch of killers?" Gage Jackson speaks up. "How long has this been going on?"

"Yes, sir, I rode with them, but this was my first time and my last. I was just holding their horses. I sure didn't rob or shoot anyone."

Spade turns his attention on Cam. "Is that the right of it, Mister Mitchell?"

"As far as I know. I found your grandson on the trail after Fox left him there wounded and bleeding."

"Well, we're a thanking you for that." Spade stands up and stretches. "Red, you show Mister Mitchell where he can bed down tonight."

"Yes sir, Boss."

Jeremy motions Cam back to the porch where he sits. "You watch out for old Red. He's sweet on Cousin Trish and he's been watching you two at the table tonight."

Cam looks over where the girl stands beside the door frame. "Why? She hasn't even noticed me?"

Jeremy grins. "Oh yeah, you tell Red that."

Cam looks up to see the girl's blue eyes staring straight into his. Touching his hat, he says goodnight then turns back to Jeremy. "I thought he was one of you Jacksons."

"Nah, just a hired hand, but he's a rough one. You watch yourself." Jeremy worries as he looks over at Spade Jackson. "Maybe I should get granddad to let you stay at the house tonight."

"Never mind, but thanks anyway. I'll be fine." Cam looks over at the girl again. "I'm a grown boy, Jeremy."

"Red."

The big man stops and turns to face Spade Jackson. "Yeah, Boss."

"Mister Mitchell has been wounded and he is a guest. You make sure the boys stay quiet tonight and let him rest."

"Yes, sir."

"I'll see you at breakfast, Cam Mitchell."

"Yes, sir."

Cam tightens the cinches on the bay gelding and the black then ties on his saddle roll and his bags. He has stayed longer at the Jackson place than he intended to, but he just couldn't bring himself to leave the ranch. He's been at the ranch three days now. His side is still sore, but he feels strong and he has no excuse to stay longer. It's time to ride. Hanging around the Jackson spread, mooning over a girl, isn't gonna get the Steeldust back. Adjusting the cheek strap on the bay's bridle, Cam takes up the reins and leads the two horses from the barn.

Jeremy walks slowly to where Cam stops near the corrals. "Well, I hate to see you leave."

"I should have ridden out yesterday."

"Why didn't you?" Jeremy grins, he knows the answer already. "Is something holding you?"

Cam ignores the question, only nods. "Tell your granddad thanks for the hospitality.

"I will tell him, but I owe you a lot more."

"You're paid up Jeremy, just live a good life."

"You mean an honest life, don't you?" Jeremy laughs. "I will and that's a fact."

"A man follows his own conscience." Cam looks over at the youngster and smiles. "You're one of the luckier ones. You get another chance at life."

"That's true enough and I thank you for it."

"Live it to the fullest Jeremy, but live it honest and straight."

"I hear you, friend." Jeremy looks over toward the porch. "Before you ride out Cam, someone wants to see you over at the house."

Cam has already seen the girl standing on the porch, clutching a flour sack tightly. Shaking hands with the youngster, he leads the horses over to the ranch house. "You wanted to see me, Miss Trish?"

"I've put you up some food for the trail, Mister Mitchell." The blue eyes stare boldly at him. "You don't have to go so soon."

"Cam's the name."

"Cam, stay a few more days." Trish smiles.

"Thank you." Cam accepts the food. "It's time I ride out."

"You're going after your horse?"

"I need to get down the road, Trish." Cam touches her hand as she continues to hold onto the sack.

"You mean you need to get after Jack Ketchum, don't you?"

"I reckon."

"You wouldn't change your mind? I know my granddad would give you a job here on the ranch."

Cam shakes his head. "No ma'am, I aim to have my own ranch and I need the Steeldust to start my herd."

"Is a horse worth your life, Cam Mitchell?"

"More than my life, if need be."

"Well, will you be back this way?" The blue eyes keep boring straight into his dark eyes without flinching, almost like she is pleading. "Someday?"

"Would I be welcome?"

"You'll be welcome with open arms anytime," she smiles.

"Then Miss Trish, you can count on it, I will be back." Cam removes his hat. "Just as soon as this business with Ketchum is finished, I'll be back as fast as a horse can bring me."

"Good." Releasing the flour sack, she lets her hand touch his lightly. "I'll be watching for you, every day."

Cam mounts the bay and dallies the lead rope on the black to the bay, then tips his hat and turns the horses. "I'll be back almost before you know I'm gone."

"You be careful," Trish smiles. "Come back to me safe."

Turning the bay around, Cam looks down at her and smiles. "You know you're beautiful."

"Am I, Cam Mitchell?"

Red slaps his chaps hard with a riding quirt as his enraged, bloodshot eyes follow Cam from the yard and out of sight of the ranch. His head turns back to where Trish stands transfixed, her eyes covered by her hand, trying to shade them from the morning sun as she stares after the departing rider. For the last three years, he has courted the girl to no avail and now a complete stranger, rides into her life and in three days, he can see, she is captivated. It isn't so much what she said, but her actions and now her eyes following him from the ranch speaks volumes.

"Seems like she's smitten with him," another hand, cleaning the barn, speaks up then laughs. "Looks like you done lost out, Red."

Only the hard slap of the beefy hand is heard as he knocks the rider backward into an empty stall. "That'll be enough, Red." Jeremy enters the barn behind the two men.

Advancing on the down man, Red stops and looks around where Jeremy stands. "You stay out of this kid. It ain't none of your business."

The dark barrel of the forty four levels at the big man as Jeremy draws his pistol. "I'm making it my business. Trish is my cousin and I won't listen to her being talked about out in a stable."

"You figure you've grown some in the britches since you've been riding with Ketchum and his scum."

"Yeah, this gun makes a man's britches real big."

"We'll see." Red starts to advance. "I don't think you've got the nerve to use it."

"Don't make me kill you, Red."

Only a snicker comes from the redhead as he takes another step. "I'm telling you boy, you ain't got the guts."

The cocking of the hammer sounds like a cannon going off in the quiet of the barn. "Don't take guts Red, just a slight touch of this hair trigger."

Slapping the quirt against his chaps, Red whirls from the stall. "You be on the lookout kid. You know, a dark night or an accidental fall from a horse."

"Is that a threat, big man?" Jeremy hasn't lowered the weapon. "If it is, I'll shoot you right now."

Red shrugs innocently. "Now, I wouldn't harm you, would I? What, just for threatening me with a gun?"

"Thanks Jeremy, you saved me a beating, I reckon." The rider rises to his feet as Red walks away laughing. "He's mean, and he's laid claim to the girl."

"I'll have to kill him someday." Jeremy lets the hammer down and returns the weapon to its holster. "He won't be getting Cousin Trish, I believe she's taken."

The rider nods. "Yeah, Red knows that too. He saw the way she looked after the stranger when he rode out."

"It's her privilege who she looks at and why." Jeremy turns and looks over his shoulder. "At least she's got good taste."

"Why don't you tell your granddad what Hacker said and get him run off the place." The rider watches the disappearing back of Hacker. "He shouldn't be foreman and still bite the hand that feeds him."

"That's true, but this is my problem, I'll handle it."

"Well, you be careful. I don't trust that redhead one little bit." The rider picks up his dropped pitchfork. "That man, he's mean clear through."

Chapter 6

$\mathcal{C}$am pulls the blowing horses in as he climbs the last steep part of the trail leading up from Jackson Basin. The ranch buildings are tiny but still visible far below, nestled in the flat, flower covered meadow. Stepping down from the bay, he loosens the girth and switches the bridle over to the black gelding. Both are powerful animals and can make the climb out of the basin without tiring, but there is no use in overworking either one. Pulling his canteen from the black, he drops the reins, ground tying the gelding and finds a seat atop a flat rock, sitting down to study the valley below. He can see horses and cattle grazing along the basin floor, even at this distance. Rays from the sun shimmer off the small creek that feeds the valley, making the wild flowers give off their beautiful colors and aromatic smells. It is a beautiful setting, picturesque in every way, a place where a man could be content, if he is with the right woman.

The breeze is slight this morning, feeling cool and welcome as it blows across his dark face. He wishes he had a pair of long-seeing field glasses that he saw in the store window in town, but never thought he would need. He never thought he would meet a girl like her either. Never would he have thought of finding any girl who would have such an effect on him in a short time. Somewhere below, in those ranch buildings, she is working, perhaps even crossing the yard or hanging out clothes on the clothesline. If he only had a pair of the glasses, maybe he could get one last glimpse of her. She affected him deeply, more than he ever thought possible.

Cam is tempted to ride back and take the offered job, but no, he cannot betray Caintuck's trust in him. Second, his pride stands in the way. He could never live off a wife's kinfolk. He knows the ranch they found in west Texas and the Steeldust is the answer. He has to recover the stallion and start his own ranch. Then, and only then, could he ride back to Jackson Basin for her with his head held high. Recapping the canteen, he takes one final look, down at the ranch buildings, longing to see her one more time, then mounts the black, turning him back to the west and the Rafter 5 ranch. He will check first to see if the two outlaws with Fox kept their word and left his horses at the ranch, then he will backtrack and find Ketchum and the Steeldust. The Rafter 5 is only days away, so he will not lose much time. Leaning down, he pulls a beautiful sunflower and smells its fragrant petals while taking one final look down into the basin.

The search for the stallion will take time, which is no problem. Cam is young, he has plenty of time on his hands. He does not worry about losing the stallion. There is no way Ketchum will part with a valuable animal like the Steeldust, nor will he damage him in any way. There is no one in these mountains that has any idea of the value of the animal, nor did they have the money if they knew. Somewhere ahead, on the long trail, he will find Ketchum and the stallion.

The small town of Gila is a wet spot in the road, a dusty, dry, and unforgiving land. The two redeeming things about the town is, it has a well-stocked General Store and the Gila Bank, which supposedly is foolproof. No outlaw band has ever been able to rob it successfully. Over the years, many have tried their luck. Boot Hill, on the edge of town, has many head markers to prove it. Down the street, a few doors, stands the Gold Nugget Saloon, which is also well-stocked with whiskey and beer. Over the years, many an outlaw has sat in the saloon, drinking their drinks. They stare across the street at the fat bank with its huge vault and the steel cages where two guards with sawed-off shotguns, wait behind a wall of steel.

Miles and Soapy rode in two days earlier and now, with their eyes on the swinging doors, they spot Sam Giles, another gang member. Giles walks into the saloon, moving up to the long bar. Motioning at him when he turns to survey the large room, which is the custom of his breed of man, they smile as he ambles over and pulls out a chair. Taking a place at their table, Giles pours himself a tumbler of Red Eye whiskey from their bottle. Smiling as he watches the strong spirits settle in Gile's stomach, making him belch.

Soapy leans forward, "what are you doing here, Sam?" Soapy looks cautiously around the saloon, looking for trouble. "Is Ketchum casing the bank again?"

"I remember the last time we tried to take it," Miles downs a whiskey. "It didn't work out too well that day. We lost two men."

"No, you dang fools, Ketchum sent me looking for you two." Another glass of whiskey disappears down the man. "Pecos and Zeke are looking east, toward Garden City and Santa Rita."

"Well old hoss, you found us," Soapy leans back comfortably in his chair. "I didn't know we were lost, Sam."

"We were wondering what happened to you." Giles downs another whiskey, then looks about the saloon. "Where's Fox and what are y'all doing here?"

"Fox is dead."

"Dead, when, how?"

"You remember the kid with the horses and the wagon, outside Garden City? Well, he shot old Len dead." Miles reaches for the half empty jug and points his finger at Giles. "Bam bam, straight through the heart, twice."

"You've gotta be joshing, got old Len from ambush did he?"

"I'll bet old Len didn't think it was a joke." Soapy looks deep into the amber liquid left in the bottle. "Nope, it was straight up, fair and square."

Giles chokes a little on the strong liquor, making him cough as he absorbs the news. "You must be kidding or were you drunk?"

"We were neither." Miles shakes his head. "Those shots weren't an inch apart or a split second between them."

"Then you're lying. Nobody alive, but Ketchum is faster than Fox. Well, maybe Doc Holliday, Earp, or Doc Mills."

Soapy looks at Giles and smiles. "We thought the same thing, but I've seen both Mitchell and Ketchum draw. I wouldn't bet a cent on who would win if they came face to face, not a plug cent and that includes the others you named."

"Y'all just stood there and watched without pulling iron?"

Miles slowly pours himself a drink and smiles at Giles. "We weren't about to commit suicide, Sam. That kid shot Len then had us covered before we could blink."

"What we're trying to tell you Sam Giles, is that we're lucky to be alive." Soapy takes another drink, his hand slightly shaking. "Mitchell seems likable enough, but he's pure rattlesnake when he gets his rattler's shaking."

"You two don't even talk sense," Giles glares at the pair.

"We do to us, and a piece of advice for you, Sam." Miles suddenly rises a few inches from his chair. "You meet with this Mitchell, you best give him a wide berth, cause three like us couldn't get the job done."

"What are you two doing here then?" Giles stares at the two men. "Why didn't you ride in and tell Ketchum?"

"We're leaving the Mogollons for health reasons."

"Health reasons?"

"Mitchell told us he'd kill us if we went back to Ketchum and we believed him."

"So you ran like scalded dogs with your tails tucked between your legs?" Giles looks hard at both of his former gang members. "I'm disgusted with you."

"You betcha we did. You ain't seen the look in his dark eyes." Miles shakes his head. "He's a dangerous man, maybe even a mite crazy. He spooks the devil out of me."

"I think you're both yellow." Giles shakes his head. "Now let's ride."

"Nope." Soapy doesn't like the man referring to him as yellow and starts to rise, but Miles holds his arm. "You think what you like, but we're through with Ketchum and this kind of life."

"Do you know where Mitchell is now?"

"No, but you ain't gonna have any trouble finding him."

"Why's that?"

"When he finds out that Steeldust ain't at the Rafter 5, he said he'll be coming after that stallion, and I believe him." Miles shakes his head. "We left two of his horses there when we passed through."

"Then we'll be waiting for Mister Mitchell somewhere along the trail."

"Sam old friend, you'd live longer if you ride west with us, out of this country." Soapy looks at the door nervously. "I'll guarantee it, this Mitchell is poison, mean, and he's riled over that horse."

Giles shakes his head and pours himself another drink. "I've been in many a tight scrape with you boys. I know you ain't yeller, but I can't believe one man can send you running like a gut-shot coyote. He's sure got you both spooked."

"Believe it," Miles shakes his head. "We're running, as far and as fast as we can, and right now."

Both men watch as their former companion stands and walks through the saloon doors without a backward glance. "Some people just don't like good advice."

"They may like it, but they don't listen so good." Miles shakes his head. "I hear Colorado calling us, let's ride."

Trish Jackson watched Cam until he disappeared into the brush of the valley then slowly turned back toward the kitchen. She didn't see the jealousy leaping from Red's eyes as he watched her from the barn door. Going back inside and closing the screen door, she finds Spade Jackson sitting at the long table, sipping on a cup of coffee, his eyes watching her.

The old prospector seems to read her thoughts as she enters the kitchen. "You've only known him for three days, Granddaughter."

"You're wrong Grampee, I've known him all my life." Trish smiles knowingly. "I didn't know it until three days ago, but he's the only man for me."

"He may not come back." The old prospector lights a sulphur to his pipe. "He may not be able to."

"He will if he can." Trish stares out the window. "When he does, he'll find me waiting."

"Are you sure, young lady?" Spade puffs slowly, thoughtfully, trying to think of something to change her mind, to keep her from getting hurt.

"I've never been as sure of anything in my whole life."

"I've known men like him before. He's wild." Spade shakes his head. "The boy could get himself killed."

Trish smiles and looks across the table at her old granddad. "Love is not measured by time, Grandfather. When he looked at me and I touched him, I knew he was the one for me. Nothing will change that, ever."

Spade Jackson is now an old man. In his lifetime, he has seen many a wild one come and go through these mountain ranges, some running from the law, some just honest prospectors. Years ago, in his younger years, when the two first met, Angus Moore was cut from the same wild cloth as Mitchell. A year or two later, Spade helped Angus escape from a lynch mob after Angus killed another miner in a bar fight. It was a fair fight, but the dead man had many friends among the Irish miners; too many. After breaking Angus from a makeshift jail in the mining camp, Spade led Angus away from the mining camps and a sure hanging the next morning.

Escaping far back into the Mogollons, where the maddened miners from the gold camp were afraid to follow, for fear of the warlike Apache. The two partners decided to split up their gold and try ranching as a healthier way of making a living. A year later, with the founding of the Rafter 5, the two partners separated. Spade brought a wife from the east, married, then stayed back in the mountains, away from town people and the trouble that surrounded town folks. Yes, Spade remembers Angus well. In his younger years, he was wild and dangerous, exactly why this young Mitchell reminds him of his old partner. Only time and age with Spade's continually watching over Angus in their first few years, had finally cooled the temper that was always simmering beneath the skin, only a word or spark away. Spade knows Angus better than any man. Even in his old age, Spade knows the fire is still there, ready to ignite at any time. It is the same hot temper the Mitchell youngster has pent-up inside him, just waiting to explode.

Mitchell is likable enough, but Spade has seen the quick fire in the young man's eyes when Red pushed him, three nights ago. No, Spade doubts Cam Mitchell will be back. He is bound for trouble, maybe death. If it isn't Ketchum then sooner or later it will be someone else. He saw it too many times before. It isn't that men like Mitchell look for trouble, it's just that trouble finds this breed of man. Spade fears for his granddaughter. He only wants her to be happy, and with a man like Mitchell, he fears there will be more danger than happiness.

The old man looks at his granddaughter and drops his eyes, nodding slowly. She has always been trapped back in the mountains and their remoteness. The girl never complains, but he knows she is lonely. For what, Spade doesn't know. Spade has sons and they all have wives, but none of them know what the girl needs or they aren't saying. He has to admit, for the first time in the last three days, he has seen another side of his granddaughter. For the first time since she has become a mature woman, she seems alive, happy with a bounce in her walk, a beautiful smile on her face, and a rich soft laugh. He hopes he is wrong about the youngster, but he doubts it. Mitchell is strong willed with a wild streak in him, like the Angus Moore. He doubts any woman will ever break him.

Sam Giles rides hard into the Rafter 5, his horse lathered, wore out, and unable to go further. Quickly turning the sweating gelding into the round corral and catching a fresh animal, he switches his saddle and without saying a word, kicks the mount on down the trail toward Echo Canyon. Only the hundred dollars in coins, sitting atop the gatepost, would explain the missing horse and the hard ridden animal left behind in the corral. It has always been an unspoken deal between Rafter 5 and the outlaws running these mountains. Nothing would be said as long as the horses are bought and paid for. Angus figures it an honest trade with no laws being broken on the ranch's part. Only once, years ago, a horse had been taken without payment, and it resulted in Angus Moore personally, tracking the thief down and hanging him.

From the beginning, the old rancher made it Rafter 5 policy not to interfere or turn in any rider who passes through as long as he doesn't steal from the Ranch. Any traveler coming down the trail to the ranch would be fed and given a bed for the night. It was the unspoken rule, no questions asked of anyone. It turned out to be an effective way of not having to protect his ranch and cattle from the many men riding the lonely back trails of the Mogollons. Outlaws like Ketchum, respect the old rancher. They know as long as they treat him fairly, he will not interfere with them or their lawlessness. As lawless and cruel as they are, they also know they don't want both the law and the hard-bitten old man on their bad side or back trail.

Giles rides hard to the southeast, letting the gelding slow to a walk or stop at the small streams he crosses, just long enough to get a drink. It is a full moon lighting up the smooth, gravel trail, well enough to permit him to travel throughout the night. Departing the Rafter 5, he doesn't know the whereabouts of Mitchell, but he pushes hard, wanting to warn Ketchum before the youngster finds and surprises him. The country he is traveling is remote and rough. Anywhere along the lonely trail, Mitchell could be waiting for him to pass, but he cannot slow down and use caution. He still can't believe Fox was outdrawn and outgunned. He has ridden the outlaw trail with Soapy and Miles and he knows them to be tough men. They had no reason to lie about the fight. Ketchum is an outlaw and riding with him is a dangerous way of life. Most men riding outside the law don't live long enough to reach rocking chair age, but for a lazy man, like Giles, it sure beats riding fence or punching cows. Giles doesn't worry about the danger. Riding the wild outlaw trail, doing and taking as he pleases, has been a good life. He sure isn't about to let Cam Mitchell ruin it.

Two nights later, after pulling the gelding in, Giles studies the quiet, dark passage that lies only yards ahead of him. Echo Canyon, with its rock walls and hard gravel trails, is amply named. Any noise at all causes reverberations to echo up and down the canyon walls with eerie sounds. Nothing passes through the canyon without giving an echoing warning of their passing. Until he clears the canyon completely, the eerie silence and cascading echoes make Giles' neck hairs stand on end, every time he passes through. Local lore of the warlike Apache, say evil spirits inhabit the canyon, the haunted ones. Only the bravest of the Apache, some like Geronimo or Juh, would dare pass through its barren reaches.

Staring at the dark mouth of the canyon, Giles remembers one time when he and Ketchum sat in the same spot, looking the narrow passage over as he is doing now. That evening, both men had an uneasy feeling, almost as if they could feel someone waiting, close to the mouth. Their feeling was right. Geronimo and his warriors opened fire on them from behind the boulders lining the canyon floor. Dismounting quickly, the two men returned the rifle fire, pouring into their position.

After an hour, just before darkness came over the canyon, Geronimo stepped boldly into plain sight, demanding to know why they were here in his mountains. A lighter warrior interpreted for the war leader, scowling as Ketchum answered. Several minutes later, after negotiating and haggling, Ketchum gave the bronco Apache all the tobacco they brought back from Gila. Geronimo smiled shrewdly, nodded, and waved his arms, sending the warriors back through the canyon. Their yipping sounds reminded Giles of a pack of coyotes after a rabbit.

Geronimo was a crafty leader. Already, two of his men were slightly wounded from the sharpshooting of the two whites who were in an impregnable position. By taking the tobacco from the whites, he prevented more of his warriors from getting killed or wounded, plus he saved face in front of his men. Now, with the gift of the tobacco from the whites for passing through his country, the Apache Medicine Man and war leader could proudly ride away from the canyon with their pride intact.

"Great." Giles gripes as the echoing of the catcalls in the canyon ceased. "Now we don't have a drop of tobacco to smoke. Why didn't you give him the whiskey too?"

"I would have if he asked for it." Ketchum breathed a sigh of relief. "You can bank on it. Letting that bloodthirsty heathen out trade us was far better than fighting him."

"Why, we had him outgunned, maybe not outmanned, but outgunned for sure."

"Maybe we did at that, maybe we didn't. I say it was better the old bandit got our tobacco than our heads." Giles still remembers Ketchum's words that long ago night, before riding forward into the barren canyon.

Kicking the gelding, Giles grins to himself. He never wanted anything as badly as he wanted tobacco that night, just one little cigarette to quiet down his nerves, after that ordeal. Never has he passed through Echo Canyon again without remembering the fight with Geronimo and never has he been without tobacco again. That night, they were lucky, the Apache Warrior was a white hater, but he was also a great leader. He wouldn't get his men killed for nothing. Pushing the gelding faster, he rides forward into the noisy passage, navigating through the dark canyon as fast as he can, safely. Breathing a deep sigh of relief, as he clears the canyon, he shudders slightly as he rides away. Ketchum's hideout is only a few miles further along the trail, hidden from sight, deep in another smaller canyon.

Reining in at a large mountain cedar tree, partially hiding a smaller animal trail, Giles looks behind him. He quickly dismounts and leads the gelding through the rocky gorge, which is the beginning of a rough trail, leading downward and leveling out onto a small grassy valley. The trail is rough and horse could easily fall and break a leg if they didn't place their feet carefully. Giles slowly works the gelding down the slippery rocks, making sure to stay on the high side of the trail and out of harm's way, just in case the horse slips or stumbles. Finally reaching the bottom, Giles looks to where he knows they always post a lookout.

"That old trail is getting rougher every time it rains, ain't it?"

"That you, Shorty?" Giles can hear the voice, but can't see the face yet.

"Yeah, it's me. It's 'bout time you got back here." The man they call Shorty appears from behind a high boulder.

"Has Ketchum been wondering where I've been?"

"Yep." The small man nods slowly. "Pacing the floor and cussing you with every breath."

"Well, I'm here now."

"Where's the rest? Where's Len Fox, Soapy, and Miles?"

"Gone, they won't be back."

"Gone where?" The guard cusses. "Ketchum is gonna love that for sure. We're shorthanded. Some of the boys are in Mexico and we've got work to do."

"Is Ketchum planning a job?"

"Maybe." Shorty shrugs. "You'll have to ask him about that."

Giles mounts and kicks the tired gelding into a slow lope across the flat valley floor. A mile further along, the small cabin and corrals sit, resting against the canyon wall, which shields them from the afternoon sun and north winds. Hidden, unseen behind the cabin, is the narrow passage, just big enough for a single rider at a time to pass through.

Ketchum and his men call it their backdoor out of the canyon. They seldom use it because of the rough terrain a rider and his horse must pass through. Nevertheless, if the law follows them here, it keeps the canyon from being a boxed in trap with no exit.

Giles reins in at the cedar log corral and dismounts. He knows he is being watched from the windows, but no one comes outside to greet him. Quickly placing his saddle on a pole sawhorse and turning the gelding loose, he shoulders his saddlebags with his possibles inside and heads toward the dark cabin. Entering the doorway, he finds five men playing stud poker at a rough board table. Three others sit near the blackened cookstove, drinking coffee. Giles nods, a little agitated at their aloofness and poor manners. He knows well enough that he was watched since leaving the canyon mouth where Shorty stood guard. He figures they could at least speak as he enters.

"About time you got yourself back." A heavy bearded man with a dark complexion looks up from the card game.

"I had to find Soapy and Miles. It wasn't easy." Giles can't meet Ketchum's hard stare. When the leader is mad or riled, no one can look into his brown eyes.

"Where were they?"

"Gila."

"What is it? You're holding something back." Ketchum stands up and walks across the room. "What were they doing in Gila?"

Giles pulls the makings from his pocket and rolls himself a smoke. Lighting up, he looks around the room. "Len's dead, Jack. Soapy and Miles are running out of the country as fast as horses can carry them."

"What?" Ketchum shakes his head as if he didn't hear what was said. "Len's dead; what happened?"

The burning cigarette is forgotten as Giles relates the story that Soapy and Miles told him. "That's all I know, except those boys won't be back, I'll guarantee it. I saw the look in their eyes and heard the fear in their words."

"He was just a youngster." Ketchum remembers Cam. "Soapy and Miles wouldn't have been that scared of him, to run like jackrabbits."

"Well, they did. If you'd seen the look in two of our best men's faces, you would change your mind about this Mitchell just being a youngster."

"Cousin Len is one of the best men with a gun I have ever seen." Ketchum rubs his face, stunned. "Nobody was faster."

"Miles said this Mitchell put two slugs dead center in Len's gizzard, quicker than you can blink." Giles looks around the room. "Where's Pecos and Zeke?"

"When they got back here, I sent them to take guns to the Apache." Ketchum strikes a match on the table leg. "They should have been back two days ago."

Giles flips his smoking stub into the charred wood box. "He's coming Jack, you can count on it; you better."

"You sound half scared yourself."

"I didn't ride two horses near to death getting back here for nothing." Giles lights another smoke. "Until we kill this one, let's just say I'll be on my toes."

Ketchum laughs shakily. He can smell the fear on Giles. "You're liable to cripple yourself standing on your toes."

"Jack, it doesn't hurt one bit to be careful."

"No, it doesn't." Ketchum looks around the room at the pitiful small amount of men he has left. "I know you're tired Sam, but I need you to take Leeds and Blake and go find out what happened to them two."

"Where you gonna be?"

"Right here, waiting on you."

Cam rides into the ranch yard of the Rafter 5 midafternoon of the fourth day after leaving Jackson Basin. He was held up for a whole day by what looked like a war party. He waited for the warriors to break camp and move on to the southwest, deeper into the Mogollons, toward Echo Canyon. The small party of Indians blocked the cross trail he was on, preventing him from leaving his place of concealment. Where the trails cross, high in the mountains, the trail was too small to pass unseen, so he had little choice but to stay out of sight and wait.

"Well, Cam Mitchell, it's good to see you again."

Cam nods and dismounts. "Bob, it's good to see you too."

"We hear you've been busy."

"Maybe a little. Are my horses here?"

Moore laughs lightly and nods. "They're here alright."

"What's so funny?"

"Couple of Ketchum's boys brought them in, course I figure you already knew that."

"What about the Steeldust?"

"Sorry, we ain't seen hide nor hair of him." Moore shakes his head. "All they said was you had your horses now and they were through with you and Ketchum both. They bought two horses from granddad and rode west like their tails were on fire."

"If you can put me up for the night, I'll head back out, come morning."

"Are you going after Ketchum or the two that rode west?"

"I told you, I want that stallion." Cam thinks about Trish Jackson. "The ones that rode west don't interest me anymore. If Ketchum would have brought the Steeldust in, he wouldn't interest me anymore either."

"You know Ketchum and Len Fox were Cousins, almost the same as brothers." Bob Moore motions to a chair. "He's not gonna let your killing Fox stand."

"So I've heard." Cam remembers Soapy's words of warning. "What's your point?"

"One of his men came through two nights ago and changed horses." Moore looks to where Angus appeared on the porch. "Ketchum is bound to know you killed Fox by now."

"You're thinking he might ride back this way looking for me?"

"Could be."

"Good, it'll save me looking for him."

Angus walks to where the two men are sitting and nods slowly as he looks Cam up and down. "You've grown some son."

"Have I, Mister Moore?"

The old head nods slowly. "In my eyes you have."

Cam knows what the old-timer is talking about. "He didn't give me much choice."

"Doesn't matter now, you outclassed him." The old prospector turned rancher, smiles. "That's what matters in the end, ain't it?"

"I reckon." Cam thinks back at the surprised look on Fox's face when the bullets hit him. "I reckon it's better than coming out second best."

Angus pushes a pup out of the way and sits down. "Old Soapy said you shot Len twice, dead center, beat him to the draw bad."

"Barely."

"An inch is as good as a mile when you get there first."

"Yes, sir."

"Put your horse up and come on in." Angus turns back to the door. "We'll talk some more."

Several riders are inside the barn working, as Cam and Bob Moore lead the two geldings through the double doors. All eyes turn curiously on the newcomer like they are seeing him for the first time. Pulling the saddles from the horses, Cam tosses them across saddle racks, then turns the geldings out, into a large corral. Looking over at the smaller corral, he recognizes the blaze face of the horse they call Thunder.

Moore props a leg on a lower corral bar and nods at the black. "Dad had us leave him up, figured you might be needing him."

"Your dad was right. My two are all used up after that fast ride over the mountains." Cam nods. "He'll need shoeing in this rough country before he can travel far."

"He's got new iron on every foot."

Cam steps up on the corral and looks the black over, shaking his head. "I'll bet that was a chore?"

"Ask the boys here, they done it for you."

Turning, Cam nods at the gathered riders. "Thank you, gents. I'll stand you all to a beer next time we blow into town."

"You earned it, Mister Mitchell, and you don't owe us a thing." Kirby speaks up. "Fox killed a friend of ours a while back."

"Well, thank you again and the beer will still be on me."

"If you insist, we'll surely wet our whistles on you then." A young rider nods. "It'll be our pleasure to drink with you."

Angus Moore sits across from Cam at the table, watching as the young man eats his supper. "Did you happen to run into my old partner Spade, on your journey?"

"Yes, sir, I did." Cam tells of finding Jeremy Jackson wounded and taking him on to Jackson Basin, saving his life. "He spoke well of you and said to tell you to come visit."

"Been meaning to and I will one day soon."

"That's the same answer I got from Mister Jackson."

"Did you get enough to eat, Cameron?" Louise walks over to the table carrying a fresh baked pie.

"I did, ma'am, and it sure hit the spot." Cam smiles at Mrs. Moore. "I have never had a better tasting venison steak."

Louise Moore blushes at the compliment. "Well, thank you Cam. Now we'll finish them off with a fresh pie."

"You're welcome." Cam looks at the steaming piece of pie she places before him. "It smells wonderful."

"I swear you've lost five pounds."

Cam smiles, "I admit I've missed a few meals lately."

"Well, we'll fix that soon enough."

"I doubt even your good cooking can fatten him up by morning Louise." Bob Moore winks at her. "He'll be pulling out, come sunup."

Surprised, she clicks her tongue. "Why are you leaving so soon?"

"I'm afraid I have to ma'am."

She waves a large spoon at him. "Then you'll have a good breakfast before you leave young man, and no arguing about it."

"Yes, ma'am."

Angus looks over at his daughter-in-law, frowning slightly, causing her to excuse herself from the dining hall and retreat to her kitchen. Looking back over at Cam, the old rancher taps on his coffee cup, absently.

"I figure that was Sam Giles that came through the other night." Angus clears his throat. "He passed through here last week, headed east in quite a hurry."

"Giles, I don't know the man."

"You will soon," Bob Moore speaks up. "He dang near rode a horse to death getting this far. By now, Ketchum is bound to know you killed his cousin, Len Fox."

Cam respects the old man and his opinions. "You're figuring Ketchum will come after me?"

Both men nod, "that's about it."

"I've been as far east as the cut off to Jackson's Basin. Would you give me the layout through Echo Canyon on to Ketchum's hideout?"

"We'll give it to you." Bob Moore speaks up before Angus can object. "Be glad to, 'cause you'd ride in there blind if we didn't."

"Well folks, it's been a long day." Cam stands up and pulls his hat from the chair. "Reckon I'll check on my horses then turn in."

Angus tosses a handwritten letter across the table. "There's the bill of sale on the black horse known as Thunder. He belongs to you young man, from mouth to tail, and welcome to him."

Cam only nods and mumbles a thank you as he reads the papers.

It seems as if the morning comes almost as soon as Cam's head hits the blankets and his eyes closed. The sun is already shining brightly overhead as he splashes cold water on his face outside the bunkhouse and walks back toward the barn and corrals. Several of the hands speak to him friendly and wish him well as he examines his two geldings. They are as gaunt and wore out as he expected them to be from the long ride up and over the mountains since leaving the Jackson spread. He doesn't cotton to the idea of riding a green broke, young horse, especially one like the black, into the mountains alone, but the horse is powerful with a lot of bottom. He would carry him further and faster than either of the two geldings Soapy and Miles returned to the ranch. With the worn down bay gelding he got from Ketchum, he has no choice. After saddling Thunder and tying his saddlebags and rifle onto the black's saddle, Cam turns toward the ranch house and the breakfast he knows would be waiting. He wants to be on his way, but taking a few minutes for one of Louise's good meals wouldn't hurt.

Stepping onto the porch after breakfast, Cam smiles and shakes hands all around. "I can't thank you folks enough for your hospitality."

Angus steps closer as he lights his pipe. "You ride light Cam Mitchell, with eyes in the back of your head."

"I'll do that Mister Moore."

"You reckon old Thunder is gonna put up much of a ruckus this morning." Bob Moore smiles.

"Well, we're fixing to see." Cam touches his hat to Louise then turns his back on the Moores. "I'll be seeing you."

Angus Moore watches as the tall, young man, walks confidently toward the barn. "I wouldn't want to be in Ketchum's boots for nothing."

"I'd have to say amen to that myself," Bob Moore agrees. "I've seen the look coming from his eyes."

Thunder unlimbers, taking a few kinks out of his back as soon as Cam steps onto his back. A hard jerk and the slight touch of sharp rowels to his flanks, quickly takes most of the fight out of the horse. The black is young, but he has learned his lessons well, from the first time the human stayed on his back. Only a few halfhearted jumps are made by the black as he crosses the small corral, then Cam swings the gate open and turns the horse east. Louise is true to her word. She fixed him a fine breakfast and a sack of food hangs from his saddle long before daylight as she knows he is in a hurry to be on the trail. Somewhere ahead, Ketchum or his men are waiting. Where, he doesn't know, but both Angus and Bob Moore insist on Cam being cautious. The mountains are as wild as the bronco Apache inhabiting them. Somewhere along the wild mountain trails, trouble is brewing.

The morning passes quickly as he rides through the rough canyons covered with blooming cactus, cedar, and all types of wild flowers. The black colt surprises Cam as he is young and green broke, but he takes to the trail like a well broke, older horse. Any other time, riding the black horse in the early morning fresh air would have been pure enjoyment, but not this morning or on this trail, where the dangers are too great to enjoy. Head down, ears thrown forward, the black travels with a smooth, ground eating, running walk that he can hold hour after hour. Most young horses, on their first few rides, away from the corrals are spooky, but not the black. Everything takes his attention, but nothing scares him.

Cam mentally calculates the miles and memorizes every water hole and small creek they cross, along with any trails leading away from the main trail he is on. Not a big trail, like a road or anything, it is still plain to follow and mostly smooth, free of any rocks or chug holes. The old prospector's words keep haunting him as he rides quietly along, keeping him alert for any sign of an ambush from whites or Apaches.

Four miles from the cut off to the Jackson Ranch, as Cam lets the black water at a trickle of freshwater crossing the trail, the horse throws up his head, sensing something nearby. Quickly dismounting and covering the quivering nostrils, Cam leads the black deeper into the surrounding brush, listening quietly until he finally locates what the black sensed. The sound of horses trotting fast along the flat trail, come to Cam's ears, warning him of riders coming straight toward him, long before they come into view. Walking the black further out of sight, inside a small stand of cedar trees, he holds the horse's muzzle to keep him from nickering a greeting to the newcomers, whoever they are. He hardly gets set when two riders come into full view, riding down the twisting trail, pushing their sweaty horses hard.

Turning the black's muzzle loose, Cam rushes forward onto the trail and levels his pistol surprising the two men. Reining in their horses hard, the riders throw up their hands and nod grimly at Cam.

"Hold on there for a minute, mister. We're from Jackson Ranch, not Ketchum's bunch." The older man, holds up his hand. "You're Mitchell. I remember you from when you rode into the Basin last week."

Cam thinks he recognizes the men, but he only saw them once. "You men seem to be in a hurry."

"We are, mister. Put down that hog leg and we'll tell you." The older rider dismounts as Cam puts up his weapon. "All hades has broken out back at Jacksons. We're on our way for a doctor."

"What happened?"

"You remember Red Hacker?" The younger of the riders leans over and pushes back his hat. "The bigmouthed, redhead that tried to ride you back at Jacksons?"

"I do."

"He tried to attack Trish Jackson when she was alone in the barn gathering eggs, then shot Jeremy Jackson when he tried to stop him."

"How bad is she hurt?"

"She ain't, except for a black eye and a torn blouse. Reckon she put up quite a fight. That's how come Jeremy found them. She was really yelling." The older rider shakes his head sadly. "Poor kid didn't stand a chance against a man like Hacker."

"Is the boy dead?"

The younger rider steps down. "He hadn't cashed in when we rode out, but he's shot pretty hard."

"What else?" Cam can tell the two men are holding back more. "Speak up man, what else has happened?"

"Red shot the old man as he rode away from the ranch." The rider shakes his head. "Mister Jackson didn't get hit too bad. The girl is taking care of him, but she needs a real sawbones for the boy and that's where we're heading."

"You boys better ride." Cam looks at their tired horses. "I've got two fresh horses back at the Rafter 5. Tell Angus or Bob Moore I said you boys are welcome to them."

"We're a thanking you, Mister Mitchell."

"The name's Cam."

"You heading after Ketchum and your studhorse, I reckon?" The older rider looks over at Cam. "We heard about the Steeldust from Jeremy."

"Ketchum and the Steeldust can wait for now. I'll be riding to Jacksons."

"Tell Miss Jackson where you saw us and that we'll get back just as quick as we can."

"I'll tell her."

Both men mount and watch as Cam pulls the black's head around by the bridle cheek. "One other thing, we saw fresh tracks about three miles back or so. Suddenly, they just disappear. We think someone might have hid beside the trail and let us ride by."

"Why would they do that?" Cam is curious.

"Can't say, we didn't have time to follow them, but they sure can't be too far off the trail, it's too narrow a canyon." The younger rider shrugs. "Couldn't have gotten far off from the trail, and there ain't no trails leading away from there."

"You think it was Red?"

"Nah, he headed southwest from the ranch like his tail was on fire." One of the riders shakes his head. "He couldn't have gotten back here that quick, not unless he sprouted wings."

"Ketchum?" Cam swings onto the black's back and holds him tight for a few seconds.

"Maybe, but that would just be a guess on our part." The rider nods. "You ride light."

Both men watch as Cam rides out of sight, and then turn their horses. The other rider takes one last look down the trail and shakes his head. "Did you see the look on his face? I sure wouldn't want to be Red Hacker when Mitchell sees the girl's bruised face."

"Me neither, anybody could tell he was taken with her just by watching them together."

The younger rider agrees, "Yep and she was doing some looking herself."

"Wonder what old Spade will think of that?"

"I'll say this, if I were him, I'd be happy about it. That's one man I'd want on my side in a fight."

"True enough." The two Basin riders disappear down the mountain trail.

As much as Cam wants the Steeldust back, he knows he has to check on Trish and Jeremy first. The black sidesteps a few steps, wanting to follow the other horses, but a spur to his shoulder changes his mind. Cam isn't in the mood for any of his tomfoolery, now it's all business. Trying to recall from his first pass through this desolate country, the small valley the two Jackson men described to him, where they saw the tracks, Cam figures couldn't be far ahead. If he's right, it is a good place for an ambush, but Cam figures whoever hid and watched the two men pass, has already traveled further his way. He hopes it is Ketchum and his bunch out looking for him, but he knows it isn't. The outlaw would have stopped the two riders and questioned them. Ketchum is a killer and an outlaw. He might have killed the men if he took the notion, but he wouldn't hide and let them ride past him.

Anywhere in the rugged Mogollons, with their rough trails, boulders and winding trails is a perfect place for an ambush. Cam worries about Trish. He can't take the time he needs to be cautious. The Jackson riders didn't know what had become of Red Hacker or his whereabouts. Hacker knows the layout of the Jackson Ranch and Cam doesn't figure the redhead would leave the Mogollons without the girl. He has to get back to Jacksons in time to help, in case Hacker doubles back to the ranch and tries to get at her again. He has to stay on the trail, riding hard, worrying about an ambush if it happens.

Suddenly, the black jerks his head up, his ears pointing forward, his attention focused fully on a thick grove of cedar trees and underbrush just across a flat mesa. Again, quickly dismounting, Cam clamps his hand across the horse's muzzle. The thick underbrush and trees along this strip of canyon is a perfect place for an ambush. There is no way of crossing the small clearing without being observed. The brushy area the black is watching is less than fifty yards across a flat clearing, an easy shot for any rifleman and Cam knows Ketchum's men are all excellent marksmen.

Tying the black with a lead rope instead of his leather reins, so he can't break loose, Cam slips quietly forward, his Winchester cocked and ready. Whoever is across the clearing has to know he is near, the same as he knows they are waiting ahead. Slipping quietly, beside a dead oak, Cam watches and waits, staying hidden and silent, while he surveys the tree line closely. His eyes never blink as he scans the underbrush and the canyon wall for several minutes. He doesn't dare move closer across the clearing, the ground is too open. Whoever waits, hiding on the other side, will have a perfect shot at him.

Suddenly Cam stiffens. A half mile across the canyon and coming openly down the trail, is several Apache warriors, heavily armed, and riding straight toward whoever hides in the trees. Cam can see the Apache are moving forward cautiously with the two lead warriors following the tracks on foot. The riders, hiding in the trees, apparently, have their attention focused entirely on him, waiting for him to show himself. Watching from his hiding place as the drama plays out, and as the warriors ride slowly forward, it dawns on him, the Apache are tracking the ones in the trees. Cam watches as the rest of the warriors dismount and advance quietly on foot, straight at the brush, leaving one younger warrior behind, holding the horses.

Cam straightens slightly. He can't believe his eyes. One of the warriors carries a white flag, something unheard of for the Apache. "You, white man in tree, you come here. Talk with us and bring girl."

"Leave this place or we will kill her right now." A gruff but frightened sounding voice, speaks back.

"You turn girl loose and we will leave you unharmed," the Indian voice answers in broken English. "You kill girl, we burn you over hot fire."

Gunfire erupts from the trees, making the warriors duck for cover as rifles and pistols spit fire and lead from the brush. A bearded white man, holding a young Apache girl in front of him as a shield, backs away from the crouching warriors, his pistol held cocked and pointed at her head.

Eight Apache men stand and walk into plain view, again holding their rifles and bows ready. The taller of the warriors, steps forward and speaks to the white. "I tell you again, if you do not harm my daughter, I will let you live white eye."

"Apache, am I supposed to believe you?" The white keeps backing up, although Cam knows the man has no place to retreat. "You back off and bring me and my partner our horses. Then I'll turn the girl loose down the trail."

"I am Juh, war leader of the Mescalero People." The warrior steps forward. "I do not lie, white man."

"Juh, yeah I know who you are." The pistol raises slightly as the white panics, his hands shaking. "I ain't telling you again. I'll kill her for sure."

"She is only twelve summers. She is innocent." The warrior steps closer. "She is my only daughter."

Cam watches the white's eyes narrow as terror grips him. The name Juh, sends chills through every white's spine. He is fixing to shoot the girl at any second. Raising his rifle, he aims at the man's gun arm, but the girl jerks the man hard as he pulls the trigger, causing the bullet to strike the big white through the heart. Every Apache head turns in surprise as Cam steps into full view, his rifle held cocked and ready across his body. Cam watches as the young girl races behind the warriors where every rifle and arrow is now pointing right at him. Walking to where the dead white is lying, Cam rolls him over, looking up at the approaching warriors.

"You have killed one of your own, white man."

"No, I don't consider this scum white." Cam looks straight into the warrior's dark eyes. "I have killed an enemy."

"You lie," Juh shakes his head. "A white does not kill another white to save an Indian."

"Like you told this one," Cam points down at the dead white, "I do not lie."

"Why he your enemy?"

"He and his partners stole horses from me and killed several men in the white man's town to the west."

"These whites ride with the white man Ketchum, who makes his camp back in the small canyon beyond Echo Canyon." Juh looks hard at the dead man. "They come to our rancheria to trade guns for our gold. This dead one and the other stole my daughter and rode away. We follow him here to this place."

"So you know Ketchum?"

"We know this one. He has traded rifles to us for yellow iron many times." Juh nods. "He is a hard man, but we must trade for the guns and bullets he brings."

Cam knows this warrior will know exactly where he can find Ketchum and his men. "He rides a grey studhorse that belongs to me. I aim to have him back."

"I understand, for I have seen this horse. He is a magnificent animal." Juh nods. "Tell me, white man, are you a man that carries metal on your chest?"

It takes Cam a few seconds to understand what the chief is asking. "No, I am not a lawman."

"Then why would you risk your life to save an Indian girl?"

"I told you, I came for the gray horse. This dead one helped steal him from me." Cam points down at the dead Ketchum rider. "Where did you see the horse?"

Juh looks back to where his warriors are listening to their words as they hold the other white prisoner. Cam can't tell if any of the others speak enough English to tell what is being said, but he doubts any did. He knows the Apache need the rifles and ammunition traded to them by the white gunrunners here in the mountains. Juh dares not betray the white who brings guns to his people, even though this one has saved his daughter's life. The wild and warlike Apache had to have guns to fight the whites and raid the Mexicans for their winter supplies.

"You will leave this place with your life. That is enough."

"I will not leave these mountains without that horse."

"Are you the son of the old one, Angus Moore?"

"No, I am only his friend. My name is Mitchell."

"You are brave, like the old one." Juh raises his hand. "Thank you for saving my only daughter. Now you will ride back the way you came, your life for hers."

"No, I ride to Jackson Basin." Cam's eyes study the warrior. "They have much need of me and I will not turn back."

Juh looks back at his warriors. "You know the other old one who lives there?"

"I know him."

"You may go in peace, Mitchell." Juh turns his head. "I cannot protect you further if you ride against the white man, Ketchum."

"What about him?" Cam points at the other white who stands trembling.

"He is ours."

"Ketchum will be mad if he dies, maybe no more guns for the Apache."

"You go now Mitchell." Juh points east. "Do not let the Apache catch you again in our land."

Chapter 7

Untying the black, Cam mounts and rides back to where the Apache are waiting, where every hostile eye focuses on him. He saved the Apache girl, but he knows, if Juh didn't hold the others back, they would have gladly killed him. He doesn't know the Indians like old Caintuck does, but he realizes he barely missed getting killed. He didn't shoot the white man to save himself. He merely meant to wound the man and to save the young girl. Her last minute pull on the white's arm, pulled the man right into his bullet and killed him. Looking over at the other white, he shakes his head.

"Save me, mister. Don't leave me with these heathens." The man pleads as the black turns away.

"There's nothing I can do for you, fella. You brought this on yourself." Cam looks back at the shaking man. "You're safer with them mister, than you are with me."

As Cam rides east, he fights the urge to look back at the warriors and the cringing white. He has heard enough about the Apache, never beg or let them smell fear. He knows the white is a dead man and there isn't anything he can do about it. Cam isn't scared, but there is nothing he can say or do to save a white who insulted and almost killed Juh's daughter, even if he wanted to, which he doesn't. Caintuck always said the Apache hate a coward and a liar, above all else. He respects an Apache's fighting ability and courage, but he doesn't fear them in the least. If it came down to a fight with the ones he rode away from, so be it, but he wasn't about to let the white shoot the young girl in cold blood.

Turning his attention back to the trail before him, he knows the Jackson riders were right about someone being on the trail, only they had mistaken the riders for Ketchum. They were Ketchum's men alright, but they were not on his trail. The two men who had taken the Indian girl, turned west on the Echo Canyon Trail, not east. Cam knows their hideout is east. He doesn't know why they didn't ride back to join Ketchum. He can only surmise they traded the gold from the Apache and then one of the whites, or both, noticed the young Apache girl on their way out of the village and took her. It is something Ketchum would not approve of, as it would ruin their trading with the Indians and his men would know that, so they rode away from the hideout. He figures the men had no intention of ever returning to the hideout as Ketchum would probably shoot them. No, the men were on their way out of the Mogollons with both the gold and the girl when Cam blocked their trail and gave the Apache time to overtake them.

Cam holds the black down to a slow walk as he studies every boulder, tree or hiding place that men could be waiting on him. The trail, turning south to Jackson Basin, materializes at almost sundown. With the sun dropping over the mountains, Cam pulls the black in and studies the dark trail ahead. He has only crossed it once. Tonight, once the sun sets, it will be pitch black and he knows he can't find his way in the dark. He remembers many trails turning away from the main trail on his last trip through the passes. If he accidentally makes the wrong turn in the dark, he would lose many hours. Ahead, he remembers a small pool of clear water, not far from where the trail branches off, there he will spend the night.

The black is young, unused to hobbles, picket ropes, or any of the conventional methods of restraining a horse from wandering away. Cam uncoils his lariat and makes a halter for the animal, which permits him to graze, but it will get Cam's attention if he becomes wrapped up in the rope. This far back in the Mogollons, he can't afford for the young horse to get crippled by a bad rope burn to his hocks or even a broken leg if he gets hung up then spooked during the night. Cam plays out the rope, giving the black enough room to graze while he holds onto the other end so he can sleep.

Digging into the flour sack of food, Louise put up for him, Cam digs out biscuits and side meat as he settles back against his saddle, holding the rifle across his lap. Breakfast was many hours behind him and his stomach starts growling. Cam doesn't smoke the Bull Durham rolls like Caintuck does or the smelly pipes Angus Moore puffs on, but he thinks it would not be a good time for any smoke. Tonight, he doesn't even start a fire for a hot cup of coffee, fearing smoke from a campfire would carry far across the land to any sharp-nosed rider or Apache warrior riding the mountains.

Leaning back, he stares up at the stars overhead, listening, as a lonely Coyote voices his sad song ringing out across the far reaches of the Mogollons. Despite his problems with Ketchum or Red Hacker, he finds the night peaceful. If only he knew for sure, Trish Jackson is safe, he could relax and enjoy the night. Cam always loved the loneliness of the mountains and alone on the trail as he listens to the night birds and hunters. Tonight is such a night, but he thinks of the girl and he can't understand these new feelings. He has known her for only three days and has spoken to her even less, but the image of her beautiful face, calm demeanor, and proud bearing, brings a warm smile to his chest. Knowing little about women or how they act, he isn't sure she has given him any reason to think as he does about her. Maybe he has mistaken her actions or perhaps she was just being friendly.

Orphaned at an early age, by the death of his folks, Cam started working the far-flung horse ranches as a wrangler before his fifteenth year. His natural ability to tame or ride a bad horse, made his reputation as a horse breaker spread throughout Arizona, even into New Mexico and West Texas. Caintuck Waters was trading horses at a local ranch and saw the raw talent the nineteen year old youngster had with a horse. The old horse trader convinced Cam to partner up with him fifty-fifty in the horse-trading business. Traveling from town to town, for the last five years together, they saved quite a nest egg, trading and selling horses, or betting on whether Cam could ride a bad outlaw horse. Later, Caintuck traveled alone, far into north Texas, keeping his promise to return with the best stallion in the state, and he did.

Cam stood on the board sidewalk, looking in awe as Caintuck paraded the gray Steeldust stallion proudly down the main street of the small town of Santa Rita, his chest thrown out and his back straight, with an old man's cocky bearing. Before Caintuck rode east, they made plans to meet in the small town in exactly two months. The Steeldust stallion was to be the herd sire of the great horse ranch Caintuck envisioned for him and Cam. The land for the ranch was located already and the bank in Gila held their hard-earned money needed to pay for it, safely in its vault. Now, after acquiring the Steeldust stallion, they were on their way.

Cam has the natural talent with broncs, and with Caintuck's knowledge of horses, they did well trading with the ranches and townspeople. Most times, when they entered a town, Caintuck was challenged by someone who had a bad horse and wanted to lay bets on whether the youngster could ride it or not. The only thing the old horse trader wouldn't bet on was a horse race. Caintuck bought and sold horses so he wasn't about to keep a horse on his string just for his running ability. If he traded for a fast horse, he was more than willing to let someone else buy the animal and run it himself. He always told Cam there just wasn't any percentage in running a horse for money. There were too many ways to lose.

Few men around the Mogollons, ever knew of Caintuck's ability with a pistol, but Cam eventually found out the old man's past. Around their many campfires, Caintuck would take a few too many nips from his whiskey bottle and start talking about his younger days. Disbelieving the tales of Caintuck's wilder days as just talk, Cam finally forced the old horse trader to pull a well-oiled forty-five from his saddlebags and prove his stories were true. In awe, he watched as Caintuck drew the weapon, then twirled, rolled, fanned, and finally fired a burst of shots that were earsplitting. Convinced of the old man's prowess with the pistol, from that night on, Cam, with Caintuck's teaching practiced with the pistol at every opportunity. The way the walnut stock feels, the burning powder smell, and the bucking as the pistol roars, spitting fire of lead, is something Cam enjoys almost as much as taming a bad horse.

Caintuck watched in disbelief as day after day, the youngster worked on his speed and accuracy with his old forty-five. The hand was just a blur as it sent five rounds into a close group that a silver dollar could almost cover. Finally, on Cam's twenty first birthday, Caintuck bought Cam a brand new forty-four and a Mexican fast draw holster and belt.

Cam was curious why Caintuck bought him a forty-four instead of a forty-five. A quick demonstration of the forty-four's superior fire-power, answered his question quickly. The forty-four has much more penetrating power than the forty-five Caintuck owns. Not that the forty-five wouldn't get the job done, the old horse trader swore, but the forty-four, he said, would get it done faster and with more range.

With the lessons also came a constant warning from the old trader, not to get a reputation with the pistol. A gunfighter lives a lonely, dangerous life. Sometime, he will face a faster gun; it is inevitable. Someone is always waiting, wanting to prove they are faster. The day may come when a killing is outside the law and then there will be a wanted poster with his picture posted on it and every lawman in the west looking for him. Cam listened, keeping the forty-four in his saddlebags while in the many towns they passed through, only buckling it on when they were in dangerous or unknown country. Only once, before shooting Len Fox, he was forced to draw on another man. A saloon drunk, poisoned with rotgut whiskey, thinking Cam was young and knew nothing of guns, because he was unarmed, tried to pick a fight. The man placed his pistol on the bar and ordered another one placed on the bar in front of the unarmed youngster. The drunk could only blink and freeze as he stared at the cocked pistol, staring right at him as he started for his pistol.

No one in the room saw Cam's hand move as he reached for the pistol. Seeing the color drain from the man's face, Cam laid the pistol back on the bar and motioned at the door.

"Git and leave your pistol on the bar while you're leaving."

The drunk could only nod, hurrying from the saloon, thankful to be alive. The town was all talk as most who knew Cam thought it was an accident, the ones telling of his speed with the pistol were drunk. That was the only time Cam resorted to a gun and later, he was thankful he didn't have to use it. Len Fox gave him no such choice.

Sam Giles sits his horse on the trail, looking down at what is left of Pecos and Zeke, the two men that were sent by Ketchum to trade rifles with the Apache four days ago. The bodies left lying in the hot sun were bloated and torn apart by animals. Giles barely recognizes the dead bodies of men he had ridden with, ate with, two men he called friends. Turning his eyes, he looks at the men with him and shakes his head. Animals prowling the night have been at the bodies of the two men, which the Apache War Chief Juh left dead, behind him. The powerful beaks of the floating buzzards did their grizzly work. Shaking his head, he looks around for someway to bury the men.

"Leeds, ride back to camp and tell Ketchum what happened here."

"What happened, other than they are dead?" The rider is confused. "What's to tell?"

"Apaches, that's what happened."

"Why were they here? It's almost five miles back to Echo Canyon and the trail leading to the Apache Rancheria." Leeds shakes his head. "Besides, why would the Apache kill the men that were supplying them guns?"

"I don't know; neither the gold or rifles are here."

Leeds shrugs. "Well, Ketchum is gonna want questions answered. I sure ain't gonna be the one to look at him and say I don't know."

Giles has seen many dead men in his line of work, but men torn up by wild animals, turns even his strong stomach. "With these men dead, we're down to six now."

Another rider dismounts and examines the trail. "Apaches killed Pecos back in the trees, but I believe old Zeke here was killed by a white man."

"What?" Giles whirls on the man. "A white man?"

"Boot tracks. Last I knew, Apaches don't wear boots." The rider points at the tracks. "Look, they're as plain as your face."

Giles nods, the high heeled boot tracks in the soft sandy trail are plain to read. Neither Giles or the other rider Blake, can be sure the white man killed Zeke. Nevertheless, there definitely was a white man here at some time when he was killed and the man rode away toward the east, unharmed. "Mitchell."

"What?'

"It had to be the one that killed Fox. His name is Mitchell."

"How is he so friendly with the Apache?"

Giles shrugs. "That I don't know. Mitchell is a curiosity for sure, a dangerous curiosity. I only know the man doesn't mind killing, and he is after Ketchum and us too, if we get between him and that gray stud. He's got to be crazy or something."

"The whole gang has been torn apart over one gray horse?" Leeds swears as he rolls himself a smoke. "Why don't we just tell Ketchum to give the horse back to this crazy psycho?"

"We're losing many men alright," Giles agrees, "I sure ain't gonna be the one to tell Jack Ketchum to give back that horse, no siree, not this old boy. I mentioned that idea to him once."

"Are we going after Mitchell or running for home?" Blake speaks up.

"First, I'm gonna get these men buried somehow." Giles looks over at Leeds. "I told you to ride."

"Those Apaches could be between us and the hideout." Leeds is scared. "For some reason, they killed two men they been trading guns with for three years now."

"Yeah, they could be and probably are out there. Now ride or Mister Leeds, you're gonna think I'm Apache." Giles whirls on the man.

The eastern sun is warm on Cam's back as it clears the Mogollons. Sitting high above the mountain trees, it already starts heating up the day. The black grazed through the night and rested so now he is ready to travel. Cam pats the smooth, coal black neck. It's hard to believe this is the same horse that was called an outlaw less than two weeks ago. Somehow, the horse was soured by human hands. He learned some bad traits, but Cam knows he isn't an outlaw. He just needed a strong, gentle hand to handle him.

Cam reins in and sits looking down at the Jackson Ranch buildings from the same spot, high on the trail, that he last observed the ranch from. Nudging the black, he starts down the gravelly trail that switches back every thirty yards or so, due to its steepness. The black is on his haunches most of the time, sliding down the trail, causing the gravel to roll freely in front of him. Cam is leaning far back in the saddle to keep astride the black and not go over his head. He dismounts and leads the horse, making the steep trail easier on both of them. Finally reaching the bottom, he mounts and kicks the black into a long lope toward the ranch.

Reining to a sliding stop in the ranch yard, he is met by two young boys carrying rifles. "What's your business, mister?"

Cam remembers the faces but not the names of the young men. "I've come to see Miss Trish and her grandfather. You boys remember me?"

"Yes, sir, Mister Mitchell, we remember you." The older of the youngsters waves his rifle. "Hand over your pistol and walk ahead of us."

Cam can hardly contain a smile, but he has to admit, the boys have him cold and don't show any fear or any intentions of letting him go into the ranch yard alone. "Here it is gentlemen."

Both youngsters study Cam for several seconds and motion him forward. "She's in the house with granddad. We'll be right behind you, so don't try anything funny."

"How is your granddad and Jeremy?"

"Jeremy's dead." One of the young men shakes his head sadly. "Trish couldn't save him."

"I'm sorry." Cam can see the tear in the boy's eye. "Where are all your menfolk?"

"They're out looking for Red Hacker." The youngster's face grows hard. "When they catch him, we're gonna hang him high, real high."

"That don't bother you?" Cam looks down at the youngster.

"Bother me, shucks after what he's done here, I'd put the rope on him myself."

Leading the black to the house with the boy's right on his heels, Cam ties the animal to a hitching rail. He hardly turns when the door opens and Trish Jackson walks out onto the porch. Recognizing Cam, the tall girl hurries to where he stands beside the black and stares up at him.

"Oh Cam, I couldn't save him." She drops her face to his shoulder, trying to hold back the tears. "I tried, but he was shot too bad."

"I know Trish, but you did your best." Cam turns her to him and looks several seconds at the badly bruised and swollen face looking up at him. "I met your riders on the trail. They didn't say you were beaten so badly."

"I'm alright now, just a few bruises." Trish takes his hand and leads him into the kitchen. "If Jeremy didn't help me, it would have been a lot worse, and because of me, he was killed."

"He died like a man, a brave man." Spade Jackson lies on a settee in one corner of the kitchen. "We're proud of him."

"I was just as proud of him, Grandfather, when he was alive."

"Trish, out here, men live and die every single day, that's just the plain truth." Spade rises slightly. "My grandson gave his life for you, Granddaughter. It's a man's place and duty to take care of his women-folk."

Motioning to Cam to take a seat at the table, she turns back to the kitchen stove and starts filling a plate with food. "Yes, Grandfather, I know how men are supposed to take care of us helpless women."

Cam can sense the strain in her voice and tries to think of something to ease the tension in the room, just as the door squeaks open and several men file slowly into the room. Looking over to where Spade Jackson sits staring at them, the oldest rider walks over to the settee and shakes his head. "Sorry Pa, we lost his tracks over in the Roughs of the Fingers."

Several times, sitting around a campfire, Caintuck told Cam of the dangers of what the old prospectors called the Fingers. A vast rock-strewn, jumble of several canyons branching out, like a hand, is how the maze received its name. The jumble of rock and canyons reminded the first white men, who discovered it, of a handful of fingers. Gravel, granite, flat rock, and shale, all combine to make tracking in its vast enclaves, impossible. The Jackson riders lost Hacker's trail almost as soon as they entered the first hard rock passes of the canyons.

Spade cusses from his place on the cot. "We'll get him. When I get on my feet, I'll track that man to the gates of Hades if I have to."

The rider who spoke, looks down at the older Jackson. "He'll surface somewhere, then we'll go after him, but tracking him through that maze is impossible."

"You're saying to just let him ride away?" Spade bites down on his pipe. "Why didn't you take Chotilla with you?"

"He's away hunting somewhere. We couldn't find him."

"I want Red Hacker and I want him bad."

"What else can we do, Pa?" The rider shrugs. "You of all people know how following a track through that mess is hopeless."

Spade shakes his head fuming. He wants Red Hacker for killing

Jeremy and attacking Trish. He knows how dangerous the man is and that he could possibly return for the girl.

"Tell me, where do these canyons, you call the fingers, lead to?" Cam pushes his plate back and looks over at the tall rider.

"Anywhere, New Mexico, Arizona, Mexico, those badlands have many exits." Gage Jackson sits down heavily at the table. "There is no way of telling where he'll head or which trail he'll take."

"Tell me, is there a trail leading through these roughs that turns back east to Echo Canyon?"

Gage nods as Trish places a cup of coffee before him. "There is. Why?"

"If you folks can point me in the right direction, I'll be riding out in the morning."

Spade looks through the smoke of his pipe at Cam. "I thought you wanted to get your horse back."

"Right now, some things are more important."

"Did my granddaughter tell you Hacker threatened to come back and get her?" Spade looks at the girl.

Cam sets his coffee cup down and looks at the girl. "No sir, she never mentioned it."

"Well, he did and I believe he will try." Spade chews on the pipe. "He'll be back when we least expect him."

Gage Jackson looks sideways at Cam then over at Trish. He has seen the look that passed silently between them and now understands why Spade asked. At first, he is shocked, knowing they have only known each other a few days at most, but the signs are there, something is between the stranger and his niece. Nodding solemnly, he accepts the plate of food she sits before him as several more of Spade's sons and other riders find seats at the long table.

"It'll just be a waste of time Mitchell. You'll wear out your horse and maybe get lost or killed." Gage shrugs his shoulders. "Probably both."

Cam looks over at Gage. "It's my horse and my life, ain't it?"

The rider smiles, "It's your funeral Mister Mitchell, but I say wait till we get a location on him, then we'll ride."

"It's a tough, wild country down in the Fingers. You'll need a guide," Spade speaks up. "That is, if you're bound and determined to go."

"You know anyone?" Cam remembers the hundred dollars Angus

Moore had given him for riding the black. "I'll be willing to pay for his services."

"I know one, if we can find him."

"Get him; I'll pay whatever he wants." Cam rises from the table. "Now, I'll see to my horse. I'll be riding out, come daylight with a guide or without one."

"You best wait Mitchell. Red is a bad one to mess with, especially if you're back there in the canyons alone." Gage Jackson toys with his food. "Besides, what's your stake in this? You don't owe us anything."

"I'm a bad one to mess with too, Mister Jackson," Cam looks hard at the rider, "I owe Jeremy."

Gage nods. "We all owe my nephew and my dad, but tracking Hacker back in those mountains is impossible."

"I'm gonna give it a try anyway." Cam stands up. "You boys guard Trish and the ranch. I'll try to run Hacker down."

Everyone at the table looks up, as Trish follows the tall man from the kitchen. Gage Jackson studies Cam's departing back as they turn to their food. "I believe him, Pa; he is a bad man."

"You're learning son." Spade lights a sulphur and refires his old pipe. "You send one of the hands to Chotilla's Rancheria. Tell his woman we need him now."

Standing back as Cam unties the black, she walks beside him to the barn. Unsaddling the horse, Cam rubs him down and puts him in a large box stall. "Is this the outlaw horse called Thunder?"

Cam nods and looks closely at her face. "He is, but he's not an outlaw anymore."

"He is a beautiful animal."

"He is and a good horse to ride." Cam studies her face. "Does your face hurt much?"

"I won't lie to you, it does smart a bit." Trish takes his hand and pulls it to her face. "You have a soft touch."

"Hacker won't hurt you again, I promise."

"I won't ask you not to go, just promise me you'll be careful." She squeezes his hand.

"I'll be careful." Cam smiles, "I have a lot to live for now."

"He doesn't look so dangerous."

"Who?" Cam isn't sure who she is speaking of Hacker or the black.

"Thunder, he seems almost gentle."

"Looks can be deceiving, Trish."

"That's exactly what Jeremy said when I said that you were very nice."

"I thought Jeremy liked me?" Cam looks down at her.

"He admired you very much." Trish smiles, "He also said you were a dangerous man."

Cam nods. "He should have lived. He would have made a good man."

"Yes, he would."

"He was far too young to die."

"So are you, Cam." Trish smiles, then slips quietly into his strong arms. "I feel safe here in your arms. Let's just leave the mountains, ride away, and be happy."

"And forever looking behind us for the rest of our lives?" Cam shakes his head. "No Trish, I have to finish this, for us and for Jeremy."

"Just come back to me Cam Mitchell, that's all I ask."

Cam is busy saddling the black early the next morning when the horse cocks his ear backward. Whirling around, the forty- four was just a blur, as Cam aims the pistol at a crouching figure behind him. A slender, dark skinned man, squats across the barn, his narrow, coal black eyes, watch every move Cam makes.

"You are fast, but your ears are not so good." The voice is low, almost inaudible. "I would rather have good ears."

Cam stares down the barrel at the squatting man, not knowing exactly what he is. Long, grayish black hair, hangs below the man's sloping shoulders and huge chest. The legs sticking out from under the loincloth are thin, almost sickly thin. The arms are the same, slender with corded muscle and no fat. It's the eyes that take Cam's attention, jet black, deep set, and wide, making the little man look reptilian. The man's cheekbones are set high in what seems like an overlarge head with a huge forehead.

Never has he seen anything like this warrior in looks, statue, or demeanor. The man didn't make a sound when he entered the barn. He seems Indian, but he speaks like a white man. The Indian can't be over five feet tall, maybe an inch or two more and Cam guesses him at less than one hundred thirty pounds.

"Don't let his looks fool you, Mister Mitchell." Gage Jackson steps from the shadows into the light, grinning at Cam's expression. "He's a handy man to have on your side."

"What exactly is he?"

"I am Navajo, not what." The small Indian seems insulted. "You can speak to me white man, I speak English."

"Sorry," Cam smiles slightly at the small warrior's gruff reply, "No insult intended."

"Old one sent for Chotilla. Say you want to go to place of the Fingers, deep in mountains." The Navajo shrugs. "Why you want go to this place? Nothing live there, not even scorpion."

Cam nods. "Do you know this place?"

"Chotilla knows, dangerous place." The little man shakes his head. "You wait here, redheaded one. He comes here, bye and bye, for woman."

"Your name is Chotilla?"

"My name is Chotilla. Squaw, she call me other names when she mad, sometimes." The warrior stands up and looks over at Cam. "This warrior pay five horses for loco squaw, maybe he more loco, what you think Cam Mitchell."

"Maybe, I'm the last to ask about a woman. I've never been married." Cam smiles. "I know nothing about their moods or anything."

"You smart man, maybe." The little Indian looks over at Gage. "You want Hacker because he say he come back for woman. Why you do this thing if you no like woman?"

Cam blushes, then ignores the question. "I'm heading into the canyons, are you willing to track for me?"

"Without Chotilla, you no find the Fingers."

"I'm going, with or without you."

Chotilla stares hard at Cam then smiles. "What you pay this one to bury you?"

"You think I'll die, do you?"

"Maybe, you young man, maybe not." Chotilla looks back at Gage then with uncanny speed he hurls his long knife into the barn post beside Cam. "You see, I'm fast too."

Gage Jackson steps forward and pulls the knife from the post, handing it back to Chotilla. "You two are getting off to a shaky start. Maybe Chotilla should go home."

"How much do you want to be paid, Navajo?"

"Five horses and white man teeth."

"Teeth?" Cam looks hard at the little man, not understanding. "You want some teeth?"

"Yes, me want bought teeth like old one has." The little warrior grins, showing nothing but gums, no teeth. "Me want eat meat, deer, cow anything that don't eat me."

"You mean store-bought teeth?" Cam has never thought about buying teeth before.

Chotilla shakes his head. "No, me want white man tooth doctor to make teeth that work good."

"You lead me into the canyon and find Red Hacker and you've got your teeth and the horses." Cam looks across at Gage. "You heard it, Mister Jackson, I'll have the finest set of teeth made for him money will buy if we get Hacker."

"I heard it alright." Gage shakes his head. "I think you're both crazy."

"We go." Chotilla turns abruptly and heads toward the door. "If you die, don't blame this one. You were warned."

"If I die little man, you won't get your teeth."

"No matter, if you die, me probably die too." Chotilla moves from the barn like the whisper of a ghost. "Dead man don't need teeth."

Cam looks over at Gage and shakes his head. "He's a character alright."

"Just remember this then, listen to him, no matter what happens." Gage nods. "I've followed him on many a trail and he's never failed us."

"What's a Navajo doing here in southeastern Arizona?"

"Chotilla is an outcast, driven out by his own people."

"What for?"

Gage looks to where the little warrior leaped lightly onto a bay gelding. "He never did say, just showed up here one day with his woman and children. He helped out around the place and came in mighty handy when we needed a tracker."

"That's all he does is track for you?"

"Hunts a little if we need meat, but he's too proud to do any physical work."

"Proud!" Cam looks at the little Navajo. "Of what?"

"Don't sell him short, Mister Mitchell," Gage grins. "He's deadlier than a rattlesnake, meaner than a bobcat with a sore tooth, and fearless as a gut shot grizzly."

"He doesn't look the part."

"Looks can be deceiving, so I've been told." Gage looks at the little warrior. "If I ever need backing, he's the one I want to side me."

Chotilla watches as Gage ties a bag of biscuits on the black and shakes his head. "White man eats too much, no catch nothing but fat belly."

"You don't eat?"

"Me eat what catch on trail, not like white eye."

"Alright." Cam tosses the bundle over to Gage. "Let's ride, Navajo."

Trish waits quietly, listening to the conversation in the barn. Now she watches as Cam and the little Navajo, who she has known all her life, ride out the back of the barn and disappear from sight. Fear clutches at her chest as she raises her arm to wave. She knows he can't see her, but she also knows Cam is as safe with Chotilla as he would be with anyone.

Turning, she waits as Gage walks to where she stands, then looks up, into his face, sadly. "I feel partially responsible for Jeremy getting killed. Now, because of me, Cam's riding into danger." Trish walks toward the house with Gage beside her. "I should have stopped him from going."

"It wasn't you, Cousin. He wants the Steeldust stud." Gage puts his arm around her shoulders. "You couldn't stop him, no more than you could have stopped Jeremy from trying to stop Hacker from hitting you."

"No, he's doing this because of me. He knows Hacker will return for me." Trish clutches her shirt. "Red Hacker hasn't a thing to do with his horse."

"You sweet on him, Niece?"

"I am," Trish nods, "You already know that, Uncle Gage."

"Something tells me the young man will be back."

Tracks of Red Hacker and the Jackson men who tried to follow him are plain in the soft trail as Cam and the small Navajo ride the mountain trails out of Jackson Basin. Chotilla rides hard, completely ignoring the tracks. Gage Jackson already told him where they lost the trail. It's good that he knows where to start looking as the jumbled tracks would waste too much time to straighten out, even for the Navajo. Cam is curious as he follows the little man. The warrior seems unconcerned the trail becomes rougher, making it harder to see tracks as they travel to the south at a jog trot. He can't see the man's eyes, only the back of the Navajo's head. He wonders if there is any life in the Navajo as he hasn't seen any movement out of him at all in the last three hours.

Finally, Chotilla reins in and sits staring at the rock strewn canyons and steep walls surrounding them, the beginning of the roughs. Cam gets his first look at the badlands. Now he knows what Spade Jackson meant when he said this is some of the worst and most treacherous country existing in the Mogollons. Raising his sinewy arm, Chotilla points out three different trails leading from the small canyon, they now sit in. Cam shakes his head in disbelief. The terrain is solid rock with small piles of rock laying about that tumbled down during heavy rains from the canyon walls. Dismounting, the small Navajo motions for Cam to stay where he is. Then he moves fluidly across the trail scanning the broken rocks laying scattered about the narrow trail. Several times, the tracker stops for several seconds, then moves on forward, his dark wide eyes searching out any sign that was left. Cam is impressed as the warrior moves like a shadow through the canyon. Not a rock or pebble is overturned, nor is there any noise made by his passing. The little warrior floats across the rough ground like a ghost.

Cam watches as Chotilla bends several times and runs his finger across different rocks like he is smelling of them before moving on. Dismounting, he runs his dark eyes across the surrounding canyon walls, then holds the horses and waits as the Navajo disappears behind a high boulder. Finally, moving at a steady trot, Chotilla reappears, coming down the trail trotting nimbly across the scattered rocks as he returns to where Cam waits with the horses. The temperature in the canyon is already rising, enough to cause a man to sweat. The air is sultry with hardly any movement, but Cam notices the Navajo shows little or no signs of effort as he rejoins him.

Shaking his head, he refuses the offered canteen that Cam holds out, then nods to the left trail, branching from the canyon. "Red Hair travels there."

"Where does it lead?"

"Many places, maybe Mexico, maybe east. Trail runs maybe five more miles, then it splits again further ahead." Chotilla uses his bony fingers to show Cam what he means.

"Can you follow him?"

"Chotilla follow this one. He not get away from Navajo." The Navajo picks up a small rock. "White man foolish. Him think rock no tell story of his passing, but they say much, tell story."

Cam looks at the rock he holds and is curious. "Tell me tracker, how do they talk?"

"Horse, him not so smart. He turn small rocks when he pass. Chotilla look close." The warrior points at the rock. "Rock darker on bottom side. Shows horse kick over rock as he pass."

"Jackson is right, you are good." Cam hands Chotilla his reins then turns to the black. "I want Hacker. I'll pay you well, but you keep after him."

"Jeremy was my friend. He always good to Chotilla." The Navajo swings easily onto his horse. "I no lose this white man, but if you no kill when we find, Chotilla will."

"I'll kill him alright." Cam's hard eyes stare down the trail. "Jeremy is just a kid. He died way too young."

"Trish Jackson, she's no kid." Chotilla halfway grins. "She much woman, strong headed."

"So?" Cam looks over at the warrior. "What are you saying?"

"I think you do this thing for her."

"You know her?"

"I there when she born. Mama die soon after. Spade Jackson tell me go find Indian woman to feed baby girl." The Navajo kicks his horse. "My squaw, she no have milk. I buy Apache woman from Cochise."

"You bought a woman like you would a cow or goat?" Cam shakes his head. "What kind of people sell one of their own?"

"Woman, she not Apache, she Mexican that Apache warriors brought back to Cochise's stronghold as prisoner," Chotilla grins. "This one give three horses for her."

"Was that a lot?"

"Squaw, she ugly, but feed baby girl good." Chotilla nods. "Yes, she was worth the horses."

Cam smiles. "I believe that. What happened to the squaw?"

"Apaches don't like Navajo people. I like these mountains so I married the ugly woman so Apache people let me live here in peace."

"That means you have two wives now." Cam is curious. "Well, did it work out okay?"

"Chotilla has three wives now." Chotilla grins. "Five little ones with the ugly one."

"You're kidding."

"No kid about something like that." Chotilla shrugs. "Chotilla have to hunt much to feed all the little ones."

"Well then, everything worked out good for you."

"Too good, maybe, Chotilla has ten babies with these women."

"Well, I guess you got your money's worth, that's for sure."

"Maybe, but now Chotilla has to work like squaw to feed little ones."

"Work never hurt anyone."

"Chotilla warrior; squaw work, not warrior."

"Times change hoss, times change." Cam grins thoughtfully.

"Bah." The little warrior shakes his head. "This one no change."

"You're Navajo, but you speak American real good."

"I learn good English from white soldier when I scout for them against the Ute people, many years ago." Chotilla grins. "Navajo learn much from white soldier, talk, gamble, cuss, and drink firewater."

"Sounds like a good education to me." Cam grins. "Well rounded."

"Good for Chotilla, me learn how to win money from soldier at fort." The Navajo points east. "Now we talk no more. We hunt red hair. Now we ride."

The country is rough, practically impassable, impossible to make good time with horses. After clearing the rough, rock strewn passes, the ones littered with the worst of the jumbled scattered rocks, the trail becomes easier to navigate. Past the roughs, riding out on a smoother trail, Chotilla points out the lone tracks of one horse traveling east at a hard trot. Pulling in his gelding at a shallow creek, the warrior studies the tracks and the direction they point, in deep thought. Sandy ground now replaces the solid granite and shale rock on the canyon floor. Cam looks up at the high mountains, still capped in snow far above where they sit, and breathes deep. Mountain pine, cedar, and an abundance of stunted black jacks, dot the landscape. Late summer flowers and green grass grow plentiful everywhere in the lush valley.

"Who owns this land?"

Chotilla leans over as his horse waters, grabbing himself a handful of the cool water and looks over at Cam. "Cochise owns all this land."

"How come he's let Spade Jackson settle in the basin without trouble?"

"Apache superstitious. Many years ago, they think Jackson bring them good luck."

"Good luck?" Cam questions, "A white man bringing Apaches good luck?"

"That's what Apache people think. He saved a small Apache Rancheria from the fever a few years back, nursing all them back to health."

"That's luck?"

"It was luck for the old one, Spade Jackson. Since then the Apache leave him in peace, except for that young hellion, Geronimo." Chotilla kicks his gelding and rides out of the small stream. "That one doesn't leave anyone alone."

"I've heard a lot about Geronimo lately." Cam nods. "Is he that bad?"

"Geronimo crazy for blood. He don't take orders from Cochise or anybody. He's wild and he hates whites." Chotilla thinks a moment, then speaks as an afterthought. "Him don't like Mexican, brown people, either."

"I know, I ran into a chief named Juh, a few days ago." Cam nods. "He spoke of this young medicine man named Geronimo and said the same thing."

"You met Juh and you're still alive?" Chotilla quips. "He's as crazy as Geronimo, perhaps even crazier."

"I was lucky, I reckon." Cam pulls loose his canteen. "You want another drink?"

"Juh, him white hater same as Geronimo. You were lucky." Chotilla pulls in his small gelding and holds up his hand, ignoring the offered canteen. "Let's hope you are lucky this time."

Cam looks along the trail and up on the ridges. "What's wrong?"

"Apaches."

"Where?" Cam looks around but can't discern anything or anybody. "I don't see a living thing."

"Soon, they come to this place." Chotilla keeps his eyes straight ahead. "Do not touch gun."

"I don't see a thing, nothing" Cam repeats, wondering if the Navajo is just seeing things or being jumpy.

"You see soon, maybe." Chotilla already spotted the warriors who are riding through the pass. "Hope this Juh, not Geronimo."

The same tall, chunky, Apache warrior, Cam met earlier when he killed the white man, comes jogging toward them with several riders strung out behind him. No weapons point at them, but Cam can see the warriors hold them ready. Catching movement out of the side of his eye, he focuses on several, higher up, looking down at them from the canyon walls.

Juh slows to a walk and reins in directly in front of Cam, his dark eyes studying the white's face. "You come Apache land again, white man."

"It is important or I wouldn't have come into Juh's land once more without permission." Cam never lets his eye blink, nor does he flinch. "I've come looking for a man."

Juh looks over at Chotilla and frowns slightly. Apache words flow fluidly from the small Navajo as he explains why he leads the white man into the vast Mogollons. "Juh knows you, Cam Mitchell. I tell him why you come again into his land."

"That he does." Cam can feel his skin crawl as the chief looks calmly at him.

"Did you get the gray horse, back yet, white man?"

"No, I've got other problems right now."

"The Navajo tells me you follow the redheaded white that rides with the one called Ketchum." Juh looks over at Chotilla. "Navajo say redhead kill and attack old man's people in valley."

"Did you say Hacker rides with the outlaw Ketchum?"

"My warriors have seen him come this way to the small cabin of Ketchum many times." Juh nods. "Many times we see this."

"I thought he worked for Spade Jackson?" Cam is surprised. "That's where I met him."

"Him do both. He work for Jackson, but Apache think he friend with bad white man also."

"The redhead killed one of Spade Jackson's children, beat a girl badly and shot Jackson himself." Cam lets the words sink into Juh's grasp. "He is a bad white, the same as the ones that took your daughter. Are you the old one's friend?"

"Juh is the friend of no white man."

Chotilla kicks his gelding closer to the Apache. "The red hair will return soon to the Jackson Ranch and steal the white granddaughter of Jackson and this time maybe he kill her."

"Is this the same white woman, the baby you traded Cochise three horses for the ugly squaw to feed?" Juh looks at Cam and laughs, "She very ugly."

Chotilla glares at the chief. "She feed baby good. Baby grow up strong."

"Baby lucky she no grow up ugly like your squaw." Juh looks back at his men then becomes serious. "White man, you were permitted to leave once and told not to return to our mountains."

"If the redhead lives, he will steal the white woman." Chotilla stares at Juh. "Let this one go in peace. Help him find the red hair one."

"I saved your daughter." Cam looks over at the chief. "That should count for something."

"Redhead big man, strong." Juh looks at Cam. "Are you strong and brave Mitchell?"

Cam is curious what the chief means. "I am strong."

"Good, we see maybe how strong."

Cam looks over at Chotilla curious. "What did he mean by that?"

"This one not know what Apache means, but he up to something I betcha." Chotilla studies the gathered Apache. "Juh sneaky warrior. I don't trust."

The Apache Chief looks first at Cam then over at Chotilla. "You can go this time white man, but do not let us catch you in our mountains again or you will die. You have been warned for the last time. This is Apache land, Cochise land, white man is not wanted."

"And me?" Chotilla grins at the chief.

"You Navajo, live only by grace of Cochise. He forbids any Apache to kill you. He thinks maybe you loco enough to buy another ugly squaw from him," Juh laughs. "Go from this place."

Cam watches as the little Navajo kicks his horse. "I will pay much for the gray horse if you find him around here."

"Apache watch for horse." Juh takes the black's reins and holds him back as he watches Chotilla ride a little distance and stop, then the chief laughs. "Navajo ugly, his squaw ugly. Juh never see children, but this one thinks little ones will be ugly too."

Cam shrugs. "I've never seen his family."

"That good, woman, ugh."

Chotilla growls as Cam approaches and the Apache start away. "One day I will cut Juh's heart out and feed it to him."

"I take it you don't like the chief very well?"

"Apache make fun of Chotilla's woman," the Navajo frowns. "She is ugly, but that is for this one to say, not another. One day he will die."

Cam follows closely behind Chotilla as they cross the valley, taking the east trail out. Only a small path, fit for goats and lizards, leads eastward, up and over the low ridge. Cam looks down at the treacherous trail as they finally scramble over the top.

"That was mighty close Chotilla." Cam pulls in and lets his blowing gelding catch his breath.

"Juh no kill, he just want see if you show fear." Chotilla nods his head. "This Navajo thinks this Apache likes you white man."

Cam knows Chotilla thinks he was talking about Juh, not the trail. "What if I showed fear?"

"Him cook you over a small fire. Maybe skin you for hide."

"Now that sure makes me feel better."

Chotilla grins. "You no dead, you should feel better."

"I was actually talking about this trail being so dangerous. Where does it lead?" Cam shakes his head, trying to change the subject.

"Trail leads to cabin of Ketchum. It comes from south, trail rough on horse."

"You mean it comes in the back side of Ketchum's cabin?"

"You know of this passage through the narrow canyon?"

"The old one told me of it."

"We go quick," Chotilla nods. "The redhead is not far ahead. Maybe already at cabin."

"Maybe Hacker is just riding to join Ketchum and get away from the Jackson Clan." Cam looks around at the trail. "Maybe he won't try to ride back to the ranch."

"That is what Juh said. I do not think so." Chotilla nods. "We will camp ahead at the small river. Tomorrow we go to Ketchum hideout."

"How far is it?"

"Two days, we be there." Chotilla dismounts near the water. "I show you where Hacker rides, then Chotilla go back to Jackson Ranch."

"Fair enough, you find Hacker and you've earned your money."

"I will take you to Ketchum's cabin," Chotilla nods. "You no forget about teeth."

"Why do you go back?" Cam is curious. "I thought you said you wanted to kill the redhead?"

"I do. He will not be ahead at cabin." Chotilla lets his gaze survey the trail. "Medicine tell Chotilla, Hacker want woman. Redhead will circle back to Jackson Ranch to steal Trish Jackson. I go there and protect her."

"How do you know that he won't stay with Ketchum?" Cam pulls in his horse and looks at the Navajo confounded. "He can't be in two places at once."

Chotilla is adamant. "Me tell you one more time, redhead, him no be at cabin with outlaw chief."

"We'll see soon, I reckon."

"Red hair scalp look good on Navajo war lance."

"I didn't think the Navajo took enemy scalps."

"This Navajo does, me like red hair." Chotilla smiles a toothless grin. "Give to squaw, make her happy."

Cam remembers what Juh said about the woman having a vicious temper. "Sounds like a good idea to me."

Red Hacker leads his tired horse out of the small passage leading up from the steep canyon trail. He catches his breath as he studies the rear of the small cabin Ketchum uses for his southern hideout. Several horses stand grazing freely on the ample grass growing on the flats of the canyon. Only a lone grey horse occupies the corral. Hacker figures it is the studhorse Mitchell spoke of, back at the basin. Red Hacker, now, no longer the proud foreman of Spade Jackson's Basin Ranch, has ridden for Jackson many years, but money speaks louder than pride. Ketchum bribed him to spy for his gang and sometimes ride for him over two years before. Greed and the lust for money turned him bad. Now he is only a spy, paid with blood money by Ketchum to keep track of the trails in and out of Jackson Basin. He could warn them in case a posse tried slipping into the Mogollons to catch the outlaw gang by surprise. Another outlaw rider is posted at the Rafter 5, making it almost impossible for Ketchum to be surprised before he could escape across the Mexican border.

Ketchum's rider, posted at the Rafter 5, has at one time, made his way cowboying and was a good cowboy. It had taken little time to work his way in with Angus Moore, convincing the Moores that he was a real cowman wanting a job, riding for the Rafter 5. Taking advantage of their trust, he worked into the good graces of Angus Moore and his grandson. Ketchum isn't an ordinary outlaw, thief, and murderer. He has intelligence along with ruthlessness to set up a good spy network back in the mountains. Eventually, he knows the lawmen in southern Arizona and New Mexico will be forced to send men into the badlands of the Mogollons in pursuit of him. By that time, he hopes to be rich enough from his bank jobs to leave this part of the country, maybe even the entire country itself. He heard of many who follow the outlaw trail and drift down to South America to retire in peace.

Finally catching his breath from the long climb out of the treacherous passage, Hacker hollers at the cabin and advances, making sure to keep his hands in plain sight. Ketchum and his gang are men on the run and as any wild thing, they are wary like a wild animal. He knows the men in the cabin wouldn't hesitate to shoot first and find out who he was later, if taken by surprise. Several rifle barrels appear, then disappear from the rear windows of the cabin as

Ketchum walks around the building and waves at Hacker.

"Red, what are you doing here?" Ketchum is surprised to see Hacker. "I thought you were supposed to be back at Jacksons."

"Trouble Jack, I had to kill one of the Jacksons."

"Why, who?"

Hacker ties his horse to the round corral, strips the saddle and wet blankets from the tired gelding. "It was the kid Jeremy Jackson that I conned into helping you on the Elcho City job. He got mad over getting shot by that posse and pulled a gun on me."

"You had to shoot him?" Ketchum looks hard at the redhead. "Why would he get mad over something that we all expect to happen every time we go on a job?"

"I don't know the why of it, but he left me no choice then I had to clear out quick or get myself hung by them crazy Jacksons." Hacker looks away, trying to conceal the lie that he can almost feel showing on his face. The redhead also fails to mention Trish Jackson, the young girl he wants so bad and attacked in the barn causing him to shoot Jeremy, which started the whole mess back at Jacksons. He also didn't dare mention he shot Spade Jackson, the deed that would forever ruin Ketchum's free run of the Mogollons. Hacker knows, with the shooting of Spade Jackson, the day of the free riding outlaw, back in the almost impenetrable mountains, is finished.

Ketchum studies Hacker's face for several seconds, then strikes a sulphur on a corral post and lights his smoke. "Turn your pony into the corral and feed him then we'll get you fed."

Relieved his lie has been believed, Hacker pulls the bridle from the tired horse and slaps him on the rump. "Sorry Jack, but he didn't leave me any choice."

"It doesn't matter Red. I've got a couple things to finish here, then I'm clearing out of these parts for good anyway." Ketchum walks behind the redhead toward the cabin door. Never would he permit even his most trusted men to get behind him. He knows the huge reward on his head is too much temptation to put on his men. "The law around here has been getting bolder and bolder. We need new stomping ground."

"What have you got on your mind, Jack?"

"I don't care what Soapy and Miles say about Mitchell cutting Len down from the front." Ketchum pulls on his smoke. "I think they were running or something. No kid like Mitchell could have taken my cousin from the front."

"And?"

"I aim to kill Mitchell for my Cousin Len, then we're gonna hit the Santa Rita Bank and maybe the Elmwood Bank then leave these parts forever."

"That's fine, those banks should be loaded, but I dunno about Mitchell." Hacker hesitates at the cabin door before opening it. "He's like a cat with nine lives."

"He's just a man, not a cat." Ketchum takes a final look at the mountains before entering the cabin. "I aim to kill him; I have to."

"He's pure poison Jack and he seems to have lady luck riding on his side." Hacker reaches for the string latch. "Why is killing him so important? Len's dead and gone, killing Mitchell won't bring him back.

"Len would do the same for me Red; it's a family thing." Ketchum nods toward the door. "If I don't get revenge for my own cousin, the men won't show me the respect I need to lead them."

"Respect? These men don't have respect for anything." Hacker shakes his head. "All they're interested in is money. Len Fox means nothing to them, whether he's revenged, or not."

"Maybe, but Len meant a lot to me. I aim to kill Mitchell if it's the last thing I do." Ketchum strikes a sulphur to his smoke. "When Mitchell's blood starts to run all over the ground, they'll have respect all right."

"Then what, after you take the bank and kill the man that is?"

"I'm riding out for good." Ketchum smiles, "I hear South America has a healthy climate for rich Americanos like we'll be."

"You want company?" Hacker has heard many men on the run say South America had a lot healthier climate for lawbreakers. "I'd like to come along."

"Sure, but keep it to yourself for now."

"Alright, Boss."

Ketchum tosses his burned-out smoke onto the ground and looks around the canyon. "You know, I ain't gonna miss this place a bit."

"Don't blame you one bit. It is kinda lonely and isolated up here."

"I've been holed up in these mountains like a hermit for so long, I'm beginning to talk to myself." Ketchum rolls another smoke nervously. "We've been living out of this cabin for five years now. I'm ready to head for greener pastures."

Hacker's mind thinks of Trish Jackson. With her by his side, the mountains wouldn't be lonely at all. "Yeah, I can see how you could feel that way."

"After next week, we're gonna live in style Red," Ketchum laughs. "Soon as I can locate Mitchell, we're heading for the big cities with our pockets stuffed."

"Why bother with him? Let's hit the bank at Elmwood and clear out."

"No, first things first, I owe Cousin Len," Ketchum growls. "I aim to enjoy killing that man."

Hacker eats his tin full of beans hungrily. At the same time, he tries to figure out a good reason for him to break off long enough from Ketchum and his men to ride back to the basin and kidnap Trish Jackson. She is in his blood. He just can't ride out of these mountains and leave her behind, no matter how much money he has. Hacker knows Ketchum is smart and would smell a lie. He has to be careful with his plans to go after the girl.

"I ain't seen Mitchell since he left the basin, but if you'll lend me a fresh horse I'll ride toward the basin and try to spot him." Hacker avoids looking dead into the outlaw chief's face. "If I get him spotted, I'll ride back and tell you where he is."

"You and him know each other?"

"Yeah, I met him once. He thinks I ride for the Jackson Ranch. Even if I ride up on him, he won't suspect anything."

Ketchum nods. "Might be a good idea. I sure wouldn't want to have him ambush us on the trail." Ketchum nods thoughtfully. "The sooner we get him located and out of the way, the sooner we can take care of our other business and pull out."

Pushing back his plate, Hacker smiles to himself. He has no intention of looking for Mitchell, but he has what he needs, an excuse to ride out alone. He isn't crossing Ketchum. The Elmwood and Santa Rita

Banks first and then off to South America with Ketchum, sounds good to him, but first he has something of his own to take care of. He has heard stories of the South American beauties, but Trish Jackson is the one in his blood. No woman could take her place. The redhead has killed for the woman. He couldn't or wouldn't ride away from the Mogollons without her. Right now, he has Ketchum's trust. The man suspects nothing and he needs him. Tomorrow, after a good night's rest and with a fresh horse under him, he will head back to Jackson Basin and take what is his, the girl.

Ketchum studies the smiling face of Hacker as he finds a seat outside the cabin door and lights up a smoke. The redhead's story is, in itself, believable, but the man double-crossed Spade Jackson, a man he should owe his allegiance. Would he double cross him as well?

"A day or so after you ride for the basin, me and the boys will head toward Elmwood, get the layout and plan the job." Ketchum studies the far-off mountains. "We'll wait on you outside the town and see if you find Mitchell."

"Alright Jack." Hacker strikes a sulphur to his smoke. "I should be able to find Mitchell if he's in the basin and be back to Elmwood in four days if I wear out some horseflesh."

"I'm leaving Frank and Mingo here to wait on the others coming up from Mexico, and then we'll all gather at Elmwood." Ketchum studies Hacker's face. "You saddle a horse and ride out, come first light."

"Sounds good, I'll be along as quick as I can."

Chapter 8

True to his prediction, two days later, Chotilla reins up behind the cabin Ketchum uses for his hideout. The Navajo tracks Red Hacker all the way from the Fingers, up through the rough passage, stopping where the trail flattens out behind the small cabin. He tracks to the same spot Hacker stopped to regain his breath and study the cabin. The Navajo leads Cam to the cabin from the south, coming in behind the hideout through the rough cut pass that Ketchum was sure few men, except the Apache, know about. Motioning for Cam to hold the horses, the warrior slips silently forward, toward the corrals and cabin without a sound. The soft, high topped moccasins, of the Apache squaw's design, touch the hard, grassy flats of the canyon without emitting a sound.

Several minutes pass before the small warrior reappears and trots back to where Cam waits. Squatting on his haunches, the Navajo plucks a blade of dry grass and looks back at the cabin as he crams it into the corner of his mouth.

"White outlaw all gone." Chotilla spreads his hands. "No one left here except two men."

"Did you see Hacker?"

"No, him already leave this place. Only two men stay in cabin." Chotilla laughs lightly. "They no watch, they sleep."

Nodding, Cam hands the reins to the tracker. "When I whistle, bring them in."

Chotilla takes the rawhide reins from Cam then crouches. His black eyes miss nothing as the young white man crosses the flat ground behind the cabin without making a sound. Pulling the blade of grass from his mouth, he nods slowly, then whispers to the horses. "Perhaps the young one is part Indian."

Not a sound comes from the cabin as Cam eases the cabin door open and steps silently into the dark interior. Stopping inside the door, to let his eyes adjust to the poor light, he is finally able to make out the sleeping forms of the two remaining outlaws. Chotilla counted right. Two men are lying in their bunks, snoring loudly, completely unaware of his presence. Whistling softly out the door, he waits, and watches the two men as Chotilla leads their horses boldly around to the front door.

"Catch any horses you can find in the canyon. Get halters and saddles on them and I'll get our sleeping friend's guns."

"They deserve to die as they sleep." Chotilla looks disgusted at the sleeping men. "These are what the white people call outlaws, bad men?"

"Maybe they will die if they're left afoot way out here with no horses or weapons."

"Good, lazy warrior no good for fight." Chotilla looks in at the men. "That maybe why Outlaw Chief Ketchum leave them here."

"We'll wake them up and ask them why he left them behind after you catch the horses and saddle them."

Cam gathers the sleeping men's weapons, leaving only one rifle and a handful of shells between them. It is a long, dangerous walk out of the mountains. Maybe they will think twice the next time they decide to take a nap without a guard. Leaning the lone rifle outside the cabin's door, Cam taps one of the men on the foot. Opening his eyes sleepily, the man instantly awakes as he focuses on the wide bore of the forty-four pointing at him.

"What the, who are you, mister?"

"Have a nice nap?"

Staring at the gun, looking him between the eyes, the man sits up slowly. "You're Mitchell, ain't you?'

"I'll do the asking and you'll do the talking."

The other outlaw sits up suddenly and reaches for his pistol that no longer occupies the place he left it. "What's going on Mingo, and who's this?"

The one called Mingo nods at Cam. "He said he's asking the questions and we better answer them or else."

"I know him. He's the one Giles warned us about, Mitchell." The rider places his feet on the dirt floor as he sits up. "Or else what, mister?"

"I left you a rifle right outside the door." Cam nods at the door. "If you don't answer real fast, I'll take both the rifle and your boots when I leave."

"Our horses?"

"You mean my horses, don't you?"

"I didn't steal your animals," Mingo whines. "I wasn't even in on that job."

Cam looks about the filthy cabin. "Where's Red Hacker?"

"Who?"

Picking up the men's boots, Cam walks to the door and gathers the rifle. "Be seeing you boys. Hope you make it out of here alive."

"He ain't kidding Frank and we sure can't walk out of here bare-foot." Mingo glares over at the other outlaw. "We wouldn't get five miles on foot before we'd be crippled or dead from Apaches."

Frank studies the boots in Cam's hand and nods. "He rode out of here two days ago, real early."

"Where was he going?"

"I heard him talking to Ketchum. He told the boss he'd ride toward the basin and try to locate you, then he'd meet with him on the trail to tell him where you were."

"Ketchum out looking for me too, is he?"

"I figure," Frank swears. "You killed his cousin, Len Fox, didn't you?"

"I killed him alright." Cam drops one boot. "Where's Ketchum and why ain't you two riding with him?"

"He rode out the day after Hacker pulled out is all we know. I reckon he went looking for you."

"Why didn't he take you two?"

"We were to wait here for some of the others coming up from the border and then meet him in Elmwood."

Cam studies the two men for several seconds, then drops another boot. "He fixing to pull a job in Elmwood is he?"

"Mister, you don't know Jack Ketchum well, do you?" Mingo stands up, only to sit back down quickly as the pistol levels on his stomach. "The boss doesn't tell anybody anything until it's done."

"Speak up, where is Ketchum?" Cam asks again. "How long has he been gone?"

Mingo breaks into a sweat as Cam picks up the boots. "There's only two ways out of this valley, mister. They went out the north trail and you came in the back way on the south trail or you would have run into them."

"What he's saying is, after they clear the upper trail, they'll have to go east or west. There's no other trail out of these mountains." The outlaw named Frank, speaks up. "His tracks will be clear enough for that redskin, you got out there, to read."

"I'll leave your boots and the rifle near the corrals. You come out before we clear this valley, I'll ride back here and kill you both."

"We hear you, Mitchell."

"Good, I don't like repeating myself."

"We ain't stupid, we hear you loud and clear," Mingo grumbles.

"You ain't stupid?" Cam shakes his head. "You ride with Ketchum don't you?"

"Yeah," Mingo nods. "Yeah, we ride with the man, you know that."

"I'll tell you like I told Miles and Soapy, if I see you in these parts again, I'll kill you on sight."

"Just like that?"

"Exactly like that." Cam turns for the door. "Your kind is no longer welcome in these parts since Hacker beat up the girl, killed the kid, and shot Spade Jackson."

Both men look up in shock and disbelief. "Mitchell, we sure didn't know anything about all that. We may be bad men, but we don't hold with hitting a woman."

Mingo looks over at Frank and nods. "That could be why Hacker was so anxious to leave here alone. I thought that was a little strange."

"Mister, he could be heading back after the girl." Frank shakes his head. "Mind you, we don't know that for sure, just guessing."

"I'll tell you something else, Mitchell." Mingo doesn't blink. "I'll guarantee you, Jack Ketchum doesn't know a thing about the girl either. Something in his past, southern born gentleman and all, no sir, he'd never permit any of us to hurt a woman."

Chotilla watches as Cam places the boots and rifle against the corral gate and shakes his head. "A Navajo would never show weakness by leaving his enemies alive and with their weapons."

"Let's ride." Cam worries about what Mingo told him about Hacker and Ketchum. Chotilla is probably right. Hacker is in this alone. Ketchum knew nothing of Jeremy or Trish and the redhead is on his way back to Jacksons. Cam takes the lead ropes of the extra saddled horses and motions to the trail. "Lead out and pick up Hacker's trail."

The trail going out of the valley is every bit as treacherous and steep as it descends through the rocky crevices. Dismounting on several occasions, where the trail is on a slant and the rock is slick and dangerous, the little warrior leads his horse forward on foot. He takes notice of the scratch marks of iron horseshoes scraping on the rocks, both coming and going from the cabin. This is the only trail out of the small canyon. There are no side trails or even deer paths leading away from the pass until they reach the bigger, east-west trail at the top.

Holding up his hand, Chotilla holds his horse, where a huge mountain cedar hides the secret passage to the canyon hideout. He surveys the trail before them and from where he stands, he can see the tracks of many horses turning to the west and none turn east. Satisfied no danger presents itself from the upper trail, Chotilla rides clear of the tree and leads his horse onto the flat trail. "All white men go this way."

"Let's go, don't worry about an ambush." Cam looks to the Navajo. "They don't know we're following them yet."

"I ride with you only as far as the cutoff to Jackson's Ranch." Chotilla mounts. "Then this warrior go to Jackson Basin fast."

"You ain't found Hacker yet. You said you'd stay until you found him."

Twisting sideways on his bareback horse, Chotilla looks back at Cam. "Clean out your ears young one. Hacker will turn off at the Jackson Trail and go after the girl."

"I figure you're right this time. We'll find him on the trail to the basin." Cam looks as far up the lonely trail as he can see. "If we get there fast enough."

"We no find him at all if you don't quit talking and ride hard," Chotilla growls. "We have fresh horses. We catch redhead."

"Let's ride these for a ways. We'll swap horses later at the cutoff to the basin."

"Bah, ride this one, that one, walk, I don't care, but let's go." Chotilla kicks his gelding into a lope.

Sundown finds the two men, one white and one red, camped beside a water hole only a couple miles from the Jackson Basin trail. Two small cottontails are roasting over the fire, one skinned and cleaned, the white way, the other whole, complete with skin, hair, and entrails, the Apache way. Cam looks on in surprise at their providence. He didn't even see either of the small rabbits hiding in the underbrush. Only the twang of the bowstring sounds and Chotilla dismounts, walking to where the small animal lies with an arrow protruding from its body.

Cam's stomach churns slightly as he watches Chotilla roast his rabbit with its hide, hair, and entrails still intact over the fire. The Navajo shakes his head in disgust as Cam skins the other rabbit.

"Ugh, young one ruin rabbit. You should no skin." Chotilla frowns and shakes his head. "Rabbit taste like dried up leather moccasin the way you put him over fire."

"You eat like you want and I'll do the same."

"You got white man tobacco to smoke?"

"Sorry, I don't smoke." Cam bites into his rabbit and motions toward the saddles laying on the ground. "Check those saddlebags. Cowboys always keep tobacco stashed in their possibles."

"These men not cowboys. They very bad men."

"They were cowboys before they took the wrong trail." Cam chews on the rabbit leg. "Take a look, see what you find."

"Here, Cam Mitchell." Chotilla rips the charred skin and what is left of the fur from a back leg and presents it to Cam. "You see, it better than one you cook."

Not wanting to insult the Navajo, Cam reluctantly accepts the leg and raises it to his mouth. Chewing slowly, he has to admit, the meat is tender and juicier than the over dry rabbit leg he cooked. "Again, you're right my friend. It is more tender and tastier this way."

"Some things Indian know better than white man."

"I don't doubt that one bit." Cam thinks about Hacker. "It seems I'm learning."

Cam watches the small warrior inspect the bags then return to the fire with the makings in his hand. "Young one won't smoke?"

"No, thank you."

"You sleep, Cam Mitchell. This one take first watch while I smoke bad man tobacco." The Navajo grins his toothless smile as he blows out smoke and looks at the cigarette. "Good smoke."

Chotilla reins in and sits his horse at the trail branching off to the south, leading to Jackson Basin. Only one set of tracks, leading south, show plainly in the gravel trail while the main group of riders continue on the trail west, leading toward to the Rafter 5. Turning his gelding, the Navajo points to the south and then to the west.

"Redhead rides alone toward the south." Chotilla studies the tracks. "Other men ride west with Ketchum."

Cam is curious, both of the sleeping outlaws in the cabin agreed, Ketchum swore to find Mitchell and kill him before leading his men on any other bank robberies. Here he is, heading west with most of his riders, away from the Jackson Ranch where he is more likely to find his cousin's killer. There is little doubt about Hacker's motives for riding south. Cam knows the redhead is heading back to Jacksons, planning to slip in unseen and unheard to kidnap Trish Jackson. He knows little of the man, but he knows Hacker is crazy, obsessed with the girl and intent on stealing her away from the ranch and her family.

"How far ahead is the redhead?"

"Maybe two days."

"That far?"

"Other men just a day ahead of us."

Cam nods. "Hacker is pushing hard."

"Redhead know this land, and he crazy for woman." Chotilla shakes his head. "He no care, him run horse to death then steal another. He one crazy white man."

"We have to hurry." Cam looks at the spare horses. "We've got fresh horses, we must push hard."

"No, we no hurry." Chotilla shrugs his shoulders. "We take time, we get there. We hurry, maybe we no get there, maybe we break leg and no can help girl."

Cam shakes his head. "I reckon you know best."

"You think Navajo know best white man?" Chotilla shakes his head. "You taste rabbit last night. You should know Chotilla know best."

Cam flexes his powerful hands. He likes and respects Chotilla, but sometimes he could choke the little warrior and his mouth. "Alright I hear you, Navajo."

"Navajo know better, we save girl. No worry." Chotilla smiles. "Mitchell young, impatient, and in love. This one chase bad man many times. Tracker must be patient like snake waiting for squirrel or rat."

"I reckon you're right."

"This one right." Chotilla slips from his horse. "We change horses now."

Red Hacker lets smoke drift from his mouth as he pulls on the cigarette and studies the buildings of the Jackson Ranch from his vantage point only a half mile from the ranch. He waits most of the day, watching Trish Jackson through his binoculars as she goes about her daily chores. Watching as she hangs out clothes, gathers eggs, then goes to the barn later in the day to milk the old Jersey cow that Spade brought back to the ranch years ago.

In the past, Hacker watched the girl on many a day when he was supposed to be working, just as he is today. He knows her habits, almost like he knows his own and he also knows the habits of all the ranch hands. On several nights, he lay in the brush and watched her window as she prepared for bed, only leaving his watching place when she blew out her coal oil lamp. He knows exactly where her room is in the house and already he has a plan figured out exactly how he will slip in through the unlocked kitchen door and kidnap the girl. His stomach growls as he thinks about the supper the family and hands are sitting down to at this very moment. Hacker hasn't eaten since early morning when he finished the last of the food he brought with him from Ketchum's hideout. It doesn't matter, his stomach is too nervous to hold food. All he can think of is getting into the house and taking the girl. He would raid the Jackson pantry for food before waking the girl and riding out. There was no hurry. He doesn't worry about getting caught. The Jackson riders weren't able to follow him after he killed Jeremy Jackson and they wouldn't be able to follow him tonight, maybe they wouldn't even try.

As dark settles over the ranch, the lights extinguish and all grows quiet. Hacker rises from his hiding spot and slips silently into the dark barn. Darkness blackens the building, giving only enough light for Hacker to find and halter the small roan mare, belonging to Trish. Leading her from the box stall, Hacker is absorbed in saddling the horse and doesn't hear the man walk up behind him in the dark.

"Who are you and what are you doing?"

Whirling with speed uncommon for such a large man, Red strikes out with the large skinning knife, he wears on his belt, penetrating the man's stomach and killing him almost instantly. Pulling the body of Jonas Jackson into a stall, he covers it with straw and takes up the mare's lead rope. Retreating to the rear of the ranch house, the redhead ties the mare and a fresh gelding to replace his wore out horse behind the building and walks quietly across the porch entering the kitchen. Quickly filling a flour sack with biscuits, side meat, and several sugar cookies, he finds in the stove's breadbox then lays the sack on the table. Stuffing two cookies hungrily, into his mouth, he moves toward Trish's bedroom door, all the while listening closely to the other sounds coming from the other end of the large house. He knows the house inside and out. The girl's bedroom is in a perfect place, at the end of the house, far away from the other bedrooms.

Slipping stealthily into the bedroom, he walks to the side of the bed where the girl is breathing shallowly, already in a deep sleep. Moonlight shines softly through the open window, permitting Hacker to clamp his huge hand across the sleeping girl's mouth perfectly. Clawing at the strong hand covering her mouth, Trish tries her best to fight away whatever is holding her fast.

"Shh girl, it's just me, old Red." Hacker eases up a little, letting her catch her breath. "You scream and I'll kill everyone in this house, that is, after I knock your little head senseless again."

Nodding slowly, she shakes slightly, then relaxes as he releases her mouth. "What do you want, Red?"

"Now that's simple Trish, I want you. I've come for you." Hacker grins in the moonlight. "You should know that my sweet."

"You're loco, Red Hacker. Granddad will follow you to hell."

"Hope not, if he does, then I'll have to kill him." Hacker smiles slightly. "You know what, beautiful, you're worth it."

"I ain't going with you."

Flipping Trish on her stomach, Hacker forces her arms behind her back and leans over, whispering in her ear. "You're going my dear, Trish. You can ride a horse in your thin nightgown or in warm clothes and a coat. It's your choice."

"I ain't your dear, you beast." Trish moans as he bends her arms more.

"If you force me to gal, I'll tie you up, then I'll kill all of them right now in their sleep."

"Alright Red, let me get dressed and I'll go with you."

"Now that's better, little darling. In time you'll learn to like me, real nice like." Releasing her hands, Hacker yanks her to her feet. "Just remember, you make one little sound and I'll kill everyone, you hear me, everyone."

"I hear you."

Trish rummages around in the dark room trying to find her warmer clothes and keep hidden from Hacker as she takes off her nightgown and slips on the woolen britches. She can only wonder how crazy the man has become to take such a chance riding into the ranch alone.

"Hurry up, woman."

"I'm hurrying." Trish wonders where Jonas Jackson is, the second son of Spade Jackson, who was on guard around the ranch tonight.

Grabbing her roughly, Hacker pulls the girl to him. "We're leaving, but you remember, you make a sound and I'll kill everyone in the house and you if I have to."

Cam and Chotilla ride into the ranch yard after sundown and pull up as several men, with drawn guns, step out of the shadows. Spade Jackson sits in his place on the porch and looks up at the two mounted men.

Not a word is spoken by any of the men standing around the yard. Cam can feel the tension as the Jackson men gather close around them. "What happened here, Mister Jackson?"

"Red Hacker is what happened." The old prospector leans forward. "He slipped in here last night while we were all sound asleep like fools in our beds and took my granddaughter."

"You didn't hear anything?"

"If we heard anything, he wouldn't have gotten her, Mitchell." Spade Jackson spits out sadly. "Not a sound, nothing."

Chotilla's face grows hard. "Which way, did the redhead ride out?"

"Southwest, I figure he's gonna try the west trail, out of the mountains, just like he did last time."

"Who follows the crazy one?"

"No one, Hacker killed one of my sons in the barn." Spade runs his hands over his face. "He left a paper, he'll kill the girl if we follow and I believe him."

Cam is beside himself. "So you're just letting him ride off with her?"

"What else could we do?" The old prospector shakes his head. "He warned us he'd kill her and I believe that lobo wolf would."

"Being dead is better than being in that man's hands."

"Is it?" Gage Jackson steps from the shadows. "Dead's permanent."

"I need a fresh horse and some provisions." Cam looks over at Chotilla. "Maybe two horses."

"We can't let you put her in danger, Mitchell." Gage Jackson steps forward. "You ain't going."

"You can't stop me, mister." Cam's hand rests on his pistol grip. "Killing me is the only way you can stop me. You willing to try?"

"You can't track him at night boy," Spade speaks up again, trying to defuse the trouble that is about to erupt. "All I'm asking is for you to hold off a couple days and let Hacker think we're not following him."

"Chotilla, are you going with me this time?" Cam looks over at the warrior. "Or my friend, am I riding alone?"

"I go," the Navajo nods. "For this, you owe me nothing."

"Okay, you go Mitchell," Gage Jackson speaks up. He sees the killing hate come out in Cam's eyes. "I'm riding with you."

Cam turns to the man. "Alright, but only you Gage. No one else is riding this trail with me and Chotilla."

"Why not, you need the help," Spade Jackson speaks up. "If you won't wait a few days, at least take more men with you."

"Three is enough, Mister Jackson." Cam's eyes seem almost blood-shot in the dim light. "Hacker is just one man, a dead man, no matter how this comes out."

Spade Jackson clears his throat. "You'll have your fresh horses come morning and good luck to you."

"I can't believe you men didn't follow Hacker." Cam is still riled as he looks around at the men. "I understand your concern for the girl."

"I wouldn't let them. You had the Navajo with you and we couldn't have followed him if we tried, and possibly we could have gotten her killed."

"I understand your thinking, Mister Jackson," Cam nods. "We'll ride out in the morning, come daylight."

"Turn your mounts over to my boys and come on in for some supper. You both look done in." Spade looks up at the Navajo. "Your people are all fine Chotilla. We took them some food yesterday and checked on them."

"Thank you." Chotilla looks over to where Cam dismounts. "Next time, you listen to Navajo maybe."

"Maybe, but how is that?"

"We should have hurried faster."

At the words, Cam can only shake his head in amazement. It was the Navajo who insisted on keeping them at a slower pace across the rough trails of the rocky Mogollons. The little Navajo kept the horses at a slow walk, counseling to ride slow and arrive at the Jackson Ranch safely, without mishap.

Cam nods agreement, but he remembers the Navajo's words distinctly. Shrugging, he pats the black on the neck. "Next time, I'll listen."

Handing the black's reins over to one of the Jacksons, he warns the young man to watch out for his teeth then steps onto the porch. Looking over at the old prospector then off into the pitch black, Cam knows Spade was right. Not even Chotilla, the great Navajo man tracker, could follow a man through the mountains in the dark of night. He has no choice, so they will wait until morning to take to the trail. His hands ball into fists as he swears, tomorrow or the day after, Hacker will be a dead man. His mind can only think of the worst for the girl, tearing at him like a jagged knife. The woman he loves is in the hands of a monster.

Cam looks to where the young man leads the black into a corral. He hates to leave the horse behind. He has come to depend on the horse's endurance and clear footedness on the trail, but the great horse must rest after traveling so many miles over the treacherous mountains. Tomorrow, he plans on wearing out some horseflesh to catch up to Hacker and the girl, and when he does, he is gonna kill the man. Never has he hated as he does now as the theft of the Steeldust pales in comparison to kidnapping Trish Jackson. His mouth tastes the bitter bile of helplessness. Somewhere down the trail, he will have his vengeance against the redhead and it will not be pretty.

"He is a good horse." Chotilla looks to where Cam is watching the black being put up, with the other horses they had ridden in relays to get there. "Maybe someday, I steal him from you."

"Tomorrow Chotilla, I want to run the redhead down." Cam looks at the Navajo, knowing the little warrior is just trying to get his mind off Trish. "I want him dead. Do you hear me, dead!"

"The girl, what of her?" Chotilla stares at Cam. "He said he would kill her if we follow."

"You believe him?"

"No, he take great chance coming back here. He no kill woman unless he knows we are close and may take her from him." Chotilla touches the blade of his knife. "By then, Chotilla be very close. I use knife on redhead before he even know Navajo anywhere near.

"So, we don't let him know we're following." Cam shrugs. "Can we do that out here in these canyons?"

"We leave before daylight, maybe two hours." The Navajo walks to where his supper sits steaming on the table. "Then we pick up his trail when light come. He running, he not wait to see if we follow."

"You're the tracker."

"I catch this one for you and me, then he die." Chotilla pulls his razor sharp skinning knife half way out of its scabbard then pushes it back in. "Him die screaming."

"He'll die alright. How I don't know, but he'll die."

"Redhead die screaming, this I tell you," Chotilla repeats himself, his dark eyes like pits of hot coals. "Kill, Apache way."

The little warrior leading the two whites to the south and west isn't the same Navajo that led Cam on their first trail after the redhead. The small warrior wears a mask of hate across his face as he pushes the bay gelding, he rides, hard. Not one ounce of caution utters from the thin lined mouth, nothing. Only driving hatred emits from of the warrior's eyes as he leads them from the ranch. Chotilla led the two white's from the Jackson Ranch as he wanted, two hours before the sun rose. The little warrior does not utter a single word as he uses only hand signs for communication and nothing vocal is forthcoming as they traverse the rough country. Gage Jackson looks briefly at the masked hatred on the face he knows so well and cringes back. Never has he seen this side of the Navajo, who he has known since he was a young man.

The horse Cam rides now, isn't the easy gaited black, but he is a good traveling horse with plenty of bottom. The Navajo is pushing hard and he knows they will pick up the redhead's tracks ahead where the trail splits. One trail heads west, eventually circling back to the settlements of Elmwood or Santa Rita. Chotilla already dismisses the other trail leading south, back into the Fingers and on into Mexico. Hacker knows the country so he is aware it is swarming with hostile Apache. Riding with the woman, it is almost impossible to travel unobserved. No, Hacker will take the woman back to the settlements of the whites and rejoin Ketchum or lose himself and Trish in the white population of the bigger towns.

Late afternoon finds Gage Jackson holding the reins of the Navajo's horse as the small warrior slowly sorts out the tracks covering the ground where the two trails separate. Slipping back and forth, like a hound sniffing out a track, Chotilla finally waves them forward to where he is studying the ground.

"Redhead and woman go this way." Chotilla points east. "We go quick."

Gage leans from his horse and looks closely at the tracks. "Some of these horses are barefoot."

"Bronco Apache follow red hair." Chotilla shakes his head in disgust. "Him stupid, he doesn't know Apache following."

Cam nods as he already read the signs and figures it was Apache horses covering the tracks of Hacker and Trish. "How close are the Apache to Hacker?"

Chotilla shrugs. "This I do not know, but they will catch red hair before we catch up to them. I just hope they don't kill red hair but leave him for Chotilla."

"Or me," Cam whispers under his breath, worrying about Trish.

Red Hacker pushes the tired horses as hard as he dares. The girl is riding on guts alone. He knows, from the look on her face, Trish is exhausted, tired as the animals. For several miles now, he watches the flicking of his horse's ears as they cross the small canyons dotting the mountains. He has an uneasy feeling, somewhere close behind, riders are closing in. He doesn't know who they are, but he figures it is the riders from the Jackson Ranch. Who else could it be, back in the isolated reaches, away from any living soul? He swears it must be that little mouse of a Navajo who he knows could track an ant across a flat skillet.

There are many trails leading off from these small canyons in different directions, but they always circle or loop back to the main trail or come to a dead end, somewhere in a blind canyon. Hacker looks behind him and shakes his head. For the last mile, his horse has been cocking his ear backward more frequently. He knows, whoever is following him, is closing in on them. Pulling his pistol, he checks the loads then replaces the weapon.

For now, there is little he can do but push on. There is not a sign of water or any cover to hide behind in the flat canyon they are crossing. The horses are tired from the long ride through the mountain passes and have to be kicked constantly to keep them in a slow dog trot. They need to rest soon, as Hacker knows there is little water or grass in the narrow passes. They have to keep going forward, hoping to find the grazing and water he needs, then he will let the horses and the girl rest.

Trish watches Hacker's actions as he continually looks down their back trail. She knows he is worrying about something, what she doesn't know. She knows the former foreman of the Jackson Ranch must be crazy, even though the years he worked for Spade Jackson, he acted normal, except for the jealous rages he went into if someone paid attention to her.

Pulling the horses in at a small pool of water, he finds in one of the valleys, Hacker dismounts and pulls Trish roughly, from her horse. "We've got to let them rest for a spell."

"At least you're still cowman enough to realize that." Trish shrugs away from his grasp. "They're about to collapse on you."

"I don't need your smart mouth, woman. We've got someone following us." Hacker pushes her roughly toward the water. "I warned them what I'd do if they tried to get you back."

Looking into his crazed eyes, Trish shivers uncontrollably. The man seems mad. "My uncles couldn't have tracked us here."

"That Navajo they keep around like a bloodhound could."

"He rode out with Cam Mitchell, looking for Ketchum," Trish lies. "He ain't at the ranch."

Hacker walks a few steps away from the water where he can see their back trail and studies the wide canyon. Satisfied, when nothing moves out on the flat land, the redhead turns toward the pool of water "Maybe they got lucky and stumbled onto our trail."

"Scared, Mister Red Hacker?"

"Shut up woman, you're the one that should be scared." Hacker whirls on her then relaxes his huge hands flexing into fists. "Like I said, we'll camp here for the night and let the horses rest."

"You want me to stand guard?" Trish taunts him. "I wouldn't run away from a nice gentleman like you."

"Don't push your luck Miss Jackson, now get some sleep."

"Yes, sir. I'll do that."

Hacker tosses her the bag of food, then unsaddles and pickets the horses near the water where several bunches of rough grass, grow wild.

Looking down the trail once again, he shivers uncontrollably. Someone is out there. He can feel them, but there is nothing he can do, the horses have to rest. Without the animals, the girl could never walk out of these mountains afoot. The animals have to rest and graze to continue. Shifting his eyes to the form of the girl, he shakes his head. How did he get himself into this mess or maybe why is the better question. Somehow he can feel it in his bones, almost sense it, he is a dead man.

The night passes slowly with only the lonely echoing of a Coyote as it pours out its sad song to the tall mountains. Trish wakes suddenly, her eyes wide with fear and shock as a dark skinned face materializes right out of the rocks, only inches from her own, as the sun shows itself in the east. With the speed of a striking rattler, the warrior clamps his hand over her mouth as she tries to scream. Dragging the frightened girl behind some boulders, out of sight, the Apache motions across the clearing before settling beside the white woman. Hearing a slight commotion that awakes him instantly, Hacker looks around to find her gone. Rushing quickly to where she was sleeping, he looks around as several warriors surround him, their weapons cocked and leveled at his chest.

"We're Jackson people, the Apache's friends. What do you want?" Hacker stares into the rifle barrels as he tries to wrench free from the strong hands of two warriors who have seized him.

The broad Apache warrior steps in front of the redhead and nods as he looks up at the big man. "Woman is Jackson, you not."

"Where's the woman, ask her?" Hacker looks about the campsite. "Ask her."

"She there," Juh points toward the boulder where a warrior steps into sight. "Chihuahua, bring woman here."

Trish is pushed bodily, to where the warrior speaking stands facing Hacker. All her life, she has heard stories of Apache cruelty and savagery and she fears the Apache as most whites in Arizona and the southwest do. She can hardly bring herself to look at the small, musky smelling warriors who surround her. Only the blank, cold look of their black eyes, stare back at her. No emotion, warmth, nothing else shows in or on their dark faces.

"You are the squaw of Mitchell, the Rough Rider?" Juh looks the woman over. "Speak; is this not true?"

"I am his woman." Suddenly her eyes show life and a little hope. The Apache leader smiles at her slightly as he turns his back to Hacker. "How do you know this?"

"Why you with this one?" Juh ignores the question. "Is this not the redheaded one Mitchell seeks?"

"Keep your mouth shut Trish." Hacker tries to shrug off the powerful hands that hold him. "Or I'll kill you."

Juh turns slowly and looks closely into Hacker's eyes as he pulls his knife. "You open mouth again, white man, and I will remove your tongue and eat it."

"He took me from my home two nights ago." Trish spits at Hacker. "He's crazy, loco as mountain cat with a toothache."

"She lies, Chief. We ran away to be married."

Juh looks over at Trish. "Does the redhead speak the truth?"

"He lies. I would rather marry a pig."

Juh turns and speaks to the other warriors who break into laughter at his words. Motioning at the fire, he toes several sticks together and nods at Trish. "You make fire and prepare food for Apache."

Knowing better than to refuse, Trish nods and piles several small sticks together, then places dry grass under the wood and ignites a sulphur. With the wood ablaze, she retrieves the sack of food Hacker had stolen from the Jackson pantry and looks up at Juh.

"There isn't much left." Trish shows him the bag. "Sorry."

"You have coffee?" The chief speaks softly. "Juh likes white man coffee."

Picking up the battered coffeepot, Trish walks to the water hole and fills it with water then returns to the fire. "I have coffee."

"Good, squaw cook," Juh nods happily. "Soon, warrior bring much food this place."

Juh is true to his word. A warrior brings in a haunch of deer meat and lays it near the fire. Tossing a knife down beside the bloody meat, he points at her and trots back the way he came. Raw meat is not new to the ranch raised girl. She has cut up many a steer that were brought in for their dinner table. Juh nods knowingly as she quickly slices the venison, separating the layers of meat so it would cook tender. Running small cedar limbs through several slices of meat, she hangs them over the fire. Stepping back, she finds a small boulder and watches the meat as it starts to sizzle.

"White man Mitchell, has good woman." Juh nods as he watches the girl. "She cook good."

"You have seen Cam?" Trish speaks to the Apache Chief.

Juh nods. "Many days ago, we meet Rough Rider and Navajo in the badland place."

"You mean the Fingers?"

"This is what your people call the bad place."

"Maybe they are following me now."

"Three men follow redhead. One Indian, two whites. They come to this place tomorrow." Juh takes the coffee from her. "My warriors say Navajo plenty mad. Face show much hate."

"Chotilla is the same as my father."

Juh laughs lightly. "Him too ugly to be your father. Him squaw ugly."

"They are not ugly." Trish frowns at the chief. "Both are beautiful."

"White woman no see so well. They ugly." Juh points at the coffee. "You cook good white man coffee."

"What will you do when they get here?"

"We wait this place, stay and watch white men kill each other."

"You can't, Chief. He must be warned."

"It be fair fight. Fight for squaw."

"What do you mean?"

"You see bye and bye," Juh laughs lightly. "One woman; two men want same woman. This no good. One has to die."

"You can't."

Juh shows her his empty cup. "You bring coffee."

"No, you get your own coffee."

Hacker watches as Trish recoils from the hard slap from the chief. "Now squaw, you get coffee quick or I give you to redhead maybe."

Trish sits back and watches the warriors gorge themselves on the half raw meat before it finishes cooking completely. She isn't hungry and refuses the meat Juh offers her, but notices Hacker was offered nothing. She felt the slap the chief gave her, but it wasn't as hard as it sounded.

She remembers the words from her grandfather that an Apache squaw is beaten soundly if she refuses to mind her husband. Treated with a rough life, the Apache women sometimes have their noses cut off if found unfaithful and trifling with another man. The lowest of warriors, up to the Chief of the Apache, must be respected by all. Juh knows, if he does not enforce his will on her in front of his men, he would lose face, for a woman of the Apache to disobey is unheard of.

The sun rises early over the rough mountain terrain and the rest of the day passes slowly. Trish watches the Apache warriors for any sudden reaction, showing they might have spotted Chotilla and Cam. For hours, she watches them sit almost motionless from their places of concealment, behind the many boulders lining the canyon wall. The warriors are only feet from where she sits, yet she is amazed that they are almost invisible to her, and she knows exactly where they are. She understands now why they are so dangerous to small hunting parties or mule trains. They seem one with the surrounding ground. Any unsuspecting passerby wouldn't know what is happening until they feel the fatal bullet or a war whoop of the Apache as they rush forward. Her mouth is dry as dirt when she tries to work her tongue and swallow. This time of year, the days are always unbearably hot. Yet, none of the warriors touch their animal hide water bags, go to the water hole for a drink, or try to hide from the sun's rays.

Silently, Juh appears beside her and holds out his water bag. "You drink."

"No, Apache no drink, so I won't drink."

"You white, not Indian. Apache go many days without water if they have to." Juh pushes the water at her again. "Drink, you brave white woman, strong woman. No shame, you drink."

Trish lifts the leather bag to her lips and swallows deeply. Nothing in her life has ever tasted as good as the stale water. Nodding her head, she hands the water bag back. Juh smiles lightly and hands her a handful of small seeds.

"Squaw put in mouth, let stay. Soon they help with thirst."

Trish looks at the small, dark seeds, then pops them into her mouth. "What about him? Can he have some water?"

Juh follows her eyes to where Hacker is sitting solemnly against a boulder with two Apache warriors guarding him. "He is Rough Rider man's enemy. You wish for him to drink?"

"I don't like to see anything, man or animal tortured, not even him."

"Soon, big redhead man fight with your man. You want him to have water and make him strong so he can defeat Mitchell?"

Trish shakes her head. "Cam would want him to have a fair chance and not weak from thirst."

"This one doesn't understand white people." Juh looks at the girl for several minutes then shakes his head. "Maybe white woman like redhead more than she does Rough Rider."

Trish looks at the Apache as if he slapped her again. "No, I don't, but he's still a human being."

"If Mitchell dies, you have to go with redhead. You say nothing because you give water, make him strong." Juh turns from her and starts toward Hacker. "You say nothing."

"I'd rather die than go with that animal."

"Yet you give him water." Juh only shakes his head. He doesn't understand whites. Maybe it is best. "I think you white people crazy."

Hacker sits beside a boulder with two rifles pointed at his chest. He has watched with veiled eyes, knowing the Apache wait here quietly for someone. He figures it is the Jackson riders, tracking him and Trish. Why they haven't killed him and fled south with the girl, he does not know. He only knows the warriors wait for whoever is coming to their place of concealment. Whether to kill them or talk, he isn't sure, but he knows these warriors, riding with Juh, are the worst of the bronco Apache, all killers and white haters. Perhaps this is an ambush that Juh wants him to see before he is killed.

Looking up at the Apache Chief, as he stops in front of him with the water bag, Hacker reaches up and takes the offered animal skin.

"You red hair, are a large man." Juh looks down at the broad faced Hacker. "You drink much."

Hacker looks at the chief curious. Why, he wonders, would the Apache give him the water bag if he is to die. "My people are all big men."

"Are you and your big people brave as well?"

"If you are going to kill me then do it and quit playing with me."

Hacker stands his ground, showing no fear. "I'm ready to die."

"Maybe you are brave, big man," Juh smiles slightly. "Men from Jackson Ranch come to this place soon. We see then."

"Jacksons?" Hacker nods. He had been right.

"Soon, we see how brave you are redhead. Maybe you are like the mountain cat, all strength and talk but no brave," Juh laughs, looking toward the canyon floor. "I hope you good fighter."

"What are you going to do with me?" Hacker hands the bag back. "Tell me you red devil."

"Soon you see," Juh turns away from Hacker. "Soon, white man."

As Hacker looks around at the Apache Warriors guarding him, he can't help see the disdain and hate that fills their eyes. Juh said they were waiting on the Jackson Riders, but why is he still alive? It's a curiosity for sure. He should have already been dead, but now he knows they have some reason for not killing him already. He always heard the Apache people did things on whims, or if they felt their medicine was strong. Whichever it is, he is still alive, for some unknown reason. Whatever is to come, the redhead swears to himself, he will not show fear in front of Trish Jackson.

Chapter 9

Halfway across the canyon floor, Chotilla reins his horse in and studies the canyon trail ahead of them for several minutes. Motioning Cam to ride forward, he nods to where the trail narrows. Gage Jackson reins in alongside the Navajo and Cam, then looks out across the canyon floor to where the two men are staring.

"What's going on?" Gage strains his eyes. "What do you see out there?"

"Me see nothing," Chotilla motions with his chin, "Apache, there."

"Are you sure? I don't see anything."

"You white, your eyes weak." Chotilla nods his head thoughtfully. "They there alright. Soon you see."

"Funny." Gage shakes his head grinning. "At least I grew to full manhood."

"Chotilla man, me got ten little ones. How many you got, Gage Jackson?"

"What are we gonna do?" Cam stops the bickering of the two and studies the canyon, as his eyes try to see anything across the flats or along the canyon walls. "I can't see a thing either."

"Apache wait there. See that one signal for Navajo to come. I go find out what they want." Chotilla nods at the pass where a lone rider rides into plain view and turns his horse in circles. "You be ready to run or fight if it is the one they call Geronimo. He will kill Chotilla maybe, if his squaw has him mad."

"Ugly squaws, mad squaws." Gage glares over at Chotilla. "Is that all you think about, you little squirt?"

Chotilla grins. "Young Jackson call me, his uncle, a squirt?"

"Sorry Chotilla, I'm just a little uptight." Gage leans forward and slaps the Navajo on the back. "No insult to my oldest and best teacher."

"Apache signal," Chotilla nods knowingly. "You wait here. Me come back bye 'n bye, maybe."

"You and old Geronimo ain't friends, huh?" Gage is watching the Apache warrior turning his horse in circles. "I thought Cochise protects you."

"No friends, Geronimo not friend of anyone." The Navajo shakes his head. "Cochise big chief, but he not here to protect Navajo. Geronimo only listen to him if he want to."

Cam looks at the little warrior who he has come to like. "Maybe I should go, you stay here."

"No, Navajo blood brother Apache. Unless it is Geronimo, they no kill." Chotilla kicks his gelding. "You go, maybe they kill. No, you stay here and watch. Be ready to run fast or fight."

"I ain't running anywhere until I get Trish back." Cam dismounts and loosens the cinch. "Not one inch."

Gage Jackson rolls himself a smoke as the Navajo starts across the canyon floor. "You want one Mitchell?'

"No, thank you," Cam shakes his head. "Never took up the habit."

"You don't know what you're missing, it helps calm the nerves." Gage rakes a sulphur across his chaps and watches as the match makes a hissing sound as it lights. "Right now, my poor nerves need calming."

"I imagine they do." Cam watches Chotilla who is halfway across the valley floor. "Thank you, anyway."

"Tell me Mitchell, are you sweet on my niece?" Gage blows smoke from his nose and looks sideways at Cam. "Is that why you're out here risking your neck or do you want Hacker that bad for killing Jeremy?"

"Bank on it. I want Hacker for killing Jeremy, that's for sure." Cam nods. "I'm here to kill the man or take him back to hang, it doesn't matter which, does it?"

"And Trish?" Gage looks down at his half-burned smoke. "Why are you here trying to help find her and not back looking for Ketchum and your Steeldust horse?"

"Maybe I am," Cam nods, "Sweet on her, that is."

"That's what I figured. You wouldn't be out here if you weren't." Gage nods. "She sweet on you too?"

"I can't speak for the lady." Cam looks sideways at the grinning Jackson. "You'll have to ask her that."

"I did," Gage blows smoke. "It's hard to believe, you two barely met, just known each other for maybe three days. Sure don't seem like enough time to me to get in a stir over each other."

"Is there a problem with trying to rescue a woman, even if I wasn't sweet on her, like you say?" Cam looks over at Gage. "She's a white woman in the hands of a crazy man. Any white man would try to help her."

"Oh, is that it?" Gage grins. "I'll tell you this Cam Mitchell, there's few white men that I know of, crazy enough to ride into these mountains looking to rescue a white woman from Apaches."

"I told you Gage Jackson, I'm sweet on her, okay?"

"You must be real sweet on her." Gage flips his burned-out smoke. "This could get you dead."

"You know, someday we're gonna have us a serious problem arguing over your niece." Cam shakes his head. "Let it go."

"Well, Pa might have a little to say about his granddaughter."

"Well, suppose we get her back and then argue over who gets to keep her." Cam turns his attention fully on the valley floor. "Okay?"

"You sure you don't want a smoke?"

"No, thanks."

"You don't mind if I have another do you?"

Cam looks over at Jackson perplexed. "Ain't you a little worried about Trish?"

"I think she's in good hands, look." Gage nods across the canyon floor. "You know Chotilla won't let you take Hacker back to hang. He'll kill him first."

"I figured that."

Chotilla disappears for several minutes, as Gage points across the valley floor, he appears again and rides into full view with Trish riding beside him. Both Cam and Gage sit with their jaws hanging open as their eyes pin on the two figures riding slowly toward them. They can hardly believe their eyes. No gunfire, no yelling, nothing, and here they come, riding in calmly like they were on a Sunday picnic.

"Does that take the cake or what?" Gage mumbles quietly, under his breath. "That little Navajo beats all I've ever seen. Man, he's something, I tell you."

Dismounting, Cam helps Trish from her horse as they ride up, pulling her close as Chotilla reins in beside them. "Are you okay? Did he harm you?"

"I'm fine." Trish hugs Cam hard then Gage. Turning to where the Navajo sits his horse, she takes his hand and smiles up at Chotilla. "Thanks to you, my father."

"What happened?" Gage focuses on the Navajo sitting his horse. "How did the Apache get her?"

"Apache War Chief, Juh surprise redhead Hacker and take him and girl captive while they sleep." Chotilla holds out his hand. "You give this one smoke."

Gage rolls the warrior a smoke and passes it over to him. "Don't you ever buy the makings?"

"No buy, Jackson tobacco tastes much better than store tobacco." Chotilla nods his head and grins as he smells the tobacco. "You got sulphur? Tobacco smoke better, when it on fire."

"It's not that store-bought tobacco tastes bad, it's just free tobacco tastes better, ain't that it?" Gage grins and passes the Navajo a match. "You sure you've got the strength to light it?"

"Me try," Chotilla smiles back at Gage then his face stiffens and grows serious as he fastens his black eyes on Cam. "Juh say you and him even now, his daughter for your squaw, but he say if you want redhead one, you come across valley and fight. If not, they let Chotilla cook him over fire."

"Hacker's still alive?"

"He is, but soon he no be." Chotilla puffs on the smoke. "Juh doesn't care who kills redhead white man, Mitchell or Navajo. When I finish smoke, I go kill redhead, then I go Rancheria"

"What you really mean is Juh wants me to kill Hacker myself?"

"Juh wants you and redhead fight with just one knife, like Apache fight." Chotilla watches Cam's eyes. "Juh wants Rough Rider to fight this fight, no one else."

"I'll fight the blowhard," Gage Jackson looks across at the Apache, "Let's go."

"No Gage Jackson, it's for this one to do," Chotilla raises his voice. "If Mitchell no fight, Navajo will."

"Why?" Cam is curious. "Why does he want me to kill him?"

"Apache no like redheaded white man." Chotilla shakes his head. "Apache Chief like Cam Mitchell. He want to see Rough Rider fight Hacker. Show how brave you are, maybe make Juh proud."

Cam starts unbuckling his pistol belt as Chotilla calls out something to the gathering warriors. Turning, he nods at Cam. "Juh is watching you, Cam Mitchell. He is pleased you meet challenge."

Cam looks at the small warrior then over at Trish. "So am I. Hacker will pay and he won't be able to hurt her ever again."

"This is so, but first you must win." Chotilla pulls on his horse's mane. "Apache like see good fight, bet much against you. They think redhead bigger and stronger. They think maybe you die, not redhead."

"Tell them thanks for the vote of confidence, Chotilla." Cam shakes his head at the small warrior. "You gonna bet on me, Navajo?"

"I bet on you, Cam Mitchell." The little warrior grins. "I bet all horses you pay me to find redhead. You still must buy store teeth, even if you die."

"That should be a good trick." Gage shakes his head that the two men could be joking at a time like this.

"I'll live, then you can buy another squaw and have more children."

"No, ten enough little ones, eat too much."

"This ain't funny, stop it." Trish places her hand on Cam's arm and squeezes. "I'm scared Cam. Don't fight him."

"Don't you see, I have to fight him." Cam looks hard at the girl, relieved Chotilla brought her out safe. "If I win, we can leave here without any more trouble from Hacker. I can take you home safely."

Chotilla looks to where several more warriors appear on foot, along the far canyon wall. "Apache waits. They say you come quick where Juh wait with redhead."

"One moment, Chotilla."

"One way or another, redhead man dead." Chotilla draws in the smoke and looks at the warriors lining up. "I will kill Hacker if you do not, but you Cam Mitchell, will lose face and much respect from Juh if you no go fight redhead now."

"You don't have to do this for me, Cam," Trish looks into his eyes, pleading.

"It's not for you Trish, it's for me and my right to live in these mountains and walk with pride among the Apache."

Chotilla hisses between his teeth. "It is not for any of you to do or not do. Juh told the others Mitchell, who he calls the Rough Rider, is a brave man. He wagered much. If Mitchell no fight redhead, Juh lose face, many horses and maybe we all die."

"Let's go, Chotilla."

"I am sorry my daughter, but this is Apache way." Chotilla holds her arm. "Among the Apache people, fighting is only way to prove he is brave man." Do not be afraid because Apaches bet against Mitchell. That is just their way. There is always much wagering on any fight among the Apache."

Chotilla looks across the canyon and watches as Juh walks out into plain sight for all to see. "I see the redhead there."

"We'll go across. Gage you take Trish home as fast as you can."

"No, Juh say woman must watch fight."

"Why?" Cam stops and looks at the Navajo. "You didn't say anything about that."

"He just say she must watch fight."

"She's going back to the ranch before I fight."

"Nobody asked me. I'm staying with you." Trish steps up on her horse. "If you have to fight because of me, I'm staying to help if I can."

"Will she be safe, Chotilla?"

"She be safe. If you die, we take her home."

"You sure?"

"No more talk, we go," Chotilla growls, throwing away his finished smoke. "Juh give word. You die brave, she be safe."

As the whites and Chotilla near the waiting warriors, Juh studies the face of Mitchell, the white he has come to like and the one he calls Rough Rider. Nodding at the Navajo as he approaches, Juh watches the small group for several minutes, saying nothing, then calling for Hacker to be brought to the front. Seeing the girl, as she comes in sight of the group, Hacker shrugs loose from the hands grasping him and straightens his shoulders proudly, as the small group of whites and their Indian escort, near. The redhead is an outlaw and traitor to Spade Jackson. He hired out to Jack Ketchum and rode with the outlaw gang for a couple years now. He isn't a coward and he sure isn't about to show yellow in front of the girl and her brother. He has worked side by side with Gage Jackson for several years. He even had a fight with the man once. There is no way he would give Jackson the satisfaction of seeing him show fear, no way.

Juh studies both white men closely as they eye each other across the rough ground. He measures each man's facial expression and grunts when neither show fear. Only hate and loathing emit from each face, but no fear. Speaking in Apache to the gathered warriors and the Navajo, he tosses a rolled up piece of rawhide to Chotilla then looks at Cam.

"You have come into my lands again, white man." Juh looks over at Cam. "You were told not to."

"I've come for my woman, not the yellow iron of the Apache." Cam nods to where Hacker stands. "Also, I want the redheaded one for shooting Spade Jackson, and for killing your friend, Jackson's Grandson."

"You wish to kill the redhead for stealing your woman?" Juh motions at Hacker with his hand. "This is what you want?"

"Hacker is a dead man." Cam looks over at Trish. "I aim to take him back to the ranch to hang by Jackson or I aim to kill him here, it doesn't matter which."

Juh laughs, "I think you hate more because he take your woman."

Chotilla holds Cam back as he tries to get to Hacker. "Someday soon, she will be my woman, but not today."

"You will kill him here, today, the Apache way?" Juh nods. "If you win, you get woman and your enemy is dead. Now you fight for your woman like Apache. Make her proud like Apache squaw."

"Turn the snake loose."

Juh shrugs. "We see Rough Rider. Now you will fight with the knife."

"What's the heathen, saying?" Hacker glares over at the Navajo. "I can't hear their whispering."

Chotilla looks at the rawhide in his hand and nods. "Him say today, maybe both of you die."

"He means for me to fight him, is that it?" Hacker laughs as he looks at his lighter opponent. "He ain't seen the day he's man enough to kill me in a fair fight."

"We see soon red hair, if your blood is as red as your hair." Juh has heard Hacker's tough words and points at the rawhide, speaking harshly to Chotilla. "Bind them together."

"What are you doing Injun?" Hacker tries to pull his hand back as Chotilla loops the braided rawhide around his left wrist, jerks it tight then knots it so it can't slip loose.

"You talk tough, white man," The Navajo grunts, slinging Hacker's hand down and motions for Cam to hold out his hand. "We see how tough you are quick."

Only a three-foot piece of braided rawhide, separate the two men, but it is unbreakable, holding the two combatants fastened together securely in their bid for life or death. Both men stand watching as a warrior, thirty feet away, stabs a razor sharp, skinning knife into the hard ground so it stands upright. The older warrior says a few words to the heavens, then turns to the combatants and nods. Hacker pales slightly as he looks down at the braided leather that ties him securely to Cam then over at the knife. Juh points at the knife, then looks over at the two waiting men.

"Whoever lives, will take the woman and leave this place." Juh looks to where Gage Jackson stands. "One of you will die here today, maybe both. The woman belongs to the winner, if there is one, even if it is the red hair."

"What's this rope for?" Hacker questions, holding up his arm at the chief.

Juh grins. "As the girl has tied two enemies together in life, the rawhide will tie you together in your death struggle. When the rawhide is cut, it means death to one of you."

Cam gathers the rough leather in his left hand and watches as the Apache Chief steps backward, away from the coming battle. Trish starts to step forward, but Chotilla grabs her arm, pulling her roughly backward. Both men bunch their muscles and still themselves for the battle ahead. Juh raises his arm and points at the knife, dropping it abruptly, causing both men to spring forward trying to reach the deadly knife. Quick as a cat, Cam trips Hacker, who is concentrating only on the knife, then wraps the rawhide around the redhead's neck attempting a choke hold. Hacker rolls sideways, slipping his head out from under the harsh rope, freeing himself then lunges to his feet. Both men start toward the upright knife, slugging at each other with their free hand.

Hacker gains the advantage for a minute and is almost in reach of the razor sharp blade only to have Cam pull him backward, physically. Pulling and tugging on the rope, both men fight with their hands and fists, kicking and clawing, anything they can do to keep the other from reaching the knife. Whoever pulls the knife from the ground and gains control of the weapon will certainly have the advantage and should win the deadly contest.

The normally tight-mouthed Apache warriors suddenly erupt in laughter and excitement, urging the one they bet on, to fight harder. Every warrior present has wagered on one of the two combatants, not because they like the man, but because they think their man will win. Gage looks down at the forty-five holstered on his side, but he knows there is no use in reaching for it. To do so would be futile and could get them all killed. That is why Juh didn't disarm him. Hacker bleeds profusely from his nose, where Cam landed a hard blow, but Hacker has landed one of his own, almost tearing Cams left ear halfway from his head. A hard drop kick to Cam's stomach brings him down, doubled up on the ground as Hacker struggles to pull the heavy muscled man toward the knife. Rolling to his side, Cam digs his heels in, resisting with all his strength as he drags across the ground by the powerful redhead, almost close enough to permit Hacker to reach the upright knife.

"Your white friend is weak Navajo, like you," one of the watching warriors yells out. "The redhead will kill him this day."

"Chotilla will bet two more horses on the Rough Rider."

"I will take your wager," the warrior laughs.

"Maybe he will wager his ugly squaw," another warrior yells out as Hacker kicks Cam, full in the face.

Suddenly, Hacker lunges backward again, toward the prone man and places a hard boot into his exposed arm. Rolling up, into the rope, bringing Hacker close, Cam wraps his legs around the redhead, tripping him backward to the ground. Crashing together like two enraged bulls, both men explode, slugging away at each other in savage fury as they roll back and forth across the ground. Both men are young and strong, in their prime, and a picture of health. Neither emits a sound, except for a grunt now and then when the other man strikes a vicious blow. With surprising speed for a large man, Hacker jerks away from Cam, springing toward the dangerous blade. Reaching and straining for the knife with his arm fully extended, Hacker finally manages to grasp the handle of the blade and wrench the knife from the hard ground. Grinning evilly, Hacker extends the sharp blade fully in front of him as he turns slowly on his unarmed opponent. Wiping the blood from his face and out of his eyes, he spits a mouthful of blood from his mouth as he rises and starts forward in a crouch.

Smiling viciously, Hacker waves the knife and taunts Cam. "I'm gonna string your guts out all over this canyon Mitchell for the girl to see their color."

Trying to stay out of reach of the knife, Cam stumbles and falls backward as the larger man steps forward and towers over him. "You got the knife big mouth."

"Now Mitchell, now I'm gonna cut your guts out." Hacker springs forward, the knife slashing toward Cam, ripping open his shirt. "And I'm taking the woman."

"You know better than that Red," Cam grins. "Even if I die, the Navajo will kill you."

Cam feigns a kick, then rolls quickly to his feet, pulling hard on the rawhide, jerking Hacker off balance, forcing him forward, trying at the same time to keep the deadly knife from slashing him.

"You cut rope red hair and you dead man." Juh reads Hacker's thoughts as he grabs at the rawhide that Cam keeps pulling him off balance with.

Both men take in great gulps of air as they circle each other with

Hacker in control of the knife, swiping the air between them. Twice, the sharp blade cuts through Cam's shirt, causing twin lines of blood to trickle from his wound and soak through the garment. Trish lets out a small moan of despair as Hacker suddenly lunges forward, the deadly blade extended at arm's length. Cam falls backward before the onslaught as Hacker continues to press his advantage, cutting at Cam several times.

"I've got you now," Hacker spits through a split lip, "I'll have your woman. Think of that Mitchell, as you're bleeding to death."

Lunging forward, Cam feels the blade cut into his side, but not before he catches the strong arm of the redhead in a powerful grasp and forces the knife away as he trips the bigger man, making him fall backward. With brute strength, Hacker kicks loose from Cam's hold, trying to regain his feet as Cam rolls across the redhead then wraps around Hacker from behind. Hacker tries to roll to his feet, but Cam clings to his back, his legs like forged iron, wrapped around the redhead's waist. Desperately, Hacker reaches behind his back and stabs at the wildcat that has him wrapped up in what seems like steel claws, which now are grabbing for his exposed wrist that holds the biting steel. Finally, all four hands of the two men clutch the knife and each other's hands and wrists. Cam manages to encircle Hacker's body firmly with his legs, making it impossible for the redhead to dislodge or roll him from his back.

In this position, behind Hacker, Cam clearly has the leverage as he applies all his remaining strength, pulling the razor sharp knife slowly closer and closer to Hacker's exposed chest. The redhead pushes back, trying desperately to hold the sharp point away from his body. Both men's arms start to shake from exertion and tremendous strain as Cam puts the last of his strength into pulling the knife into Hacker's chest. Hacker is at a disadvantage. Trying to push the ever-nearing knife away takes all his strength as he strains holding the knife back from being forced into his chest. Cam's position behind the redhead, gives him a great advantage over the bigger, stronger man, if he can hang on. Arching himself backward with all the effort he can muster, Cam slowly forces the knife, inch by slow inch, toward the exhausted redhead's chest. Both men's arms shake from the exertion they are applying, knowing the end is near.

The Apache warriors, who bet so much, yell loudly with wild enthusiasm, as they suddenly see the turn in the struggle and shake their heads in disbelief as the knife touches the redhead's chest. To defeat a larger and stronger opponent, the Rough Rider has fought like a wildcat. His savage ferocity is the same as the Apache who watch in respect at his bravery.

"Now Hacker, this is for Jeremy," Cam breathes hard and exerts all his remaining strength. "Taste the cold steel big man, as that boy did."

Trish turns her head as Hacker rolls onto his side, trying to dislodge Cam, who still clings to his back, even after taking several severe cuts across his sides. Feeling the blade's pointed tip as it enters his body, Hacker screams in terror and pain. Cam forces the sharp blade slowly, inch by inch, deeper into his heaving chest. Hearing Hacker's final gurgle and feeling Hacker's dead body stiffen, then go limp as the blade pierces his heart and lungs, Cam pushes the big man away. Juh walks to where the two men lie on the ground, one dead, the other too exhausted to move and cut the rawhide rope that binds the two enemies together. Pushing Hacker's limp body still further from him, Cam staggers tattered and bloody from the ground, regaining his feet to face Juh.

"You have fought bravely today Rough Rider, like an Apache." The War Chief pulls his own knife and holds it in Cam's face, who doesn't blink or flinch. Slicing his own hand Juh picks up Cam's bloody hand and holds both of their palms together for all to see. "Apache and whites, see this man. He is the Rough Rider, a brave warrior, and now he is the blood brother and son of Juh. No one in this land, Indian or white, will harm him or he will die by my hand. Juh has spoken."

Cam touches his bloody chest, then touches Juhs. "There will always be peace between us, my uncle."

As the aftershock of the hard fight, and the loss of blood from several bleeding cuts, saps what strength he has left, Cam looks over at Trish and Gage. Reaching out, as he grows dizzy, Cam grasps Gage's hand and with Trish's help, both ease the exhausted man to the ground, leaning him back, against some rocks. Pushing water into the girl's hands, Gage watches as she washes his wounds.

"Is he hurt bad, Trish?" Gage watches as the girl examines Cam.

"He Rough Rider, he no hurt bad." Juh stares down at Cam.

"He's sliced up some and has lost blood, but he has only two serious wounds." With a sigh of relief, Trish washes the blood from the wounds. "He's young and strong. He'll be okay, but he'll carry these scars the rest of his life."

Gage looks over her shoulder and watches as Trish tries to stem the blood running down the wounded man's sides. "Those cuts look bad too me."

"They're nasty looking, but not deep. He's just exhausted is all." Trish smiles as Cam opens his eyes and looks up at her. "Hi there."

"Howdy Doc, am I gonna live?"

"You just might, and maybe a long time if you'll listen to your doctor."

Cam nods slowly. "What does my doctor say?"

"Your doctor says you should quit this kind of stuff." Trish rips up a shirt and starts wrapping the more serious cuts where the knife penetrated his sides. "Your future wife, Mister Mitchell, not your doctor, says you will quit risking your life like this."

"Yes, ma'am." Cam blinks as her last words sink in. "My future wife?"

"There." Trish looks at her handiwork, then gathers what few pieces of cloth she has and stands up. "Yes, Mister Mitchell, your future wife, if you want me."

Cam doesn't have time to answer as Trish walks away toward the water hole, out of his sight. Hearing a horse walk up, he looks back to see Juh staring down at him. "We go, Rough Rider. We come someday, visit you at Jackson Ranch."

"I owe you, Juh. You will always be welcome." Cam nods tiredly up at the chief. "If I can ever do anything for you, anything, just ask."

"We will meet again, my son." Juh looks at the bandages Trish made from his tattered shirt. "You have good woman. She make good squaw. You keep always, she make you happy."

Cam follows his eyes to where Trish talks with Gage. "I'm a lucky man and I will keep her always."

"She is a lucky woman," Juh smiles. "She has my son for a husband, the one I call the Rough Rider."

Chotilla watches curiously, as the Apache crosses the canyon floor with his warriors and disappears. Never has he known a bronco Apache to help a white man as Juh helped Cam today and the Apache Chief is one of the wildest of the Apache. Kicking his gelding, he leads the horses close to where Cam leans against the rock wall. "We go now, reach Jackson Ranch tomorrow."

Gage looks over to where Trish is washing Cam's face and shakes his head. "He needs to rest here today, he's weak."

"When wounds stiffen up, he be very sore, much fever, weak. Chotilla shakes his head. "We go now, while he can still sit on horse. Maybe he live to fight again"

"He's right, Uncle Gage." Trish stands up and frowns at Chotilla. "We need to go now before the fever sets in, but I'll assure you, he will not fight again, ever."

"We see, bye 'n bye, missy."

Chotilla leads the small party into Jackson Basin before noon, just as he predicted. With a full moon, he can follow the rough trails through the jumble of canyons, taking the shortest way back to the Basin. They only make a few short stops to give Cam a much-needed drink, and then the long night ride continues. With the coming of the warm sun, the fever seems to settle into the wounded man's stiff body, making him reel with pain and fatigue. Both Trish and Gage ride, flanking his horse, holding the wounded man upright in the saddle.

Gage lets out a war whoop as the smoke from the Jackson Ranch shows in the distance. "We're home, little daughter."

Several pairs of hands reach out to help the almost unconscious man from his horse as they stop in front of the ranch yard. Following Trish's directions, they carry him quickly into the house. The blood soaked bandages cover Cam's entire chest and sides, making the ranch hands shake their heads and look dubiously over at Gage. Only a shrug comes from Jackson as he pushes the men back, out of the bedroom, ignoring their unasked questions.

Chotilla watches as Cam is carried into the house, then motions at Spade. "Me no help here, go Rancheria, see squaws and children."

"You'll get your horses and probably more, old friend, if I read that boy in there right," Spade Jackson smiles. "We checked on your family and sent food. They're all fine."

"For this I thank you, old one." Chotilla swings up on his gelding and takes the trail south, into the high mountains, without a look back. "Apache warriors owe Navajo many horses. They stupid, bet on redhead one."

"You think they'll pay off?" Gage is curious.

"You bet chum. Chotilla get horses or maybe Apache scalp," The Navajo holds up a bloody red scalp, "Like this one."

"He scalped Hacker," Gage is struck. "We didn't even notice."

Spade Jackson spits and then nods as the Navajo rides off. "I'll guarantee, the Apaches did."

"How is he this morning, Granddaughter?" Spade Jackson steps into the dining room and looks over to where Trish is boiling water.

"He's hungry as a bear and recovering," Trish smiles.

"About time, it's been a long week, but I knew he would." Spade picks up his coffee cup as she turns from the stove. "He's young and strong."

"Yes, he is, and very handsome," Trish beams.

"Gage says you're taken with the lad." Spade looks over the brim of his cup, staring openly at her. "He says the boy got himself all cut up fighting for you."

"I don't think the Apaches gave him much choice about whether he was to fight or not." Trish smiles down at her grandfather. "The Apaches used me as an excuse to force him to fight, but I think they really wanted to test his courage."

"Does he have courage, girl?"

The girl's blue eyes look toward the bedroom door dreamily. "He was very brave, courageous like the knights of old."

"You gonna marry the boy?"

"I am, if he asks me," as she smiles over at her granddad.

"No matter what I say?" Spade looks mischievously at his grand-daughter. He knows how headstrong, she has always been, since child-hood, and she only grows more set in her ways as she ages.

"I'm marrying Cameron Mitchell when he's well enough to ride to Garden City, no matter what anyone says, Grandpa." Trish looks straight at Spade without batting an eye, "Anyone."

"Well, he's a good man from what I see," Spade grins. "You have my blessings. He'll make you a good husband."

Trish smiles and hugs her grandfather happily. No matter what, she is going to marry Cam Mitchell, but with Spade's blessings, it makes her even happier. "Thank you, Grandpa."

Chapter 10

Two weeks have passed since the bloody duel in the canyon. With Trish's constant care, Cam slowly mends and regains his strength from the fight with Hacker. The sun is shining brightly when Caintuck rides into the ranch yard and reins up to the front porch where Cam sits resting in a rocking chair. Rising gingerly, the young man walks to the edge of the porch and nods. Caintuck studies the thin, wild looking caricature, standing on the porch in front of him and shakes his head.

"Lite down and rest yourself stranger," Cam smiles over at his old friend as he sees the distrustful look Caintuck is giving the Navajo.

"Heard you were here, laid up for a spell." Caintuck shifts his weight in the saddle. "Figured to find you dead from the stories I've heard. What in tarnation is that?"

"Now who would you hear something like that from?" Cam ignores the question as Caintuck points at Chotilla.

"A few days ago, a couple of riders from the Rafter 5 rode into Garden City, where I've been cooling my heels and waiting for news about you and the Steeldust." Caintuck grows serious. "They came into the saloon and started telling about you leaving them in the Mogollons without their boots or horses."

"They wouldn't be called Frank and Mingo would they?"

"I believe that was their names alright," Caintuck nods. "Said you were a devil of some kind and had an Indian siding you."

"Well, they were partially right." Cam looks over at Chotilla and grins, thinking back of the two sleeping men in Ketchum's cabin. "To answer your question about Chotilla here, he's English, the best tracker and friend a man could want. I'm proud to have him at my side."

"He don't look like any Englishman, I've ever known."

Cam laughs when Caintuck doesn't catch the joke. "No, he's a Navajo." Cam looks over at Chotilla. "This is my friend, Caintuck."

The little Navajo only grunts a greeting, not attempting to rise or shake hands. The dark eyes study the horse trader, never taking his eyes from Caintuck as he watches him dismount. "Me see this one, many times."

"He don't seem too impressed with you, Caintuck," Gage laughs as he walks up. "You two know each other?"

"Don't seem that way does it." The horse trader shakes his head. "Can't say I've ever seen him before."

"What else have you heard?"

"They said the Apache War Chief, Juh is bragging all over the Mogollons. How you, his adopted son, the Rough Rider, killed a redheaded feller in a knife duel and said you were cut up bad."

Chotilla nods. "Me hear this at Rancheria from squaw. She say Juh tell everyone about big fight in canyon. He proud."

"They also say Ketchum wants to meet with you real bad."

"Ketchum, huh." Cam shakes his head. "How bad does he want me?"

"I reckon bad enough to get himself captured by the Rangers if he goes through with the crazy caper he's planning." Caintuck unfolds a heavy piece of paper. "Read this."

"Everyone knows Ketchum is a wild one. What's he planning now?" Gage Jackson walks out on the porch and is listening to the conversation.

"This." Caintuck hands Cam and Gage a paper flyer. "The one called Mingo gave it to me. Said Ketchum printed in Elmwood, just before he robbed the bank."

"Well Chotilla, I guess old Mingo lied to us. He made it out of the mountains alright, without any boots."

"Him say he no can walk out of mountains without boots." The Navajo shakes his head in disgust. "We should have killed them as they slept."

"So you rode way out here to check on me?" Cam reads the paper slowly then straightens stiffly in his chair.

"Yeah, reckon I did at that." Caintuck reaches for his cigar. "You see anything of the Steeldust?"

"I've been lazy, I reckon. I ain't got around to finding the stallion yet." Cam looks over at the door. "Other things came first."

"I know the stud's in good shape." Caintuck ties his horse and steps up on the porch, finding himself a chair. "I also know where the horse is."

Cam starts to lean back, but stops as he hears the news. "Where is he?"

"Ketchum is waiting, biding his time at a ghost town east of here called Silver Pass." Caintuck pulls up a cane backed chair and lights up his stubby cigar. "He's got the stud with him."

"How'd you find out?"

"Silver Pass has been played out of silver for several years now. No one lives there anymore. An old miner named Jules Moss passed through there. Seen the lights and corrals full of horses, so he crept in close and recognized Ketchum and his bunch sitting there big as brass."

"He actually saw the Steeldust there?"

"Yep, he did," Caintuck nods. "He said that horse was bright as a shiny new gold piece, standing alone in a corral."

"Came and told you, huh?" Gage Jackson lights himself a smoke then seeing Chotilla licking his lips, hands the smoke to the Navajo. "Here you little beggar."

"Me no beggar, Gage Jackson." The head nods happily. "Me smart, no have to buy expensive tobacco at white man store long as you buy."

"Chotilla, I swear."

Caintuck shakes his head as he watches the two men bicker over the cigarette then turns to Cam. "When old Jules reached Garden City and found out I was in town, he looked me up and described the stud to a tee," Caintuck nods. "You've become famous, boy. Seems like everyone in the Mogollons knows the story of you and how you're looking for the Steeldust."

"I expect they do by now." Cam sits heavily into the rocking chair, thinking of Fox and Hacker. "Word gets around."

"It does, especially when you're leaving dead bodies lying everywhere."

"Fox came after me."

"Everyone has heard of you killing Len Fox and how you beat him in a stand up fight. Two of Ketchum's men cleared out of the Mogollons like a turpentined tom cat after you killed Fox and put the scare in them. They talked plenty about how crazy you were and that they were clearing out of the mountains and Arizona for good." Caintuck pulls out his old corncob pipe. "It's also on every pair of lips in the country that you shot a white man that was trying to kill an Apache girl."

Cam nods, wondering how anyone found out about Juh's daughter. "Word does get around."

"Yeah, Ketchum's men loafed around Garden City for a couple days, then just up and left one night." Caintuck looks at Chotilla again. "Before they left the saloon, they told everyone that would listen about the killings."

"Must have been Frank and Mingo. Still can't figure how they found out about the killing over the girl?"

"Yep, that was their names alright," Caintuck laughs. "I believe you walked two inches off their bare feet. They were still limping and not able to wear their boots."

"I should have killed them." Cam leans back in the big rocker. "Wonder how they heard about the girl?"

"Said a man named Giles was there and seen it."

"They lied, weren't a white there, just me and the Apaches."

"And the dead man," Caintuck adds.

Cam looks over at Chotilla and shakes his head. He heard Angus Moore speak of a man named Giles on his last visit to the Rafter 5. "What do you think Chotilla?"

"White man named Giles ride with Ketchum, bad man." The Navajo looks into the blue smoke of his cigarette. "Me see, many times."

"I know he wasn't there when I killed the white man."

"Over an Indian girl?" Caintuck looks at Cam. "Why?"

"Because of an Indian girl, Caintuck, not over an Indian girl, there's a difference." Cam nods. "Could be he came along later and was good enough to read the signs."

"You could be right. They said one of Ketchum's men, named Giles, recognized your boot print and said you gunned the man in the back." Caintuck shrugs. "It could be the Apache told Ketchum about you helping the girl when they went to trade for guns."

"Giles must have read the signs," Cam nods. "I wouldn't think Juh would do anymore trading for anything after his daughter was almost killed."

"Young one, wrong this time," Chotilla chuckles. "Guns more important to Geronimo and the Apache, than small squaw."

Caintuck looks over at the little Navajo then back at Cam. "Killing a white man over an Apache isn't well thought of out here boy, even if he were an outlaw."

"He had it coming. Weren't no other way to save the girl." Cam moves slightly. "I'd do the same again."

"Why did you want to save an Apache?" Caintuck thinks like most whites in Arizona, the Apache are vermin to be rooted out.

"She was just an innocent kid." Cam shakes his head at Caintuck's accusations. "I didn't aim to kill him, but it happened."

"Tell me, did the Apache Chief, Juh help you against this other man like it was told?"

Cam nods absently, thinking back to the fight with Hacker and the wily Apache Chief. "He did for a fact. Why, I don't rightly know."

"Spade Jackson is thought of highly by the Apache, that's probably why." Caintuck puffs on his cigar. "I've heard he's helped them a lot over the years with sickness and such."

"Juh no help Mitchell because of friendship with Jackson," Chotilla speaks up. "He help his adopted son."

Caintuck looks over at the little Navajo confused. "Now what's he babbling about?"

"Chief Juh adopted Cam Mitchell into his clan and made him his son," Gage speaks up. "I seen it myself, blood to blood and all that."

"You're kidding. I've heard of it, but never seen such a thing myself."

"I ain't joking Caintuck," Gage laughs. "There sits a bona fide Apache warrior."

Coughing roughly from inhaling to much acrid smoke, Caintuck shakes his head. "Shucks, looks like a white man to me."

"I should have killed Frank and Mingo," Cam repeats. "They wouldn't be spreading these wild tales like they are."

Caintuck shakes his head slowly. "No Cam, it would have come out sooner or later."

"How's that, dead men wouldn't be telling their lies."

"Let them talk, this way is better. Everyone will hear and won't blame you for the killings," Caintuck puffs smoke, "except maybe for this adoption business. You know, Juh is not exactly thought of as a saint around these parts."

"Where is this town, Silver Pass?" Cam changes the subject away from the Apache.

Spade steps onto the porch in time to hear the question and smiles as he finds Caintuck sitting on his porch. "It's east of here about forty miles as the crow flies, Cam."

"Spade Jackson, you old rock hermit." Caintuck grasps the old miner in a hard handshake.

"How long has it been, Caintuck?"

"Ten years, if it's been a day."

Cam watches the two old men. "This Silver Pass, is it another hideout that Ketchum uses?"

"I think it probably is," Caintuck shakes his head. "I figure it was his bunch that robbed the bank at Elmwood. I can't figure though, why he ain't heading back this way, to his old hideout."

"Elmwood?" Cam knows the town, but the bank is small, not really worth the trouble. "What happened there?"

"Ketchum robbed the bank and shot up the town, that's what happened," Caintuck shakes his head. "Man, he did some meanness there."

"The man sure gets around. I reckon he's heading back to his hideout now."

"Nope," Caintuck shakes his head. "We killed one of his men, but before he died, he said Ketchum was waiting for some gun hand, named Red Hacker, to bring him word to Silver Pass about your whereabouts."

Chotilla grunts, then looks over at Caintuck. "Redhead, Hacker, won't be bringing word about anything now."

"What's that supposed to mean?" Caintuck looks curiously at the Navajo. "He talks in riddles."

"Hacker's dead, Caintuck." Spade lights his pipe. "Cam here killed him."

"He's the redhead we've been telling you about." Gage looks at Cam, "The redhead that Juh helped with."

Caintuck looks over at Cam and shakes his head. "You sure been doing a lot of killing boy."

"He needed killing if anyone ever did." Cam tells the story of Jeremy being killed and Trish being kidnapped by Hacker.

Chotilla pulls his long skinning knife and makes a gurgling sound as he pretends to pull it into his chest. "Redhead, him no steal woman again, I bet."

"He crazy or what?" Caintuck looks nervously at the Navajo.

Gage finishes the story in its entirety, including the part the Apache played back in the box canyons of the Fingers. "No, he isn't crazy, but he is a tightwad for sure."

"What tightwad, Gage Jackson?" Chotilla questions the word.

"Sounds like you and the Apache have gotten pretty thick." Caintuck rocks back and forth in deep thought.

"Could be, but without them, I'd probably be a dead man now," Cam acknowledges. "Is that a problem, Caintuck?"

"It could be, but it's not the only problem we've got now."

"Ketchum?"

"Mingo said Ketchum went loco since you killed Fox and now he's taking his meanness out on the town of Elmwood." Caintuck strikes a sulphur to his cigar, filling the porch with the rich aroma of tobacco smoke. "They killed five men, including the banker, who wouldn't open the safe."

Spade shakes his head. "Ketchum has never bothered us or the Rafter 5. This could change things. He's is a bad one for sure."

"I'd be on the watch, were I you, Spade." Caintuck looks at the old prospector. "He's liable to do anything now."

"What's he after, Caintuck?" Cam looks over at the horse trader. "Mingo said he'd never have gone along with Hacker kidnapping the girl."

"You boy, that's what." Caintuck passes Cam a poster. "Like this poster here says, he's inviting you to meet him at Garden City in broad daylight for a showdown."

"A showdown, you mean a gunfight?" Cam shakes his head. "In Garden City, where he'll be recognized? Why?"

"For killing his Cousin Len Fox, for one thing, and according to that poster, you also killed several of his men."

"Fair fights, all of them."

Spade shakes his head. "Fair fight to a man like Ketchum, doesn't matter one thing. He wants you dead and he wants an audience to see it."

"He wants to meet me in full daylight, with every lawman in Arizona and New Mexico after him?" Cam shakes his head. "He is loco, gotta be."

"He's planning that way, for a fact." Caintuck sucks on the pipe. "The Ketchums are proud people from the mountains of Tennessee. You killed his cousin and made a fool out of his men. He can't let you get by with that."

"Why not, would he rather get caught in broad daylight on the streets of Garden City?"

"You've hurt what he thinks is his self-respect." Caintuck eyes the Navajo narrowly. "To him, without his self-respect, men will no longer follow him."

"The law, what about them?" Cam looks over at the old horse trader. "They'll be all over Garden City waiting on Ketchum to show."

"I've wondered about that myself," Caintuck scratches his beard. "The man may be crazy for revenge, but he's smart. If he says he's gonna meet you in Garden City, you better believe, he'll be there."

"What if I don't show?"

"You didn't finish reading that paper." Caintuck motions to the flyer. "I'll tell you, he said he'll kill the Steeldust right there on the street and then ride into the Mogollons to look for you and anyone who hides you."

"He is crazy."

"From what I've heard from George Mason, before I left town, he said if you're willing to fight Ketchum, the law may be willing to let you two settle your differences by yourselves." Caintuck flips ashes from his smoke. "He figures this is the only way out of this mess without a lot of killing."

"Save them the trouble and chances of getting killed," Cam shakes his head, "Is that it?"

"It may be something like that," Caintuck nods. "I figure Stark will be there, and together, he and Mason will get Ketchum, dead or alive, after you and him get through shooting each other up."

Spade shakes his head. "I never heard of the law letting a known killer and bank robber ride into their town for a showdown."

"This is the Mogollons Spade, you know that." Caintuck shakes his head. "Not much law, except local. They want Ketchum anyway they can get him."

"I'm their man, huh?"

Caintuck nods. "Mason is smart. He knows Ketchum's a killer. If the law interferes and says no to the fight, they know he'll just fade back into the mountains, then he'll be back robbing and killing as always."

"It could be a trick to get Ketchum into Garden City," Spade speaks up. "Could be Mason won't let it go as far as a fight."

"No, Spade old friend, I don't think so." Caintuck looks over at the old prospector. "I believe George will keep his word."

"So they sent you out here to show me the poster?" Cam looks down at the rolled up paper he holds, "Is that it?"

"I got this one from Mingo. These things are hung up all over town." Caintuck holds up the poster and looks at it again. "I figured I better come find you before Ketchum's time limit is up, and he rides back this way."

"What else does it say?" Spade looks at the paper.

"Nothing much, just that Ketchum challenges Cam to a stand up gunfight." Caintuck offers the paper to Spade. "Old Ketchum has the gall for a fact, but the man's cunning as a coyote after a rabbit."

"You know I can't read a word, old hoss."

"I can." Trish stands in the doorway where she is listening to every word. "Cam's not fighting anyone for any reason. He's finished with all that now."

"Don't figure he's got much choice, missy." Caintuck looks at the girl, he remembers, who has now grown into a beautiful woman. "If he don't ride into Garden City, Ketchum will come looking for him here. That is, after he kills the Steeldust."

"What?" Trish didn't hear the first of the conversation. "He's threatening to kill the Steeldust stud."

"Yep, if Cam don't ride into Garden City before sundown on the twentieth of the month, he swears to shoot the horse dead, right on main street."

"I know him, he'll do it too," Spade joins in. "Ketchum is mean clear through."

"No man can be that mean." Trish walks to where Cam sits. "That poor horse hasn't done anything to him."

"He's just making sure Cam fights." Caintuck looks at the girl. "Can't you see that?"

"There has to be more to it than that, more than me killing Fox."

"I doubt it, those Tennessee hill people are a tight knit family. Also, he doesn't want to have to dig you out of these hills where you have friends, Apache friends, that is." Caintuck strikes another sulphur to his cigar and puts in a little dig, looking over at Chotilla. "Moreover, what he wants most is for the whole town and state to know he killed you straight up and he aims to have the whole town as witnesses."

"What will that prove?"

"If he gets it done and gets away free, it'll put the scare in everybody in these parts, which is exactly what he wants to do," Caintuck shakes his head. "You might say, he'll rule the roost in these parts for sure."

Cam looks sharply, over at the old horse trader. "You think he had anything to do with Hacker coming here to kidnap Trish? His men, Frank and Mingo, said he didn't."

"Could have been, but I doubt it," Spade shakes his head. "We've always left Ketchum alone up here and he does us the same. I doubt he even knew about Trish. No, it was Hacker's play and his alone, but now Ketchum's pride is at stake and he's got to get revenge."

"He'd kill a valuable animal like the Steeldust, just to get to me?"

"That horse means nothing to him at all," Caintuck shakes his head. "He's a mean one, and from what this Mingo said, he's gone crazier than a bedbug."

"Make him come here into our country," Trish looks over at her grandfather. "We've got good men here."

"That won't work girl," Spade shakes his head. "Tomorrow, next week or next month, he'll bide his time, then he'll slip in here and start picking our people off one at a time, from hiding, and his men are all excellent shots."

"He's right, Trish," Cam reaches out his hand to her. "Can't you see, I've got to go. There's no other way."

"You're still weak from your wounds." Trish turns, walking slowly past Chotilla on her way into the house.

Following her from the porch, Cam takes her arm gently. "Trish, wait."

Turning, she slips into his outstretched arms. "I can't bear the thought of you getting hurt again, I can't."

"You heard Caintuck, there's no other way."

"I know it, but is the Steeldust worth it?"

"It's not the horse. It's you, your folks, and the men of the Rafter 5." Cam looks down and touches the tears on her cheek. "Ketchum is a killer, a sick man. He'll come here looking to kill, and he will."

"I can't believe he'll walk into Garden City and take a chance of getting caught just because his pride has been hurt."

"Like Caintuck said Trish, the man's loco." Cam shakes his head. "He may even be insane."

"When are you going?"

"According to the poster, we've got ten days before his deadline."

"Garden City is five days away, hard riding."

"I'll let Caintuck rest a couple days, then we'll head out."

"I'm going with you."

"No!"

"No arguing, I'm going." Trish shakes her head at him. "When this is over, then we'll be married."

Cam smiles down, into the beautiful, worrying face, nodding slowly. "Yes ma'am, we will be married, I promise."

Trish looks over to where Caintuck is still talking with Spade. "You think he'll let you get to Garden City in one piece?"

"From what his men told Caintuck, before they rode out, he wants to kill me in a stand up fight in front of the whole town. He ain't likely to do anything to lose face again," Cam shakes his head. "No, he won't ambush me, that's for sure. Ketchum wants to kill me in Garden City for a big show and his pride."

Chotilla watches and listens outside an open window as Trish pleads with Cam then silently slips away in the dark. The girl is like a daughter to him. Over the years, as a baby, she spent many days with his woman and his children. The old Apache woman, who nursed her after her own mother's passing, was the only real mother she ever knew. Both, the woman and Chotilla, love her as their own. Through the window tonight, he had seen tears running down her face for the first time, tears that don't belong on one so beautiful. He knows, if anything happens to the young white man, the girl would lose the happiness she has found with him. Turning back, to look through the window as he mounts his horse, the Navajo strikes his chest and rides away.

Five riders, including Spade, Gage, and Trish, along with Cam and Caintuck, ride into the Rafter 5 Ranch, five days later. Both Angus and Bill Moore walk from the barn and raise their hands in welcome. Angus and Spade dance a jig and hug on each other for several minutes before noticing they are being watched. Blushing, they smile happily and turn to where the others stand watching.

Angus looks over to where Cam dismounts. "So you're gonna do it, huh boy?"

"Yes sir, I expect I am." Cam is curious. "Who told you?"

"Caintuck, when he passed through a few days back."

"Ketchum is a bad man, a killer, and he's fast with his gun." Angus shakes his head slowly. "Me and the boy seen him gun a man once in Tucson, many years ago. The other gun slick didn't even clear his holster before Ketchum shot him dead."

"Don't count me out before I get a saddle on him," Cam grins.

"Just letting you know, is all, no offense intended," Angus nods.

"You want to try to win those boots you wanted?" Cam makes reference to Angus calling Thunder a killer and betting on the horse against him. "I've still got my hundred dollars."

"No, I've learned my lesson," Angus smiles, stroking the neck of the black, who Cam has ridden back from Jackson Basin. "I wish you luck, Cam Mitchell."

"How's my horses." Cam looks over at Bob.

"Fat and sassy."

"You know Ketchum has a man posted here on the Rafter 5?"

"He had a man here. I hung him last week after the boys came by and brought your horses back."

"They told you who he was?"

"Yep." The hard crusted old rancher shakes his head. "They were scared after they told me. Said something about telling you they were even with you now. We started watching and guess what? We caught him and two others rustling our cows."

"Just like that, no trial?"

"Them cows walking away from the Rafter 5 was the trial. Nothing else was needed, except a rope." Angus winks at Spade. "That's the law of the Mogollons, ain't it Spade?"

"For a fact, pard." Spade nods. "That's how it's done."

The sun breaks magnificently over the mountains as the men walk out on the front porch after breakfast and take seats along the wall. Caintuck looks off at the mountains and shakes his head in wonder. Only the place he and Cam discovered in the wilds of the Pecos Country, back in Texas, touches the old horse trader's fancy as this place does.

"This has to be the prettiest spot in all the Mogollons." Caintuck sips slowly on his morning coffee and looks at the cloud covered slopes. "The Basin is pretty also, but there's just something about this place."

"Yep, it is." Spade nods, "He beat me out of the place."

"I did not, you old rock goat," Angus blusters. "We flipped for it, as I remember."

"You did something to that coin."

Angus shakes his head. He has heard the same halfhearted arguments from Spade many times before, over the years. "Yeah, I flipped it."

Caintuck smiles, looking to where Cam sits quietly against the cabin wall. "We've got to be riding, if we're gonna make Garden City before the twentieth."

"I know, we'll ride out soon as Trish is ready."

"We'll be riding in with you boys." Bob Moore looks over at his grandfather. "That is, if you don't mind me and granddad tagging along with you."

"It's a free country, the more the merrier," Caintuck grins. "You're more than welcome."

"Let's get saddled up." Cam stands up and starts for the barn. "We've got a long way to ride and a short time to get there."

Chotilla rides his horse as hard as he can, reining in at his wickiup, arriving almost at dark. Quickly summoning four of his squaw's young nephews to his lodge, he converses silently for several minutes, then watches as they bridle his horses and ride away without a backward glance. He has to know Ketchum's whereabouts, and the wild Apaches, like Juh, Geronimo and several others, will know. Far back in the Mogollons as they are, the Apache watch every pass for the pack trains of the Mexican traders from the south or the white eye gold seekers of the Americans. He knows if anyone knows of Ketchum, it would be one of the wild ones. The wily Navajo sends the young warriors to the rancherias of the head chiefs to find out Ketchum's whereabouts. Now all he can do is sit back and wait.

For three days the small warrior stalks his wickiup, playing with the children he is so proud of and watching the trails to his small Rancheria. He knows he has little time to find Ketchum before the outlaw rides into the white man's town of Garden City. Hearing the shrill whistle of his oldest son, who he sent to watch the trails, Chotilla jumps to his feet and runs from his lodge. Only one nephew appears, riding a tired horse up the steep grade.

"You found out where he is?" Chotilla speaks in Apache.

"Yes, Uncle," the slender young warrior of about sixteen summers nods. "Geronimo says he is camped at the place the whites call Sand Springs."

"You have spoken with Geronimo?"

"Yes, Uncle, we met in the yellow canyon."

"What did he want for such information?"

"He just wanted to know what a Navajo wants with the outlaw, Ketchum."

"Did you tell him?"

"No, Uncle. You didn't tell me what you wanted with the white man."

"The Springs are one day's hard ride from Garden City." Chotilla thinks quickly to himself. "You have done well, Nephew. The horse is yours."

"Do you go there?"

"I go."

"I will ride with you."

Chotilla looks over the young man's shoulder to where his woman is beating pinion nuts into a pulp for flavoring her stew. "The squaw nods her approval."

"You would be welcome to ride with me," Chotilla nods. "We may have to kill."

"I am Apache."

"Catch fresh horses, we go."

Quickly gathering his weapons, a skin bag of water and another of food, Chotilla speaks briefly to his woman then trots swiftly to where the young Apache waits with two fresh horses.

"We must hurry, Nephew."

"There will be a full moon tonight, Uncle. We will make good time."

"We must catch the one called Ketchum before he leaves Sand Springs." Chotilla kicks the gelding into a hard lope. "We go."

For three days, Chotilla rides hard, stopping only long enough to rest the tired horses briefly. "When the sun comes again, we will be there." Chotilla dismounts and turns his horse loose. "We will go from here on foot."

"It is still a far run, Uncle." The young warrior looks doubtfully at the older Navajo. "Many miles."

"Maybe you are too old to run that far?" Chotilla looks at the young warrior and smiles. "We go on foot from this place, Nephew. In the dark, we would not want the horses to give us away if Ketchum moved his camp."

The iron muscled legs and deep chests of the two warriors, carry them steadily throughout the night, bringing them to the place called Sand Springs while it is still dusky dark. Daylight hardly runs the darkness from the place of the deep pools of water when Chotilla and his young Apache nephew, called Bajo, crawls closer to the nearby rocks surrounding the cool springs. Four bodies lay rolled up in their bedrolls, fast asleep. Chotilla picks out the sleeping form of Ketchum, a man he has seen many times as he passed through the mountains coming and going from his hideouts.

"These are the ones you seek, Uncle?" Bajo whispers quietly.

"Yes, Nephew."

"They have many guns." The youngster eyes the weapons draped close to the sleeping men. "They are also poor warriors to sleep without a guard."

"Come." Chotilla moves forward, shaking his head. The sleeping men remind him of Frank and Mingo, back at Ketchum's hideout. "They are foolish men. They will soon pay for their foolishness."

Circling quietly around the camp, even the picketed horses don't hear or smell them as the two warriors slip atop the rocks, above the sleeping men. Looking cautiously down on the men, Chotilla spits in disdain at the lazy whites then notches an arrow.

"You will kill the one with the red blanket when you see my arrow strike the first one." Chotilla looks at the nervous youngster. "For my sake, Nephew, don't miss. Your aunt would never forgive you."

"I will not miss, Uncle." Bajo shakes his head. "The fat one under the blanket would be hard to miss, even for a Navajo."

"Even for a Navajo, Nephew?" Chotilla grins.

Chotilla slips down from the rocks and approaches the sleeping men to within an easy bow shot. Looking up at the young Apache, he nods, then draws back the powerful, ash bow slowly and releases the arrow. Since boyhood, he has been trained with the deadly bow and arrow, and he is an expert with it. Hardly has the arrow taken flight when he has another quickly notched and ready. Neither man moves or makes a gurgle as the metal tipped shafts penetrate their chests, killing them instantly. Again, both bows strike the third man, leaving only Ketchum alive. Soundly asleep, he isn't aware that his men have been killed while he lies sleeping in his blankets.

Picking up a rock, Chotilla walks to within fifteen feet of the sleeping outlaw chief and tosses the rock, striking Ketchum's blanket. Rolling to his feet, the outlaw rubs the sleep from his eyes as he looks at the small Indian standing in front of him.

Pointing to the dead men, Chotilla smiles as he tosses down his bow and points to where the arrow sticks from the outlaw Frank's chest. "Your men are all dead white man. They like sleep too much, lazy warrior, dead warrior."

"You, I know you. Why did you do this?"

"For my daughter."

"Your daughter?" Ketchum is confused. "We don't know your daughter."

"The one from Jacksons, you sent the redhead, Hacker to harm." Chotilla stands taller, growing. "Trish Jackson."

"I never sent Hacker to do anything but find Cam Mitchell." Ketchum pulls the tie down from his pistol. "I don't even know where Hacker is."

"Him there," Chotilla points off to the west.

"He is supposed to come and find me." Ketchum slowly loosens his shirt that has tightened around him as he slept.

"I don't think him come, no come."

Ketchum looks at the small warrior. "Why not?"

"Redhead one dead," Chotilla hisses. "You dead now too, no harm daughter anymore."

"You're crazy."

"No, me Navajo, from the Bear Clan of the Shash People." Chotilla watches the outlaw's eyes. "Chief Nani Chotilla, murderer and outcast of the Navajo. Now I have come to kill the mighty Ketchum."

Ketchum is curious, as the small warrior doesn't appear to be armed, yet here he stands alone, taunting an armed man, only fifteen feet in front of him. Looking quickly around for any other warriors, his hand blurs toward the pearl handled pistol. The pistol barely clears its holster when Ketchum's eyes open wide as he paws at the knife shaft protruding from his chest. Trying his best to raise the heavy pistol, he finds his arm can't obey. The gun seems so heavy, it wouldn't come up.

Staggering two steps forward, he shakes convulsively then falls to the ground, dead before the arrow from above enters his side. Chotilla retrieves his knife and rolls Ketchum onto his back. "You were slow white man, but at least you brave, no coward."

Quickly taking the full black scalp, Chotilla motions to Bajo, then over to the other dead whites. The young Apache watches in awe as Chotilla scalps the black haired Ketchum and ties the bloody trophy to his horse's mane.

"Apaches do not scalp their enemies, Uncle." Bajo shakes his head. "Why do you do this?"

"Neither do Navajo, but I have to prove this one is dead. How else can I do this?" Chotilla grins and pulls up the blood soaked hair. "Without this?"

"What do you wish me to do?"

"Bajo has done well today. He is great warrior. Take from them whatever you want, their horses and weapons."

"Everything is mine, Uncle?" Bajo looks around in shock. "I will be rich."

"Everything you want, except the gray stallion."

"You do not want anything here from these whites?"

"Take whatever you wish and return to the Rancheria."

"Where does Chotilla ride?"

"Below, to Garden City."

"What do I say when I return to the woman?"

"Tell your aunt I will return soon," Chotilla looks as the young warrior starts to gather his trophies, "Bajo will say nothing of where you found these guns and horses."

"They were just wandering in the mountains loose, Uncle," Bajo smiles. "I found them."

"That is good."

Darkness finds the small party unsaddling alongside a beautiful, fast running, mountain stream. Quickly gathering dead wood, the men toss together a fire and fill their beat up old coffeepot with coffee beans and water. The rich aroma of boiling coffee filters around the campsite as the men roll out their bedrolls using saddles for headrests. Trish fixes a quick meal of side meat, pan gravy and biscuits while the men water and hobble the horses. Small talk sounds across the camp, underlying each man's true thoughts. Jack Ketchum is foremost on their minds. They know the man is dangerous. They aren't sure Cam Mitchell is fast enough to take the outlaw. Every man around the camp wants Cam and Trish to have a full life. Each would have faced Ketchum for him, but they know only Cam stands a chance against the fast gun of the outlaw.

For some unknown reason, the coyotes, occupying the mountains, raise their voices in unison, seemingly joining in with the men around the fire in their thoughts. The yips and moaning howls of the wild dogs seems lonely and sad, almost like the thoughts of the gathered men. Trish shivers despite herself as she can't shake the dread of the upcoming fight. There is no way around it. Even if Cam is faster, there is a good possibility that a hard case like Ketchum could get lucky and find his target before he dies. She looks over to where Caintuck and Cam have their heads together in a low conversation. She knows the old man is good with a gun. She figures he is trying to give Cam last minute advise before he faces Ketchum.

Seeing her watching them, Cam turns from Caintuck and walks over and sits down beside her. "You should be asleep."

"I can't sleep, my love. We'll be there in two days." Trish pulls the blanket open and leans over to him as he pushes closer. "I would be so happy if only this night was far behind us."

"When we reach Garden City, we'll get you a new dress and a hot bath." Cam smiles and takes her hand in his. "Then I'll take you to Jericos for a fine supper."

"I don't want a bath, food, or a new dress." Trish pulls him to her. "I just want you. Hold me Cam, hold me tight."

"It's gonna be alright Trish," Cam takes her into his arms, "I promise."

"Don't tell me that." Trish turns her face so he can't see her tears from the glow of the campfire. "You can't be certain."

"Nothing will happen to me."

"Why do things like this have to happen at all?"

"Trish there's always a Ketchum in a man's life somewhere down the road." Cam pulls her close. "Always."

"A man like you has to stand up to him, is that it?"

"Like I told you once before, back in the canyon, a man can't live if he's labeled a coward."

"Let's marry as soon as we get there." She wants to change the subject, lighten the mood.

"No Trish, when it's all over, then we'll marry."

"If anything should happen to you," she buries her face in his chest. "Oh, Cam."

"Nothing is going to happen. Now please, you go to sleep."

"Stay here with me." She holds him. "The fire is so romantic. Listen to the coyotes, they're serenading us from their lofty places up high."

"Your grandfather will shoot me." Cam touches her damp face.

"He's full of hot air," Trish smiles and snuggles closer. "Besides, he's already asleep."

Garden City is alive with people as Caintuck leads the small party into the west end of town and stops his horse at the livery sitting at the outskirts of the town. Shaking his head, he looks up and down the streets in shock at all the people that have come into town. Saddle horses, farm wagons, and buckboards of every nature, line the wide, main street. Many others sit under the large oaks, lining the small creek outside Garden City, eating on picnic lunches.

Spade and Angus both shake their heads. "Looks like the hanging we seen in Prescott, back in the fifty's, don't it Angus?"

"Looks like every living person in two states is here to watch," Caintuck mumbles. "Came for the show, I reckon."

"The posters are all over the territory. They've all heard about the big challenge, you old horse thief." The town smithy walks from the stable barn and looks at the riders, focusing on Cam. "It'll be the biggest show since Gettysburg and I see you brought the main attraction."

"I didn't bring anybody, Harvey, but we're here." Caintuck spits.

"You seen anything of Ketchum yet?" Angus Moore looks down at the fire and coal smudged man.

"Nope, and I don't expect to."

Caintuck looks sharp at the man. "What do you mean?"

"He won't be here. The Rangers got wind of this little set-to and have a whole company of star toters here, just waiting for him to show his ugly face."

"When I left town, George told me he was gonna let Ketchum and the boy settle their own affairs, without interference."

"Mason don't have any say so in the matter, now that the Rangers have shown up." Harvey looks off, toward town. "You might say the Rangers have taken control of Garden City, for now."

"They're not gonna let me and Ketchum go at it?" Cam looks down at the man.

"They don't care one hoot, whether you and Ketchum kill each other," Harvey spits. "They think they have a chance to catch Ketchum here and they're sure not gonna miss it."

"You don't think he'll show with all those Rangers in town."

"Would you show Caintuck, if you were the most wanted man in two territories?"

"I ain't Ketchum. I've said all along, the man's crazy loco, he'll show."

"They want Ketchum bad for the mayhem he did in Elmwood a couple weeks back," Harvey argues. "He's made a fool of them for going on five years now, even killed one Ranger and a few men back in the Mogollons. They're scattered about town, acting like farmers or cowboys, figuring Ketchum won't recognize them for what they are."

Angus and Spade both shake their heads. "He knows, Jack Ketchum may be crazy, loco, mean or whatever you want to call him, but he ain't stupid. He's had men in this town watching for the last two weeks."

"You think he'll come in tomorrow, Harvey?"

"Can't say, Ketchum may be meaner than a rattlesnake, but he's not gonna fool around with the Rangers," the stableman shakes his head. "He's been running free around these parts many a year because he's smart. He sure ain't gonna walk right into their hands now."

Angus Moore shakes his head. "Ketchum will be here, I'd bet on it."

"Ain't a chance, old-timer, there's too many lawmen in town." Harvey looks at Angus. "He'll pass this time and wait for another."

"Well, in that case, I reckon we took a long ride for nothing." Caintuck sighs in relief.

"No, we haven't," Trish speaks up with a smile. "We're gonna have a bath, new dress, a wonderful dinner, and then a wedding."

Spade Jackson laughs. "In that order, Granddaughter?"

"Exactly in that order, Grandpa."

Cam looks over to where Caintuck and Angus are frowning. "What's wrong?"

"I know Ketchum. He ain't gonna back off just because a few Rangers are in town." Angus shakes his head. "No sir, the man is crazy, but he's also cagey as a fox."

"Speaking of foxes, he ain't about to let killing his cousin, Len Fox, go, no sircc. He'll be here. His pride will force him to come," Spade Jackson speaks up.

"I'll tell you what I'm gonna do." Caintuck dismounts and leads his horse into the livery.

"What's that?" Cam looks over at the old horse trader.

"I'm gonna wet my whistle, that's what." Caintuck looks toward the far-off saloon.

"That's just great Caintuck, you old horse thief, go get drunk when we need you," Angus frowns.

Caintuck grins. "Well Angus, I'll tell you, it ain't about drinking, but I sure ain't gonna find one of Ketchum's men in a church house, now am I?"

"You know what?" Angus grins. "I think I'll have myself a drink too."

"No, you boys go have supper with Cam and his fiancé." Caintuck shakes his head. "Whoever is here, and someone will be, is more likely to approach me if I'm alone."

An hour later, Cam blinks in complete shock, as Trish enters the dining room of Jerico's famous eatery. At first glance, he doesn't even recognize her. The rough corduroy pants, flannel shirt, and boots are replaced with a full-length, light blue dress with a sash and a large bow around her small waist. A smaller blue ribbon ties her long, thick hair, back in a ponytail and a small bracelet decorates her bare arm.

"Don't pass out in shock Cam, it's me."

Luckily there are no flies in Jericos, as Cam's mouth drops open in complete shock of her beauty. "I ain't gonna pass out Trish, but I could, you're so beautiful."

"Pssh," she laughs. "You've just never seen me in a dress before."

"That's not true," Cam protests his innocence. "You wore a dress at the ranch, but it sure didn't make you look like you do now."

"Keep talking Mister Mitchell, you're getting yourself mired deeper."

Cam blushes and looks for a waiter. "Yes ma'am, I think we should eat."

Minutes later, Trish looks up and smiles as the others enter the eatery and walk to where they are sitting. Seeing both Cam and Trish, all cleaned up in new store-bought clothes, the others look down at their own dusty, trail worn clothing.

"You lovebirds mind if us old people sit with you or should we get another table?" Spade smiles down at his granddaughter.

"Don't be silly, Grandfather." Trish frowns at him and motions to a seat, "Sit down."

"Caintuck still over at the saloon?" Cam looks around the room for the horse trader.

Bob Moore removes his hat and sits down. "He was still over at the saloon when we last saw him."

"It's over." Angus looks around at all the people in Jericos. "Ketchum wouldn't dare come into this town with all these people here."

"Don't sell that man short, Angus." Spade Jackson looks across the table at his old partner. "If he decides to come, he'll be here."

"I saw the look in that man's eyes when he killed that gunfighter in Tucson." Bob Moore picks up his coffee cup as the waiter pours it full. "He's a cold blooded killer. He enjoyed killing that man."

"You think he'll still come here?" Trish looks at Angus Moore, hoping he'd say no.

Cam interrupts the conversation. "Let's order, the food here is the best in the territory."

Spade sees he is trying to take the conversation away from Ketchum and their troubles. "Are you sure boy, I'm so hungry I could eat a rock lizard."

"Those things are poisonous Angus, you know that," Spade shakes his head. "I'll surely order you one if you want me to."

"Poisonous? Why I survived on them things for a whole month when the Apaches chased me back into the Mogollons a few years back." Angus looks around the table at the curious faces.

"A whole month?" Trish looks at Angus, "What happened?"

"Well, I died, of course," Angus laughs. "They're poisonous, haven't you heard?"

Trish knew, as soon as her mouth opened, she shouldn't have asked. "Well, if I had one right now, Mister Moore, I'd order it up for you."

"No ma'am, a good thick steak and potatoes will do fine," Angus smiles. "I believe I've had enough of those lizards to last me a spell."

"Uh huh." Trish looks over at Cam and winks.

As the waiter takes their orders and retreats from the table, Spade looks over at his old partner. "Angus, do you remember the last time we were in here eating?"

"Yep, I do." Angus nods, thinking back to the day Spade's mail order bride arrived. "Just like it was yesterday, not thirty some odd years ago. It was the day Maggie came in here on the mail hack, from back east."

"She was a beauty." Spade hesitates to think a second, looking over at Trish. "She was as pretty as her granddaughter here."

"Yes, she was," Angus laughs. "I even offered to swap the Rafter 5, lock, stock, and barrel for her that day."

"I'm surprised that dad didn't swap you," Gage Jackson laughs. "As much as he likes that ranch."

"No." Spade smiles and looks over at Cam. "Anything but her. Just one look is all it took to land me. I was smitten."

Cam knows exactly how Spade feels. He, too, remembers the first time he looked at Trish as she doctored his side. Some things are just meant to be. Time doesn't matter when the heart and eyes speak. Sometimes, one look is all it takes, a man is snared, trapped, and there's nothing he can do about it. Something clicks for both of them and they are mad about each other.

The skinny waiter places the plates of steaming food around the table and then clears his throat. "Enjoy your meal folks, it's on the house."

"On the house?" Cam looks up at the man.

"Yes sir, our compliments to Miss Jackson and you, sir, on your marriage," the waiter smiles. "We haven't seen Miss Jackson in years, but we remember her when she was much younger. You sir, are the luckiest man we know."

Cam is relieved. He thought the man was going to say something about the upcoming fight and ruin the mood of the evening and the fine set table. "Thank you, sir."

"Enjoy."

Chapter 11

$\mathcal{D}$ishes and silverware rattle throughout the room as everyone enjoys their meal, except for Trish, as she is worrying and feeling uneasy. Spade Jackson is seldom wrong about his judgment of men and if he says Ketchum is coming, the man is. Either here in Garden City or somewhere on the trail, the outlaw will put in an appearance. For years she lived an isolated life on the Jackson Ranch. Now, happiness with a man she adores is within her reach and a crazed outlaw is something that can ruin it. Barely touching her food, she listens as the men make small talk, but she knows they are as worried as she is.

"You're not eating," Cam leans over slightly and speaks to her. "Is the food not to your liking?"

"I'm not hungry."

"You need to keep up your strength for our wedding," Cam smiles knowingly. "Then we're heading for the Gila Bank and then east into West Texas to our new ranch."

"I can't wait to see it," Trish smiles. "Caintuck said so much about it, I can picture the land and beautiful streams in my mind. It must be majestic, just majestic."

"You believe that old horse thief?" Spade speaks up. "Both of you should come back to Jackson Basin and start your new life there with your family."

"No, Grandpa," Trish lays her hand on Spade's. "Cam has his ranch dreams the same as you had yours, remember?"

"That country is a long way from here gal," Spade shakes his head. "Besides, my dream was to find a mountain of gold."

"Yes, it is a long way from here," Cam pushes back his plate. "We'll come visit."

"There's land here, boy. You and Caintuck need to look at it," Angus pushes into the conversation. "You have friends here. Out there is nothing."

"Caintuck has his heart set on that land, Angus. We're going, but we thank you for the offer."

"I'll never see my grandchildren, never." Spade pulls out his pipe, "Trish, what is to become of you?"

"Grandfather, you make it seem like the end of the world," Trish laughs, temporarily forgetting Ketchum. "Wish us luck."

"I do, Granddaughter, the best of luck," Spade smiles softly.

"I would have found that mountain of gold for you Spade, if you hadn't of taken up ranching," Angus speaks up, pointing his fork at his old partner.

"You, find gold?" Spade sputters. "Hah, you couldn't find your own mule on some days."

"That's your opinion."

"Okay, okay," Trish holds up her hand, laughing. "You've managed to get my mind off Ketchum, now finish your dinner, and we'll all have a drink."

Caintuck enters Jericos and walks to the crowded table where the topic turned to bad horses and away from Jack Ketchum. Pulling out the last unoccupied chair, he pours himself a cup of coffee from the pot sitting in the middle of the table. All eyes watch him intently, curious as they wait for him to speak.

Looking over at Cam, he takes several sips of the hot coffee then sets the cup down. "Ketchum's right hand man now, since you killed Fox, is a man named Giles."

"We know him," Angus and Bob both speak up. "He's a bad one."

"Yeah, and he knows both of you," Caintuck waves off the waiter.

"He said he'd kill all of you if you interfere in this set-to."

"So Ketchum is coming?" Cam looks hard at Caintuck.

"Giles says he is."

"What about the Rangers?" Gage speaks up.

"Giles said they'd take care of it, come morning," Caintuck shrugs. "He seems confident."

Trish grips Cam's arm. "No."

"It'll be alright, I promise," Cam pats her hand. "I'll never lie to you, never."

Shaking her head slowly, she tries to smile. "I believe you, but I'm so scared."

"So am I, but we're gonna have our ranch."

Pulling Caintuck off to one side, after seeing Trish to her room, Cam looks around for any prying eyes before speaking. "How's he gonna pull it off, did Giles say?"

"Nope, just that Ketchum plans on meeting you on the street, come morning."

"You believe him, Caintuck, or is it just a bluff?"

Caintuck shrugs. "With a man like Ketchum, you never know for sure, but I believe, if he can get past the Rangers, he'll show."

"How is he gonna do that?" Cam shakes his head. "I'm seeing Rangers behind every shirt in town."

"I know what you mean. If I were him, I'd be making tracks out of here, plenty fast," Caintuck pulls out his pipe. "Those Rangers ain't nobody to fool with."

"Apparently, Ketchum isn't either."

"No, I reckon you're right about that."

Cam looks about for the others who have retreated to the saloon. "You know that day on the trail when all of this started, Ketchum didn't seem too bad a feller."

"Don't kid yourself boy, he's a bad one," Caintuck puffs and looks at Cam. "The worst kind, he lulls you into thinking he's okay, then bam."

"I know, Caintuck. I'll be ready for him this time, if he shows."

"If he don't, we're pulling out for Texas soon as you and Trish are knotted up." Caintuck stands up. "I'm tired of this silliness."

"You're tired?" Cam shakes his head. "What about me? Shucks, I've got more stitches in me than a hand-sewn blanket."

"Let's go get our tonsils wet down."

"No, I'm turning in, it's late."

"Can't figure how you can sleep at a time like this."

Cam smiles. "Easy, I just get in bed and close my eyes."

Caintuck shakes his head as he walks across the street to the Rainbow Saloon where the others are already well ahead of him. He knows Cam is fast with the forty-four, but what he doesn't know is, how fast is Ketchum. He heard stories, just like everyone else, but only Bob Moore and Angus have actually seen the man draw a gun but that was several years back. Caintuck knows Ketchum is middle age now. How much he practices, he doesn't know, but Cam is younger, his reflexes must be faster. Caintuck shrugs as he pulls out a chair where the others sit. Hopefully they will get lucky and Mister Ketchum won't show.

"You get those two, off to bed?" Angus looks around at Caintuck.

"Yep."

"We should be asleep ourselves." Gage downs a warm beer.

"How can you sleep?" Angus shakes his head. "I'm telling you, Ketchum will be here and he ain't about to miss this little set-to, no sir."

"Well, we can't stop him from coming. It's up to the Rangers if they decide to let the fight take place, then it's up to Cam."

Gage looks around the table. "I can't figure it."

"What can't you figure, boy?" Spade questions.

"Why he would come into Garden City in plain daylight like this." Gage looks over at the door expectantly. "I've never heard of a man putting his head in a noose just because of pride."

"It's simple, the man's run free so long, he thinks he's indestructible and he just may be," Spade shakes his head. "Roll me a smoke boy, my hands seem shaky."

"Tell me Caintuck, are we gonna let the boy face him alone?" Gage Jackson looks at the old man.

"We have to, unless Cam asks for our help but he won't or unless some of Ketchum's bunch gets into it." Caintuck shakes his head.

"Why not?" Spade questions. "You wanna get him killed?"

"No, I don't want to get him killed, you old rock hound, but the boy has pride too. We sure can't take that away from him in front of the girl and this whole dang town."

"Pride, pride is a stupid word," Angus spits the word out. "Well, I hope his pride doesn't get him killed."

"Don't sell him short, he's tougher than you think." Caintuck leans back in his chair. "In my prime, I wouldn't have wanted to face him, no sir."

"Ketchum is no longer in his prime." Spade looks across the table. "Is that what you're thinking?"

Caintuck shakes his head. "I don't think it makes a bit of difference."

"He's that fast is he?" Angus questions. "I remember the day in Bisbee when you shot it out with King Steelman."

"King Steelman?" Bob Moore puts down his drink and looks over at Caintuck. "You're the man that downed Steelman?"

"He's the man," Angus grins. "I saw it with my own two eyes. Old King was dead and he didn't even know it."

"You were supposed to keep your mouth quiet about that shooting," Caintuck looks over at Angus, "Big mouth."

"Why didn't you want anybody knowing about you facing a man like Steelman?" Gage Jackson remembers hearing of the gunfighter.

"If you get a reputation with a gun, every young punk in the territory comes looking for you."

"How did you keep the territory from finding out who killed him?"

"Your old granddaddy helped," Caintuck grins. "Until now."

"It happened over a spilled drink." Angus rubs his chin, remembering. "A bar girl in a saloon called The Dragon Lady, accidentally spilled some whiskey on Steelman's pants while he sat playing cards, then he knocked her to the floor. King Steelman was a bona fide dandy, of sorts. He sure didn't like his clothes messed up. Anyway, Caintuck was a young man back then, not too smart, you know. He up and tells Steelman to pick her up and the rest is history."

"That's it?"

"Yep, other than bullets flying and King Steelman cashing in, that's about it."

"Caintuck killed a man for slapping a bar girl?" Gage grins, looking over at the old horse trader. "She must have been something to behold."

"Let me tell you," Angus grins, taking a sip of whiskey. "They didn't call her the Dragon Lady for nothing."

Caintuck smiles. "She was something, wasn't she Angus? Wonder what became of her?"

"They say she's got herself a huge mansion in San Francisco, overlooking the harbor." Angus laughs, "Probably spending all the gold we spent in her place."

"Then what happened?"

"Nothing much, we beat it out the door just as the local town marshal got there," Angus grins. "He started barking questions and I told him the man who done the shooting was a kid called Blue Diamond."

"Who's that?"

"Beats me boy, but every gunfighter in Arizona looked for him for years."

"If Mitchell is faster than you were and you gunned down King Steelman, then why don't you want him facing Ketchum?"

"I don't want him getting the reputation of killing Ketchum, but if he has to, I believe he's up to the task." Caintuck stares hard at Bob Moore. "Killing a man like Jack Ketchum only calls for more and more killings."

"If you think Cam Mitchell hasn't got a reputation with a gun, after killing Len Fox," Spade picks up his coffee cup as he looks over at Caintuck. "You're crazier than Ketchum."

The wedding was canceled after Caintuck brought word about Ketchum. Everyone sitting around the dining table lost the festive mood that normally surrounds such a happy occasion. Both Cam and Trish want to postpone the wedding until after Ketchum and this craziness settles. Trish only shakes her head worrying, but she says little else concerning Ketchum. She knows Cam has no choice. Either he meets the outlaw here, in front of the whole town or Ketchum will try to ambush him on a lonely back trail somewhere in the mountains. It is inevitable, Ketchum is bound and determined to prove to everyone, he is the better man. His pride, as he sees it, had been tarnished. According to his law, the only way to settle it is for one of them to die. Why the law permits this, she does not know, but she knows enough about Ketchum to realize he will carry through with his threat.

Years have passed since his upbringing on the southern plantation, instilling the aristocratic carriage and pride in him so the passion of a gentleman from the south, persists. Losing his father, grandfather, and the ancestral mansion and lands, after the Civil War was lost, Ketchum had become embittered and enraged against anything law abiding. Most consider Ketchum a robber and killer, but in his own eyes, he is still the southern gentleman of years past. He was the one who lost everything. Union soldiers killed his father on his front porch as they tried to push their way into the large mansion, confiscating the entire plantation, down to the last chicken. No, Ketchum, in his own eyes, was owed all he took, innocent of any wrongdoing.

Only doors down from Cam's room, Trish lies awake in her room, worrying about Cam so there will be no sleep tonight. She wants to go to him, to reassure him, to give him strength, but she knows she will only add to his worries. He needs his rest to try to regain his strength from the long ride from the Mogollons. Turning on her side, she looks out the open window and sends a silent prayer up to the heavens. If he dies, she knows she could not stand living. For once, in the short time with him, she finally found happiness and contentment.

George Mason walks down the board sidewalk of the dusty town and stops before Jericos, where Caintuck, Spade, and Angus found themselves chairs. The familiar old pipes of the men send small puffs of smoke into the morning air giving off their aromatic smells. Fishing his pocket watch from under his gun belt, the Sheriff checks the time then clicks it shut. The cold blue eyes of the lawman drift slowly over the busy town street, then look down at the three friends.

"It's ten o'clock, boys." Mason's voice seems nervous, even shaky. "He should be riding in."

"Where's your ranger friends, George?" Caintuck looks up at the lawman.

"They're around here somewhere, I suspect."

"You're gonna let Ketchum ride in here, kill that boy and not try to help?" Spade knocks the ash from his pipe. "Just like that?"

"I gave my word, Spade, and I'll keep it." Mason looks annoyed at the old prospector.

"George Mason gave his word, and you're gonna keep it." Angus spits into the street.

"You boys know Ketchum robbed and killed all over Arizona and New Mexico. If he comes in and the boy doesn't kill him, we will," the Sheriff shrugs. "I know this is an unorthodox way of doing things, but if he comes in today, well, one way or the other, we'll have him."

"Whether or not the boy gets killed, doesn't matter." Spade shakes his head. "As long as you get your man, is that it?"

"Spade, I know Mitchell is fixing to marry your granddaughter and I hope nothing happens to him, but we've got to get this killer anyway we can." Mason looks away from the staring faces, guiltily. "From what I'm hearing about this Mitchell, if I were Ketchum, I'd ride out of the country as quick as I could."

"That's what this whole mess is about," Spade speaks up. "Ketchum ain't about to run and lose face, no sir."

Angus looks up as Bob Moore and Gage join them. "Tell me George Mason, since when does the law let an ordinary citizen do their dirty work for them?"

"Normally we wouldn't Angus, but this ain't normal times." Mason strikes a sulphur on the upright post and lights a smoke. "Mitchell and Ketchum started this mess and I gave my word to leave it be until they settle their own affairs, man to man."

"Just that simple, is it George?" Caintuck speaks up.

"To me, it's that simple Caintuck, and you know it." Mason looks down at the old horse trader. "Just that simple."

"So Sheriff, you figure Ketchum thinks he is gonna walk in here, gun Mitchell down, then ride out free as a bird." Bob Moore shakes his head. "It ain't gonna be that simple, he knows it and mister you know it."

"We gave our word that he wouldn't be confronted until after he and Mitchell settle their differences. After that, if Ketchum survives, he's open game."

"He knows that?" Caintuck looks incredulously at the Sheriff.

"He knows it. We sent word by Giles and Mingo," Mason nods. "We didn't say anything about him riding out of town free and clear.

We just said we wouldn't confront him until after he met Mitchell."

"Crap!" Spade swears. "This sounds like the wild west days of twenty years ago."

"I thought the Rangers were running this show now?" Gage speaks up. "What happened to that?"

"I gave my word boys, that's it." Mason shakes his head. "This is my town, my jurisdiction, and the Rangers were told to stay out of it until I give them the go ahead, then we'll take Ketchum."

Spade stands up slowly as every eye turns on him. "Well, here's my word George Mason, and you've known me for nigh on thirty-five years. If Ketchum kills that boy, I'll kill you if it's the last thing I ever do."

"I didn't think Mitchell meant that much to you, Spade."

"No, but my granddaughter's happiness does."

Mason opens his watch one more time, then turns and walks toward his office. All eyes watch his broad back as it disappears from sight. Ten minutes later, every head turns as Cam and Trish walk from Jericos to the porch beside them. Spade smiles and stands up, never has he seen his granddaughter look so radiant. Even in this hour of stress and fear of the confrontation that is soon to come, she seems content.

Cam looks over at Caintuck and nods. "Well sir, it's almost eleven. He's supposed to be here before twelve."

"He's here." Caintuck nods up the street where the Steeldust stallion trots out from a side alley with no rider. As one of the split reins slips from the arched neck, the well-trained stallion stops and stands still. After the people quickly leave the street, nothing stirs, as every board-walk is vacant. Every man on the porch studies the horse, and then surveys the empty street. Nothing moves except for a dust devil, stirring up the broad street.

"Why ain't he coming out?" Gage Jackson lets his hand rest on the large pistol at his side. "What's he waiting on?"

"In his own due time, he'll show himself." Caintuck leans back in a chair and relights his cigar. "He just wants folks to get all worked up real good, before the show."

"Mister Jackson, you and the boys take Trish and wait inside until this is over." Cam motions for them all to go back inside.

Chairs scrape as everybody stands and starts for the open doors of the restaurant. Only Caintuck sits, leaning back in his chair, puffing calmly on his cigar. "You watch his eyes Cam, watch his eyes."

"Go inside, Caintuck."

"Reckon not young'un, not this time." Caintuck pulls his forty-five and rotates the cylinder, checking the chambers and replacing the weapon. "I'll just watch from here."

Chapter 12

Caintuck sits up straight, making the chair slam down hard on the board sidewalk as Chotilla rides slowly from the alley, just as Giles and Mingo walk out from the Rainbow Saloon across the street. Both men stare intently across the street at Cam and Caintuck, unaware of the Navajo riding down the street, straight toward them.

Cam waves his hand for Caintuck to stay where he is, then steps into the street. "You keep clear of this Caintuck."

"Not likely, boy." The old horse trader steps into the street beside Cam, his smoke hanging from his grizzled mouth. "I'll take the fat one. You take Mister Giles, if Ketchum don't show."

"I reckon you get the fat one called Mingo, all to yourself. Peers to me like Chotilla done killed Ketchum." Cam points briefly to where the Navajo stops, holding up the black scalp and the silver mounted pistol belt with the pearl handled pistol, the trademark of Jack Ketchum.

"Well, what do you know, I 'spect he has. I doubt he'd loan his hair to that Navajo," Caintuck grins. "He must be some kind of man to kill Ketchum."

"He is." Cam starts forward, just as Giles looks to where Cam points and notices Chotilla sitting his horse in the middle of the street, holding up his grizzly trophy.

"Take them Mingo; Ketchum's dead," Giles yells as he pulls his pistol and fires.

Gunfire erupts and resonates up and down the board fronts of the buildings of Garden City and through Jerico's front doors. Trish holds hard onto Spade's hand as the last shot rings out and then all goes quiet. Jerking loose from her grandfather, she races outside to find Cam bending over Caintuck who is leaning on one elbow.

"Dang it Caintuck, I told you to stay out of it." Cam holds the older man in a sitting position.

"I ain't hurt. I had a bee sting hurt me worse once."

"Yeah, well a bee sting don't make you bleed like you are now, you old fool." Cam looks down at the bloody pants.

Caintuck shakes his head and shrugs in pain. "Yeah, yeah, wait until you get an old man down, then kick him."

"Oh, shut up."

Trish kneels beside Caintuck and examines the wound as Spade, Angus, and the others run from Jericos. "Take him inside and pull a couple tables together, and for Pete's sake, be easy with him."

Cam helps lift Caintuck, amazed at how light he is, then lets the others carry him inside as he looks down at Trish and smiles.

"It's over, Miss Jackson. Now we can have our wedding."

"I'll see to Caintuck first." She looks over to where Chotilla sits his horse. "It's only a flesh wound. He won't need a doctor."

"I'll go see Chotilla," Cam nods. "I believe we owe that little man a great deal."

"Tell him," Trish waves at the Navajo. "Tell him I love him and honor him as I would my father."

Cam walks over to where Chotilla sits his horse, holding the Steel-dust. The dry, bloody scalp and silver gun belt dangle from his left hand. He looks up at the Navajo, and the coal black eyes, seem to smile as he approaches. "The old one is not hurt bad?"

"No, just a crease to the leg."

"He is an old man. He should have let you kill both of the bad ones." Chotilla tilts his chin. "Much honor you kill these whites."

"Just like Chotilla let me kill Ketchum?" Cam grins.

"Chotilla no old. I have ten children." The Navajo straightens his head proudly. "Soon, one more come."

Cam has to laugh, as he figures, from what Spade Jackson said about meeting the Navajo many years before, the warrior must be at least sixty years old. "How many more after that?"

"That is for the Gods to know, not Chotilla."

"Oh, I was of the idea that you had something to say about it."

Chotilla smiles smugly. "Me young man."

Cam looks back at Jericos. "Come young man. We'll go see how an old man is doing and get you something to eat."

"No, this one goes home now, see ugly wife. Me gone too many days." Chotilla hands the reins of the Steeldust to Cam. "You and her be okay now. All bad men dead."

"Yes, we will, thanks to a mighty big man and good friend."

"That good, me go."

"Thank you, my friend." Cam extends his hand. "Thank you."

"You good man. You take care of my daughter."

"I will, and she told me to tell you she loves you," Cam smiles. Even under the darkness of his skin, Cam can see the small warrior is blushing. He knows Indians aren't so free with their feelings.

"Chotilla will see her again someday."

Cam lays his hand on the reins of the Navajo's horse and looks up at the little warrior. "We go to Texas to build a horse ranch. You and your family are welcome to come with us."

"Chotilla, no cowboy," the Navajo shrugs. "No work cow."

"Who knows, we may need a tracker from time to time."

"This one think about it, but only as tracker," Chotilla nods. "You give Navajo many good smokes, maybe come one day."

"I'll leave a map with Angus, if you change your mind."

"We see," Chotilla nods. "You still owe me teeth."

"See that sign right over there?"

"I see where big teeth are smiling."

"You'll have to come in and see the man. He'll fix your store teeth."

"White man, no fix teeth for Navajo." Chotilla shakes his head. "Maybe scalp Navajo."

"You come in. I'll make sure to tell him all about you before I leave this town in the morning."

"I do this thing, if Cam Mitchell say, okay."

"If you come to the Pecos Country later, you be careful Chotilla. Where we ride is a dangerous country."

"For Indians?"

"Yes, and for everybody else."

"Wilder than the Mogollons and the Apaches?"

"Maybe wilder."

"This place sounds good. Maybe I come, but have to ask squaw first." Chotilla shrugs. "Woman may not leave Apache land."

"I thought the man was the big chief in his family."

"Big chief on war trail, yes. In wickiup, no." Chotilla grins. "This one likes to eat."

"Good-bye, my friend," Cam extends his hand. "Thank you for everything."

"You listen to Chotilla; have many little ones and you live long."

It's Cam's turn to blush. "Good-bye, Chotilla. We'll be in Gila in a few days. Bring your wife and ten children there and ride with us to our new home."

Chotilla extends his left hand that holds the bloody scalp and gun belt. "These are wedding presents for my daughter."

Knowing the Indian put much pride and thought, differently of such things, he doesn't want to insult the man that has befriended and helped him so much, so Cam takes the grizzly trophies. "Thank you, my friend. They will make her proud."

"Always be strong, young one."

Cam stands holding the Steeldust, watching as the little Navajo rides down the alley and from his sight. He shakes his head as he never would he have thought Chotilla would kill Ketchum and maybe save his life. He has much to thank the Navajo for. Leading the stud, he walks down the street and ties the horse up, placing the scalp and gun belt under a blanket in the rear of the wagon. He will bury them properly when they leave Garden City. Entering the eatery, just in time to hear Caintuck hollering and raising a ruckus, he knows the old horse trader is alright.

"Does it hurt, you old horse thief?" Cam looks down to where Caintuck is lying on a table.

"No, it don't hurt, you dang fool, it tickles." The old horse trader cusses.

"Then what are you hollering about?"

"That woman of yours is refusing to let me have a drink," Caintuck grumbles. "Tell her, will you. All she wants to put down me is that pig swill she cooked up."

Cam remembers Chotilla's last words. "Nope, she's the boss of the wickiup."

"Now what's that supposed to mean." Caintuck puffs up, like a toad. "You saying I've got to drink something a sick billy goat wouldn't?"

"It means she's the boss of the house."

"Great." Caintuck looks longingly at the whiskey bottles behind the bar. "This relationship is starting off with a bang."

Cam looks over to where Trish is putting away her medical bag and smiles. "Can you walk, old man?"

"Probably could, if I had a drink," Caintuck shrugs. "Why?"

"I'm in need of a best man to stand up for me at my wedding," Cam smiles. "So far you've done a good job today."

"What about the drink?"

Cam looks over to where Trish holds up one finger. "One."

"One doesn't even tickle a man's gizzard."

"Take it or leave it."

"I'll take it," Caintuck frowns as a small shot glass is filled with the amber liquid. "A man could die of thirst around here."

Two days later, after the wedding and a rousing celebration, a large covered wagon stands fully loaded with everything they need for the long trail into Texas to their new ranch. The old wagon, Caintuck used in his horse-trading business for years, he traded for a newer, larger wagon. Caintuck has been limping around on a crutch, trading horses, and saying his good-byes. The Steeldust, along with five other well-blooded mares, and a couple riding geldings, stand tied alongside the new wagon. Spade, Angus, and the boys, wait sadly alongside the wagon, dreading to see the small party pull out.

"Caintuck, there's plenty of land here for a horse ranch," Spade speaks up as Trish hugs him. "I'll even give you some land."

"Not for me, old friend," Caintuck shakes his head. "You know how you felt when you and Angus first laid eyes on the Rafter 5 valley."

"I remember and so does Angus." Spade shakes his head. He knows he is gonna miss her greatly. "I don't blame you for going, one bit."

"That's the way I feel about the land I found in Texas, many years ago."

"Texas is a long way from here," Angus speaks up sadly.

"It's not far. A good horse run away," Caintuck smiles.

"That'd be a heck of a horse."

"Yes, sir. That's exactly the kind of horses we intend to raise."

Cam helps Trish onto the high wagon seat, beside Caintuck, and shakes hands all around before mounting the Black. "We'll come back to see you all soon."

"You take care of my horse, you young rascal," Angus reaches over and pats the black's neck, shaking hands with Cam.

"And my granddaughter," Spade speaks up.

"I will, both of them," Cam looks up at his new wife.

George Mason kept his word to Ketchum and did not interfere. Watching the gunfight from his office, he waited until the last shot was fired, then walked over with his deputies and several Rangers to remove Giles and Mingo's remains. Now, as he watches the wagon, getting ready to depart, he steps closer to the edge of the porch and looks over at Cam.

"How do we know Ketchum is really dead? Wait for him to kill again?

"He's dead George or the stallion wouldn't be here alive, you know that."

"Maybe it's a trick of some kind." Mason rubs his chin. "I ain't sure."

Turning the black, Cam rides to the back of the wagon and brings the scalp and gun belt, wrapped in the blanket, back to the Sheriff. "Here's proof. If you don't recognize the hair, you're bound to know that silver mounted gun belt and the pearl handled pistol."

As he unrolls the blanket, Mason blinks, nodding his head, sighing in relief. "It's Ketchum's alright."

"Then we'll be seeing you, Mister Mason."

"One other thing, Mister Mitchell. You know Ketchum had a large reward on his head?" Mason looks up at Caintuck. "Who do I get it to?"

"Give it to Spade over there." Cam nods to Spade Jackson. "He'll get it to the right party."

"Well, I need a name to put on it for my records," Mason persists. "Tell me who it was, if you know."

"I'll tell you this Sheriff; he's the biggest little man I've ever met. A five-foot giant of a man."

"Are you daft or what, man?" Mason shakes his head. "That tells me a lot."

"Good-bye, Sheriff." Cam waves and kicks the black. "Ask Spade, he knows the man well. You wouldn't believe me."

Trish leans from the wagon, waving and looking back at the family she is fixing to ride away from. Then, she looks at Cam and smiles. As Caintuck clucks to the team and the heavy wagon lurches forward, she waves one final time and turns her attention to the east and the land of west Texas and the Pecos River. Excited and filled with happiness, her thoughts turn to her new family and down the road. She is heading for a new life and adventure.

The End